HUGH MACLENNAN was born in Glace Bay, Cape Breton, Nova Scotia, in 1907. He took his B.A. (1928) in Classics from Dalhousie University, then travelled as a Rhodes Scholar to Oxford University where he obtained another B.A. and his M.A. (1932); he completed graduate studies in Classics at Princeton University, where he received his Ph.D. (1935).

MacLennan returned to Canada in 1935 to accept a teaching appointment in Latin and History at Lower Canada College in Montreal, which remained his home. In 1951 he accepted a position in the Department of English at McGill University, where he taught for three decades.

Barometer Rising was MacLennan's first novel. His seven novels as well as his many essays and travel books present a chronicle of a Canada that often mediates between the old world of its European cultural heritage and the new world of American vitality and materialism.

MacLennan's many honours include five Governor General's Awards and nineteen honorary degrees.

Hugh MacLennan died in Montreal, Quebec, in 1990.

Hugh MacLennan

EACH MAN'S SON

With an Afterword by Alec Lucas

M&S

Copyright © 1951 by Hugh MacLennan
Copyright © 2003 by the Estate of Hugh MacLennan
Afterword copyright © 2003 by Alec Lucas

This book was first published in Canada by the
Macmillan Company of Canada Ltd. in 1951.
New Canadian Library edition 2003

National Library of Canada Cataloguing in Publication

MacLennan, Hugh, 1907-1990
Each man's son / Hugh MacLennan ; afterword by Alec Lucas.

(New Canadian library)
Includes bibliograpical references.
ISBN 0-7710-3483-0

I. Title. II. Series.

PS8525.L54E23 2003   C813'.54   C2003-900372-8
PR9199.3.M334E23 2003

We acknowledge the financial support of the Government of Canada
through the Book Publishing Industry Development Program and that of
the Government of Ontario through the Ontario Media Development
Corporation's Ontario Book Initiative. We further acknowledge the
support of the Canada Council for the Arts and the Ontario Arts Council
for our publishing program.

Typesetting by M&S, Toronto
Printed and bound in Canada

McClelland & Stewart Ltd.
The Canadian Publishers
481 University Avenue
Toronto, Ontario
M5G 2E9
www.mcclelland.com

1 2 3 4 5   07 06 05 04 03

Except a corn of wheat fall into the ground and die, it abideth alone: but if it die, it bringeth forth much fruit.

Prologue

CONTINENTS ARE much alike, and a man can no more love a continent than he can love a hundred million people. But all the islands of the world are different. They are small enough to be known, they are vulnerable, and men come to feel about them as they do about women.

Many men have loved the island of Cape Breton and a few may have hated her. Ericson was probably the first to see her, Cabot landed on her, and after Cabot came the French. She seemed harsh and frigid to the firstcomers, but the moment the French saw her their imaginations were touched and they called her the Royal Isle. After a while they built on her eastern rim the master fortress of Louisburg to dominate Nova Scotia and guard the St. Lawrence.

When the wars began, the English and the New Englanders came up to Cape Breton and for a time she was as famous as Gibraltar. Louisburg fell, the French were driven out, the English and Americans went home and for a third of a century the island was vacant again.

Then across the ocean in the Highlands of Scotland a desperate and poetic people heard of her. They were a race of hunters, shepherds and warriors who had discovered too late that their own courage and pride had led them to catastrophe, since it had enabled them to resist the Saxon civilization so long they had come to the end of the eighteenth century knowing nothing of the foreman, the boss, the politician, the policeman, the merchant or the buyer-and-seller of other men's work. When the English set out to destroy the clans of Scotland, the most independent of the Highlanders left their homes with the pipes playing laments on the decks of their ships. They crossed the ocean and the pipes played again when they waded ashore on the rocky coast of Cape Breton Island.

There they rooted themselves, big men from the red-haired parts of the Scottish main and dark-haired smaller men from the Hebrides, women from the mainland with strong bones and Hebridean women with delicate skins, accepting eyes and a musical sadness in their speech. For a long time nothing but Gaelic was spoken on the island until they gradually learned English from the handful of New England Loyalists who came to Nova Scotia after the American Revolution.

To Cape Breton the Highlanders brought more than the quixotic gallantry and softness of manner belonging to a Homeric people. They also brought with them an ancient curse, intensified by John Calvin and branded upon their souls by John Knox and his successors – the belief that man has inherited from Adam a nature so sinful there is no hope for him and that, furthermore, he lives and dies under the wrath of an arbitrary God who will forgive only a handful of His elect on the Day of Judgment.

As no normal human being can exist in constant awareness that he is sinful and doomed through no fault of his own, the Highlanders behaved outwardly as other men do who have softened the curse or forgotten its existence. But in Cape Breton they were lonely. They were no part of the great outer world. So the curse remained alive with them, like a somber beast growling behind an unlocked door. It was felt even when they were least conscious of it. To escape its cold breath some turned to drink and others to the pursuit of knowledge. Still others, as the Puritans of New England had done earlier, left their homes, and in doing so found wider opportunities in the United States or in the empty provinces of western Canada.

But if the curse of God rested on the Highlanders' souls, the beauty of God cherished the island where they lived. Inland were high hills and a loch running in from the sea that looked like a sleeve of gold in the afternoon sun. There were trout and salmon streams lined by sweet-smelling alder, water meadows and valleys graced by elms as stately as those in the shires of southern England. The coast was rugged with gray granite or red sandstone cliffs, splendid with promontories, fog-bound in the spring when the drift ice came down from Newfoundland and Labrador, tranquil in summer, and in the autumns thunderous with evidences of the power of the Lord.

So for several generations the Highlanders remained here untouched, long enough for them to transfer to Cape Breton the same passionate loyalty their ancestors had felt for the hills of home. It was long enough for them to love the island as a man loves a woman, unreasonably, for her faults no less than for her virtues. But they were still a fighting race with poetry in their hearts and a curse upon their souls. Each man's son was driven by the daemon of his own hope and imagination – by his energy or by his fear – to unknown destinations. For those who stayed behind, the beast continued to growl behind the unlocked door.

Daniel Ainslie was one of those who stayed. In the year 1913 he considered himself a freethinker, a man who was proud because he had neither run away nor sought a new belief in himself through hard liquor. But he did not know – how many of us can understand such a thing – that every day of his life was haunted by a sense of sin, a legacy of the ancient curse.

Even when he tried to find strength by denying God's existence, he lived as though the hound of heaven were snapping at his heels. Even when he displayed his knowledge and intelligence as a priest displays his beads, he felt guilty because he knew so little and was not intelligent enough.

In one way or another he was forced to discover, as most of us do, that a man can ignore almost anything in his life except the daemon which has made him what he is and the other daemon which gives him hope of becoming more than any man can ever be.

One

THE SHADOW OF a promontory lay forward on the sea like that of a giant resting on his elbows with the back of his neck to the late afternoon sun. Facing the sun over the water was a second-quarter moon, white in the cobalt mass of the sky.

Two small figures sat in a cove under the promontory, a woman and an eight-year-old boy. The red smock of the mother, the white shirt and green pants of the boy – the pants secured by cloth braces with large white buttons – were bright between the cliff and the giant's shadow on the sea. The tide was moving into the cove and now the water was breaking not many yards from the boy's feet. The whole place was awash with sound as the cliff caught and magnified the noise of the wind and water, echoed the screams of sea birds and reverberated with the occasional thunder of a big wave. Feeling the air rushing cold out of the sunshine into the shadow, suddenly conscious of the rise of the whole sea, the boy turned to his mother.

"The tide's coming in, isn't it?" He was proud of his knowledge. For a few moments he watched to see if the next wave would obliterate the mark of the one before. "What makes it change like that?"

She pointed to the white wafer of the moon. "There is what does it."

He looked at her with bright surprise. "The moon? How?"

"It pulls the water up the shore and then lets it go back again."

"Mummy, that's just another of your stories." His eyes were twinkling.

"No, it isn't. I read it in a book. All the stars in the sky pull on each other all the time. In every direction at once. The earth is pulling on them, too. That's what we're on – the earth. And when the moon comes around on our side of the earth it pulls and pulls and the whole sea is lifted up against the land and that's what the tide is."

He looked up at the moon and again at the water, and as she watched his face she wondered what he was thinking about. She was pleased because she had been able to answer such important questions so well. He watched the moon for a long time and then turned back to his play. It was no ordinary child's castle he had built in the sand, she thought. It was like the picture of the castle he had seen in the book she was reading to him. There were four walls with towers on the corners, a courtyard within and a drawbridge over a moat. The drawbridge was a chip of driftwood which he had just finished inserting.

But the boy's attention wandered while she watched him. The sea and the sky were too big and he was getting sleepy. He turned his head as a gull flew out from the overhang of the cliff and then he looked far, far up the beetling rock to the flecks of white where birds rested in crevices of the rock.

Mollie MacNeil looked too young to have an eight-year-old son. Her body was slim and her pale skin made her seem fragile, just as the eagerness of her smile showed how vulnerable she was. She had a Celtic delicacy of skin with a rose flush over her cheekbones, and as she leaned back with her chin tilted towards the sky her face seemed even more fragile than her body. It was the younger-than-normal face of a woman who has lived for years with a child and for a child.

Without warning, a strident steam whistle blasted the air. There was nothing in sight which could send forth such a sound, but the scream of the whistle shot up into the sky and filled it. Birds flew crying out of their nests in the cliff as the noise hung wailing in the air, but neither the boy nor his mother moved. They knew the whistle came from the colliery half a mile inland and they heard it with only part of their senses. It had always marked hours in their lives.

When the sound died away she rose with apparent reluctance and pulled down her rumpled skirt. "There is the end of the day shift, so you know how late it is."

He watched her wrap a heel of bread in a piece of newspaper before putting it into a basket, along with a partly used jar of molasses and the empty bottle in which she had brought milk. Her dark hair and lovely eyes were reflected in his as she smiled.

"Think how good it will be when we get home this time! Did I tell you what we have for supper tonight?"

His face broke into a delighted smile. "Pork pie!"

"One whole one for you and another for me. I got them at the store only this morning so they'll be lovely and fresh." The wind riffled her hair and she pushed it back out of her eyes. "Come now, Alan. It is always longer going home."

"Will we stop at the spring in the woods?"

"Today there is no time for that. The spring is behind the doctor's house and that is on the other side of where we live."

"But you said it was the best water in the world."

"So it is, but we will save it for another day."

He turned to look back at the sea, trying to understand what his mother meant when she had told him about the moon. Then he saw something which had not been there before. It was a schooner emerging from behind a bluff of land; close-hauled on the starboard tack, it was standing out to sea against the humping waves.

"Look!" he said. "There is a really big ship. Where is she going?"

"She would be bound for Newfoundland, probably."

"What's that?"

"It's a great big island out there."

"I can't see it."

"Of course you can't. It is too far away for you to see it."

"Could Father see it if he was here?"

"Not even your father could see that far."

"Mummy?" The boy's face was grave as he forgot about the ship. "Where is Father now?"

She set her basket down on the sand and the smile left the corners of her mouth. "But I have told you, Alan – I have told you over and over again." The smile reappeared to encourage him. "See if you can remember all by yourself."

"Father has gone out into the world," he said, as if repeating a lesson.

She clapped her hands. "Now tell me the other thing. Why has he gone out into the world?"

"He has gone away to do things for us. And when he comes back everything will be good. We will go into the store and get whatever we want and people will be proud of us and we will live in a fine house and be different."

She bent and caught him, pretending she found him too heavy to move, and the child laughed and leaned back against her until she gave a jerk and swung him to his feet. A long rush of water slid up the beach, splashed against the sand house and washed part of it away. Another ground swell followed and both of them scampered into the recesses of the cove as they saw a sudden hump of water arch out of the sea, lurch forward into the shadow of the giant's shoulders, its crest whipped by the breeze so that it came at them like dark horses with streaming white manes. It burst on the sand, thundered within itself and hissed after the footsteps of the

woman and boy, and when it ebbed the sand house had disappeared. Nothing was left but a cold mound trickling with
water, and on the edge of it, white and glistening, was an
empty conch shell that had not been there before.

The boy darted back while his mother turned towards the
path running slantwise up the side of the cliff, her basket
swinging from her hand. As he followed her he slipped the
shell into the pocket of his shirt.

At the top of the cliff they paused, breathless, and looked
back over the sea. Its blue was deeper than the blue of the sky
and the black hull and white sails of the schooner were tiny
on its surface. Waves three miles long swelled in from far out
and burst in lines of slow, lazy foam down the length of the
coast. The woman and the boy stood watching until the distance made their eyes ache and then they turned inland. A few
sheep, their shadows spindle-legged on the common where
they pastured at the cliff's edge, looked up and baaed at them.
They walked over the treeless pasture, climbed a stile and
descended on the other side to a rough path which led them
homeward through a low growth of brush and brambles.

Before them to the right stood the colliery. Black and mon-
strous it bulged against the western sky, a huge mountain of
coal with the bankhead seemingly on top of it, a trestle beside
the coal bank supporting a square-boilered locomotive with
a short train of cradle cars behind it. From this distance the
train looked like a column of black ants that had crawled up
the stalk of a gigantic plant and died there.

This was the visible colliery. Without framing their
thoughts, both Mollie MacNeil and her son knew that what
they saw behind the wire fence was merely the product of
the last two weeks of work. A hundred fathoms beneath the
ground they were walking on ran the seam. Galleries like
the tentacles of an octopus branched out beneath the floor
of the sea itself, and it was in these galleries that the men of

the families in their neighborhood went down each day and came up again. They also knew that theirs was only one of some fifteen collieries which circled the town of Broughton. They felt lucky because theirs was so close to the sea.

Mollie and her son skirted the colliery fence, its enclosed area quiet as a church since the men had quit work, and finally they reached the main road which came from Broughton and then, after passing the colliery fence, made a right-angled turn and ran down a steep slope to a bridge over a bubbling brook. Between the bridge and the colliery, for a distance of two hundred and fifty yards, crowded so close together they looked like a single downward-slanting building with a single downward-slanting roof, were the houses of the miners' row.

Mollie looked at Alan and smiled. "There now," she said. "We're almost home."

Somewhere in the row was a door which they called their own, but nothing distinguished it from the doors to right or left of it. Each house was a square with a triangle set on its top. There were two doors side by side in the front of each one and on either side of the doors were single windows behind which lurked small parlors. The houses were divided in two by a common wall between the doors, behind each parlor at the back of the buildings was a kitchen, and upstairs under sharply sloping roofs were the bedrooms. The houses had all been painted the same fierce shade of iron-oxide red when they were built by the coal company; two families shared each sloping roof; all of them used a rickety board sidewalk which ran between the low doorsteps and the road. Between the sidewalk and the road was a deep ditch overgrown with thistle, burdock and coarse grass, and down the center of the road, making a right-angled turn at the corner by the colliery, ran the tracks of the tramline which bound the collieries to their heart in Broughton.

Tonight as Mollie and Alan passed the tram stop and went their way down the board sidewalk there was activity along the whole row. Before each house, beside each low doorstep, a washtub had been set on a stool. In front of each tub a miner just back from the pit crouched, stripped to the waist, while his wife, working hard with both arms, scrubbed the coal dust off his face, neck, back, shoulders and arms. Mollie and Alan passed them one by one and Mollie exchanged greetings with some of the wives. There was a loud splashing of water and a grunting and spitting from the men as the two figures went by, but the boy saw no adventure in the scene. It had been this same way every night of his life when the weather was warm.

In the kitchen that evening, after they had finished their supper, Alan took the sea shell from his pocket and held it against his ear.

"Mummy, listen!"

He handed her the shell and she also held it against her ear. "All shells sound like that," she said. "They remember the sea."

"How can they remember? They're not alive."

Her face lightened as she thought of an answer. "It was in the book we read with the birds and snakes and fish. It said that the first things that ever lived were in the sea. Are you listening, Alan? That means the shell is so old the noise in it is the oldest sound in the world."

She was pleased because he seemed to be satisfied and for a moment she watched him as he listened to the shell. Then she looked at the alarm clock on the shelf over the table and told him it was late and past his bedtime. He got up and went upstairs slowly, knowing that because it was Saturday night his mother would be going out. Under the sharp slant of the roof he took off his shirt and hung it on a nail. Then he took off his pants and finally his shoes and stockings. He laid his shoes side by side on the floor by the head of his cot and carefully pressed down the creases in his pants before he laid them on a wooden chair. He turned the socks inside out and laid them on the back of the chair and finally took a flannelette nightgown from under his pillow and put it on. The shell went under the pillow where the nightgown had been, he scrambled into bed and pulled the covers up to his chin and lay on his back.

"Mummy," he called. "I'm here."

A moment later he heard the stairs creak and then she came in and looked quickly to see how well he had disposed of his clothes.

"Now," she said, and smiled at him as she sat on the edge of his cot. "You're all ready for sleep."

"No. I'm not sleepy."

"But that is the time you grow, and think how strong you must grow if your father is going to be pleased when he comes home."

Alan's voice was muffled. "Does Father remember me?"

"Of course he does."

"Donald's father doesn't have to remember him. He comes home every night."

She slipped off the edge of the cot and sat down on the floor beside him, to make her serious face on a level with his. "Look at me, Alan."

He turned on his side to face her.

"Now, don't ever, ever forget. You have one of the most special fathers of anybody you've ever heard of. He is not like Donald's father, coming home every night with the pit dust all over his face so you can't tell who he is."

The boy began to smile.

"Archie MacNeil," she said the name proudly. "It is something to be the son of the bravest man in Cape Breton." She stood up and looked down at him. "But you must do your part and grow strong so he will be pleased when he comes home. It is hard for a boy not to have his father with him every night. It is hard for me, too. But think how much he misses us. Your father is so special that he had to go out into the world to do his work."

She touched his lids with her finger tips, but he was still unsatisfied. "Don't go yet, Mummy," he said.

She sat down on the side of the bed again.

"Mr. Camire doesn't come home with the pit on his face."

"Mr. Camire is different, too. He is a Frenchman from France, and he had a fine education."

"But he just lives in Mrs. MacPherson's house beyond the bridge."

"I know. But that's because he is a stranger here and he has to learn English better. I've told you all about it, Alan. Mr. Camire was a sailor and his ship was wrecked not far from here. You remember how excited everybody was when she went on the rocks."

The boy frowned. "I sort of do." He began to pleat a fold in her skirt. "Do you like Mr. Camire, Mummy?"

"He's a very nice man. He's kind as kind can be. Don't you like him, too?"

"If he's kind, I do." He smiled up at her. "If you like him, I like him too. I like everybody you like, Mummy."

She got to her feet. "Now then – it's time for you to sleep."

"Mummy?"

"Alan, I've got to go." But she laughed at him.

"Dr. Ainslie doesn't have the pit on his face. Is Father like Dr. Ainslie? I wish I could remember him, too."

She hesitated before she answered. As she walked to the door she said, "No, your father would not be like Dr. Ainslie at all."

"Is he stronger?"

"Oh, yes. He is much stronger."

"Is he better than Dr. Ainslie?"

"The questions you're asking me tonight!" She made a face of mock despair. "He is just different, Alan. Lots of men are different. Dr. Ainslie is a surgeon and he is a very fine, clever man. Some day perhaps you will be a doctor yourself. That would be wonderful, for he is the best doctor in town. Think of it! He studied so hard he went away to be a doctor in the United States and then he came home to help us here."

"Mr. Camire says Dr. Ainslie has a bad temper."

"Oh, he means nothing by that. Mr. Camire hardly even knows him."

"Mr. Camire doesn't like anybody but you."

"That is just his way. He is a Frenchman from France and he is lonely here without his friends. Now then, close your eyes and drop right off to sleep. And when I'm gone Mrs. MacDonald will look in, just to make sure you are safe and sound."

Two

DOWNSTAIRS the late light of evening was in the little parlor when Mollie pushed open the door. It was a room they had seldom used when Archie was home, but he had been away four years now and she had turned it into a workroom. In the center of the floor was a frame with a partially finished rug mounted on it and a debris of materials on the floor where she could put her hands on them as she worked. Against one wall stood a dresser with her best china displayed on its smooth top. In front of the window stood a solid table holding a glass lamp. Two rocking chairs, which Mollie now skirted in order to look at herself in the mirror that hung over the open coal grate, filled the room. There was one other piece of furniture in the corner, a tall whatnot reaching three quarters of the way to the ceiling.

She was touching a piece of chamois to her nose when she heard the grinding of wheels and knew the streetcar had cleared the bridge. Quickly she put on her hat and left the house, but when she reached the sidewalk she saw the tram as it stopped at the corner seventy-five yards up the row. There was no point in hurrying now. The tram took on its passengers, turned the corner and went on its way into Broughton. It would be half an hour before the next one followed.

Mollie went back into the house and stood quietly in the hall, wondering whether she ought not to work some more at the rug instead of going into Broughton to see the moving picture. But tomorrow was the Sabbath and this was the one night in the week she called her own; to break the routine she had made of the last four years was hard to do. It was the routine that had helped her forget how long four years could be.

She went back into the parlor and took off her hat. She looked at the rug and even picked up the hook, then she laid it down again. She touched a match to the wick in the lamp, turned it low, and then stood for some minutes considering her reflection in the mirror. She did not think she had changed much. Archie would find little difference in her if he came home now. An idea crossed her mind and she looked about the room until her eyes found a small framed photograph on the top shelf of the whatnot. She took it down and went back to the mirror, comparing her reflection with the girl in the picture until she admitted to herself that she had changed a great deal. She looked no more than a child in that wedding photograph as she stood hanging on to Archie's arm. They had both been so young; Archie twenty and she three years younger. She looked at Archie's thick hair and remembered the way it felt when her fingers brushed it the wrong way. He had never been able to part his hair, it had been so stiff. Even in that poor picture his eyes looked hurt and exposed, and no wonder, she thought, with the life his father had made for him. She had been the first person in all Broughton to understand and admire Archie – before he became a hero whom nobody understood and everyone admired.

She put the photograph back on the whatnot and then sighed without realizing she was doing so, as she passed the palms of her hands down the neat curves of her hips and flanks. For the first time in four years a thought opened wide in her mind as she tried to examine it. Would Archie ever come home? It was more than a year since he had sent any money and eight months since she had even received a postcard from him. But she knew where he was at the moment, and that was a lot more than she usually knew about him.

Did Archie ever intend to come home? She put the thought away again as she pulled open a drawer in the table by the window and took out a piece of newspaper which she had folded and stuffed in there the day before. Spreading it out flat on the table, she turned up the lamp and began to read it slowly, beginning with the Halifax dateline under the banner on the sports page. Archie's name was often to be found in this column, but never before had there been so much.

Up from New York comes word that Archie MacNeil's next opponent is being groomed for a shot at Jack Dillon's light-heavyweight title. They say this boy Packy Miller is quite a slugger and you can get odds at four to one that he'll beat Archie, and two to one he'll win by the knockout route. The fight's to be held in Trenton, New Jersey, by the way, Miller's home town.

If these odds are anywhere near right, all we can say is that Archie has gone a long way over the hill. We saw Packy Miller in Boston last fall, and the boy who fought that night couldn't have stayed in the same ring with the Archie MacNeil who flattened Tim O'Leary two years ago that great night in Providence.

Mollie remembered the fight with O'Leary, remembered what Archie's victory had meant to the men of Broughton and all the collieries roundabout. They had been as happy as though something beautiful had come into the lives of them all. She read on.

Archie's decline from the status of top-line contender to a trial horse fighting for peanuts calls for some pretty sharp questions about how well he's been managed. A long time ago – three months after the O'Leary fight to be exact – this column noted that Archie MacNeil was battling at the rate of once every ten days. What fighter can stand a pace like that? He was sent in at catchweights against George Chip before his left eye was healed from an old cut. Chip was ten pounds lighter, but he also happened to be the middleweight champion of the world, and what he did to Archie's eye that night wasn't funny. To our way of thinking, that particular fight was the turning point in the career of the boy from the mines.

Make no mistake, this boy Packy Miller is no George Chip. The odds may be heavy, but we have a hunch that Archie is going to win this one. He better had, because if he can't beat Miller there's no place else for him to go.

Mollie read the last sentence over again and tried to realize that the words referred to her husband. When she and Archie were married there had been no question of his becoming a prize fighter. That he was a brave and a good boxer she had known; so were lots of other boys in Broughton. She had even known that he was fierce, unpredictable, hated his work in the mine and sometimes got roaring drunk. So did many others. But she had always been able to quiet him and control him until he was calm again. Alan was too little to remember the excitement when his father won the middleweight championship of Canada in a fight in Halifax, thereby astonishing and delighting the whole of Cape Breton Island. Then the fat man with the bowler hat had come up from the Boston States to offer him big money for fighting.

Mollie closed her eyes and clasped her hands as she remembered the man. He had been so dreadful and Archie had not been able to see it. He was fat and pasty and his voice was a thin falsetto. He had only half a nose, and when she asked Archie what had happened to it, Archie laughed and told her that somebody had bitten it off years ago. That was the first time she had felt a whisper of fear that she might lose Archie. His lovely body – wide in the shoulders, narrow in the waist with rippling muscles all over – this was to be turned into a punching machine by an ugly fat man whose name was Sam Downey.

But to the men of Broughton, Archie was a hero. When he gave an exhibition before going away, six thousand Highlanders – men who had been driven from the outdoors into the pits where physical courage had become almost the only virtue they could see clearly and see all the time – paid to watch him fight. They loved him because he was giving significance, even a crude beauty, to the clumsy courage they all felt in themselves.

Mollie stuffed the newspaper back in the drawer and went out to the kitchen to look at the alarm clock. The next tram was due in twelve minutes, but she wanted to get out of the house. She left the door unlocked so that Mrs. MacDonald could come in later in the evening, and began walking slowly towards the corner.

It was a far different scene now from the one which she and Alan had passed on their way home from the beach that afternoon. The miners' row was quiet. The sun had set and the long afterglow of a June evening was flooding scattered clouds with red and saffron and then with bronze. Below the clouds the earth was darkening fast and the whole area seemed uncannily silent with the men in town for Saturday night.

"And where do you think *you're* going?"

Mollie started at the bitterness in the voice and brought her eyes down from the sky to see the withered face of Mrs. MacCuish staring at her from the steps of a neighboring house. The old woman's husband had been killed in a mine accident fifteen years before, and one of her sons was married and two others had gone to the States. The old woman sat alone on her steps smoking a clay pipe and looking up and down the row. Mollie disregarded her because it was said that she was no longer right in her mind.

"All day long you do nothing at all whateffer and in the nights you enjoy yourself. You whill pay for it when himself comes home."

Mollie was relieved when she had passed the old woman and was out of earshot, for the old voice was thin and high. Other women sitting on their doorsteps spoke to her in kind soft voices and she answered them. The women were always on the steps on a fine evening like this when their men were in town. They sat there in the gathering twilight whispering like spirits, some of the older ones speaking in Gaelic, the others in English with a strong Gaelic accent. As she passed the fourth house, Mollie saw that the women on the steps were turning to look farther up the row where Angus the Barraman, another MacNeil though no relation of Archie, was kneeling on the ground in front of a washtub. His wife stood over him, and everyone in the row knew this meant that Angus had escaped his wife before she had been able to get her hands on his pay and had got drunk before he had even washed the coal dust off his face. As Mollie neared them she could hear Mrs. Angus scolding and Angus grunting back at her through a foam of suds.

Something she said which Mollie couldn't hear must have been more than he could take, for suddenly he rose in a rage and heaved over the tub. The water splashed her skirt and her shoes as he stood there, lean, angular, wet and only half-washed.

Out of the suds came his voice. "Hold your tongue, woman, or by Chesus, I whill be angry at you!"

"Your own wife," said Mrs. Angus, ignoring the water at her feet, "and efferybody looking at you, and efferybody able to hear you, moreoffer!"

"You and the lot of them!" the Barraman shouted. "There iss a place where you can go!"

"And what whill Father Donald be saying when I tell him where the pay hass gone this week?"

"Father Donald hass my permission to buggerize hisself iff he would say a man cannot spend hiss pay without the old woman foreffer asking where it goes. Would I be saying no to Red Whillie when he iss happy?"

"Red Whillie! So it wass him you wass with? I might haff known it."

Angus picked up the tub in both hands and smashed it down on the ground. The wood was too well seasoned to break, but the tub bounced and hit his wife on the foot and she began to jump up and down on one leg, holding the ankle of the other.

"Into the house, by Chesus," Mollie heard Angus roar, "or I whill show you what else I can do!"

Mrs. Angus gave him a bitter look before she turned her back and limped into the house. As the door slammed behind her, Angus the Barraman sat down on his front step, the suds beginning to melt on his face and the wet coal dust like a black scum patching his naked chest and flanks. He sat there with his chin in his hands staring across the road at the field beyond, and Mollie took care not to look at him as she passed, for when the Barraman was sober he was always conscious of his dignity and she did not wish to embarrass him now by watching him when he was at a disadvantage.

When she had passed she could hear him begin to croon a Gaelic song to himself. It was as soft and plaintive as the cry of a sea bird lost in the fog.

The reason for the tart remarks Mrs. MacCuish had made became apparent as she neared the lamppost with the white band around it, at the corner. Louis Camire was standing under it, and from his position she knew he had probably been waiting for some time.

"Hullo!" she said when she reached him, letting him see that she was glad to find him there.

"I thought maybe you would be going into town tonight," he said without emphasis. "*Mon Dieu*, it is a miserable place, that theater, but it is a place to go."

She noticed that Camire was wearing his best suit, the one he had bought in Sydney which always made him look more foreign than when he was in working clothes. Compared to the bulky Highlanders of Broughton, he seemed a very small man. Even with his padded shoulders he looked frail, but she knew he was wiry and quick, for he had already earned the reputation of being able to take care of himself.

"You look verree nice," he said in his strong French accent. "Some day I would like to buy you fine clothes." He shrugged his shoulders. "But there are no fine clothes 'ere. What a place!"

"It is not so bad as you think it is," she said.

She forced herself to look away from him. For four years she had been alone except for Alan; it made her afraid of the look in his eyes. She still knew little about him. It was believed that he had run away from France to escape military service. It was an explanation which satisfied those who could think of no other reason why a young Frenchman should have been sailing under the Italian flag and then elected not to return with his mates from the wrecked ship. Whenever Mollie asked him about France his voice became wistful. His father had a business in an ancient town in the south of France, he said. Some day he might go back to it. He said he was a socialist and that a great revolution was coming. For a time he had tried to advance himself in the local of the union, but he got nowhere with the men, who were friendly enough to him personally while they dismissed him as a foreigner who talked too much. To Mollie he talked about many things she could not understand, and he wanted to talk about other things she understood only too well. That was why she was half afraid of him. She knew he wanted to be her lover and she knew he was even more lonely than she was herself. On an evening like this she tried not to think about the feeling he gave her.

"'Ow is the boy?" he asked.

"Oh, we had such a lovely afternoon on the shore! He is asleep now. At least I hope he is." Her expression changed. "Louis, something is the matter with your eyes! They're all red."

He shrugged. "Coal smoke is not an ointment for ophthalmia."

"You ought to see Dr. Ainslie."

"I would have to be very sick before I see 'im."

"But Dr. Ainslie would help you. He is the best doctor in the whole town."

"Me, I think 'e is a son of a bitch."

"If you would know him," Mollie went on eagerly, "you would not think so. He is the kindest man. Alan goes to play by the brook near his house and the doctor lets him. Whenever Mrs. Ainslie sees him she always speaks to him." As Camire made no comment she added, "Mrs. Ainslie is very fond of children, I shouldn't wonder."

Camire rolled a cigarette, twisted the end, lifted his foot and scratched a match on the sole of his pointed tan shoe. He spoke through a puff of tobacco smoke, his eyes squinting as some of the smoke got into them and irritated their already smarting membranes.

"This wife of the *docteur*," he said, "she is another thing. She 'as a figure like a statue before the Hôtel de Ville in my town." He made generous curving movements with his hands. "But what does she do with a figure like that, eh? Not one damn thing. No children. Name of God! Or maybe it is the *docteur* that is no good."

Mollie broke into a soft musical laugh. She knew it was only his way, to talk like this.

"There is nothing the matter with Mrs. Ainslie," she said. "Or with the doctor, either. Everybody knows they have had bad luck."

He pointed his cigarette at her. "According to you, there is nothing the matter with anybody. You like them all. When some woman 'as a baby, you go in to wash her dishes for her." The cigarette kept jerking towards her to emphasize his points. "That *docteur!* Sometimes 'e says good-morning. So that makes 'im a lovely man." Again the cigarette jerked. "That is why you are always the underdog."

She wanted Camire to be happy, and she wanted him to like her and to understand that people here were kind no matter what people were like in France.

"No, Louis – the doctor is a special man. He knows more than we do and he works so hard he sometimes goes two or three whole days without even sleeping."

Camire shrugged his shoulders. She could not understand why he made things so hard for himself and it troubled her.

"This *docteur*," he said, "'e talks to people like dirt."

"He's just tired, and everybody knows he has no patience with nonsense."

"'E thinks 'e is better than everybody else. Does 'e say *Mister* Camire? Does 'e say *Mister* MacDonald? No. But who pays 'im? The workers pay 'im. Every month thirty cents comes off their pay for that fine 'ouse 'e lives in. You are the bosses, but every time 'e comes along, what 'appens? You take off your caps and thank 'im for doing what you pay 'im for." Camire kicked a pebble with his pointed shoe. "Let me tell you something. There is no future in being the underdog."

She put her hand on his arm to quiet his excitement. "But, Louis, nobody here is an underdog."

"No?" He looked at her with a scorn she knew was not for herself but for the ideas she held. He pointed to the hideous mass of the bankhead towering up to the sky on his right. "Who owns that?"

"The company owns it, of course."

"And 'ow much money would the company make if you did not let yourselves be underdogs? This is Saturday night.

At MacDonald's Corner there will soon be at least fifty men fighting each other. Do they fight the company? No, they fight with their fists against each other, every Saturday night, for the sport."

"But nobody wants another strike. Four years ago there was a terrible strike. And the men like fighting. It makes them feel better to show each other what they can do."

His short silence made her hope that he might be trying to understand her point, but when he spoke again she sighed.

"You admire this *docteur*," he said, "because you think the education is a fine thing, and 'e 'as maybe just a little bit of education. At the same time you admire that *salaud* Red Willie MacIsaac because *le bon Dieu* gave 'im a body ten times too big for the brain of the mouse that 'e 'as in 'is 'ead. You –"

"But nobody admires Red Willie!" She was laughing at him.

"So you stay the underdogs. Because you think it is better to be Scottish than to 'ave some sense. You think it is better to 'ave the big fist than to 'ave the big brain."

She pressed his arm with her fingers. "Louis, you don't understand. Everybody admires Dr. Ainslie because he has a very big brain. The men know he likes them even when he scolds them. They know he wants them to improve."

He looked at her with exasperation. Then his eyes softened and he drew closer to her, folded her hand under his arm and stopped talking. They stood quietly for several minutes waiting for the tram, but the long slope down to the bridge remained empty and there was no sound of wheels grinding in the distance.

"When I made shipwreck," he said more quietly, "I said to myself, so – this is a new country and I am sick of waiting for the revolution to change things at 'ome. I will stay 'ere. So I stay, and what the 'ell do I find? I find it is older than France. There is no organization. Labor in France – that is something. It 'as organization. But 'ere you do not even know the most necessary thing. The men who run the world, they are sons of bitches, and you do not know that." Then he smiled at her and his eyes were liquid. "But you are 'ere, too, and you are something else. Me, I am the one man in this place that knows what you could be."

She knew it was better to smile than to say anything. The loneliness in his eyes was so great she wanted to stroke his forehead to take the look away.

Three

SUNSETS were always lovely in the grounds of the big red house on the other side of the bridge where the doctor lived. The afterglow filtered through white birches and the light westerly air was fresh with balsam; it had reached the doctor's house from the hinterland of the island without crossing a single colliery on the way. Shadows of trees lay in a net over the white gravel of the drive leading to the main road. The grassy intervale on the east side of the house was brimming with darkness and soft with the sound of a brook. The water bubbled around a tree-lined curve at the bottom of the inter-vale, ran true for seventy yards, turned again under the bridge and disappeared. It was hard to believe, in the grounds of the doctor's house, that the beginning of the miners' row was less than a quarter of a mile away.

While Mollie had been preparing to leave her house, the doctor's wife had already gone out of hers and now was standing on a patch of lawn on the south side, surveying her roses. Margaret Ainslie was a tall woman, almost statuesque, with a singer's chest, a narrow waist and splendid curving hips. Her skin was creamy and her hair a rich chestnut. Her lips were full and soft, but that Margaret herself was not soft was apparent from the line of her chin. For all the oval grace of its curve, her chin was a strong and stubborn one. Fine lines about her eyes showed how often she laughed, and the lift at the corners of her mouth revealed her essential optimism.

When she bent over the rose bed to cut some flowers, her movements had the decisive simplicity of a woman who has always known what she wanted. Tonight she wanted two red roses and a white one and she was frustrated by the illogicality of nature. Her red roses had bloomed ten days before her whites, and now her fine Frau Karl Drueschkes, more creamy white than the skin of her own shoulders, were virtually wasted. One white rose with two or three reds was magnificent; a white rose alone looked drab. But the Frau Karls were now opening and there were no other roses ready to be cut, so she snipped two of the white roses and took them into the house.

In the kitchen she put them in a blue Delft vase and started towards her husband's office. Coming out into the hall with the vase in her hand, she saw the surgery door open and the library door closed. This meant that Daniel Ainslie had finished reading the article in the *British Medical Journal* and had shut himself up in the library to study Greek. Margaret's face took on the strangely serene expression it always showed when she was annoyed or frustrated. She had scarcely seen her husband all week and now she knew it would be at least three hours before she saw him again.

She sighed and entered the surgery. It was a grim room, but one she respected, for she had some notion of the quality of the work that was done in it. Its walls were brown and two of them were lined with bottle-crowded shelves. Most of the bottles contained drugs and medicines, for in Broughton there was no central dispensary and the various colliery physicians dispensed the drugs they prescribed. Behind a white screen in one corner were the burners and scales and test tubes of a small laboratory. On other shelves was a sinister array of bottles containing anatomical specimens from Ainslie's numerous autopsies – sections of diseased livers and kidneys, of arthritic bones, of a rheumatic heart, an appendix or two, tonsils and various other organs which Margaret could identify only by inspecting the labels. Beneath the shelves of drugs was a black leather couch with a white sheet folded neatly at its head, on which thousands of patients had stretched out for examination.

Margaret went to her husband's desk and tidied it, looked at his engagement pad and saw that it was clear for tonight and reflected ruefully that in his practice a clear pad meant nothing. Saturday night was always busy, though there was generally a lull between dinner and eleven o'clock, when the first petty casualties from the brawls in Broughton appeared at the surgery door with hangdog faces, black eyes and broken noses.

She set the two white roses on his desk and was about to leave the room when the telephone rang. She picked up the receiver and spoke into the telephone and as she listened her eyes fell on the three photographs which had hung on the wall over this desk all the ten years of their life together. One was Lord Lister, another was Sir William Osler, and the third was Ainslie's chief and her own dear friend, old Dr. Dougald MacKenzie, the chief surgeon in the Broughton Hospital.

"All right, Miss MacKay," she said into the phone. "I'll tell the doctor right away."

She hung up the receiver and left the room, and now the serenity had left her face because she was sorry for her husband. During the past three nights he had slept no more than a total of eleven hours, not counting the hour or two he might have dozed in his carriage. This morning he had performed five operations and then he had made his calls and seen patients in his surgery all afternoon.

She opened the library door and saw Daniel's head turned sideways as he looked up a word in the huge Greek lexicon on the left side of his desk. She hated that volume as a woman hates her husband's mistress. She feared it because it stood for something in his nature she could never touch. Why a brilliant doctor who worked as he did should feel impelled to become a master of Greek she had never been able to understand, especially as nobody else in town except Dr. Dougald and the minister could read a line of the language.

"Dan, I'm sorry, but Miss MacKay just called. It's the wife of the new manager at Number Six."

"Oh!" But he did not turn around. He shifted his head from the lexicon to the text and made a note in the margin.

"I told Miss MacKay you'd go in right away."

"All right." Still he did not move.

"Dan – will you be all night?"

"Probably. It's her first and she's got a bad heart."

"Then I might as well spend the night at Mother's. But I do wish you didn't have to go."

He was still bending over his Greek, squeezing the last moment from it, when she left the room and went upstairs. When she came down again she found him moving about in the surgery. She sat on the black sofa and waited while he packed his worn doctor's bag.

"If it weren't for that woman," he said, "I could have got through at least a hundred and fifty lines tonight. I set myself the whole of the *Odyssey* for this year and it's June already and I've only done five books so far."

Margaret tried to laugh. "Dan, for goodness' sake – what you need is a rest, not more Greek. Why don't you call in a locum and take a trip somewhere? You haven't been away for six years."

"What's the use? Unless I put at least two thousand miles between me and this practice, I'd be called back in less than a week."

She knew he was keeping his emotional distance from her. They had quarreled far too much lately, Margaret thought, and she knew now – had known it clearly since talking with Dr. Dougald last Thursday – that much of the misunderstanding had been her own fault. Now more than anything else she wanted him to stay home and after a while go upstairs with her where they could lie warmly in bed together like other people and she could show him how much she loved him. But he was tired so much of the time and his hours were so irregular. Beyond that, he had never been an easy man to love. There seemed to be a diamond in him in place of a heart.

Yet as she followed his movements as he went between instrument cabinet and his brown leather bag, she knew her judgment was wrong. It was only his surface that was hard; inside was a hungry tenderness which she seemed powerless to answer. Inside Dan Ainslie was a humility so basic and profound it frightened her. No matter how good his work might be, she knew it would never be good enough to satisfy him. Not once had it occurred to him how strong was his own personality; how much men and women were moved to try to earn his approval. In his own eyes he was always falling short of an ideal she had never seen clearly enough to understand. He grumbled about the stupidity of others and wounded nearly everyone by his surface rudeness, and of course it never occurred to those he hurt that this was one of his ways of finding fault with himself.

Margaret smiled, but he was too engrossed to notice her change of expression. If it were not for his work, she thought, he would be intolerable. He was one of those rare doctors who invariably seem able to take a patient's ills upon themselves. She knew this and she reverenced the devotion which made him exhaust himself. There had been innumerable nights when she lay awake upstairs and heard his feet pacing the floor, back and forth from the surgery to the hall, the library, the dining room, while she had lain helplessly alone in bed knowing that he was doing more than ponder a case. He was trying to *be* his patient, to find a way to convince him that he would not die.

As he bent over his desk to make a note on his pad, a lock of hair fell over his forehead and he brushed it back with a gesture unnecessarily quick and impatient. He had soft black hair which he was ashamed of because his father, whom he had both feared and revered, had been a burly, red-haired Highlander. The dark hair came from the rarely mentioned mother who had died when Daniel was ten. His lithe physique came from her, too, and his large, dark eyes which tonight looked like those of an animal who has been chased for miles and knows he has still farther to run.

With an abrupt movement he straightened his shoulders and clenched his fingers on the handles of his bag. "All right," he said. "Are you ready? I didn't take the harness off the mare. I knew something like this would happen. All I have to do is back her into the shafts."

They went out together, the surgery door clicked behind them, and while Ainslie prepared the carriage Margaret stood on the white gravel drive and looked up at the sky. Colored clouds, darkening fast, were sailing seaward over the treetops and the sound of the brook was as soft as sleep. It was an hour of day that always made her feel lonely, and the persistent wish for children filled her once again. When Ainslie led the horse by the bridle to the door, she stepped into the carriage and they drove out to the main road, turned left, passed over the bridge and settled back against the seat while the mare plodded up the steep slope in front of the miners' row. They passed the women on the steps and Angus the Barraman still sitting half-naked with the suds on his face. Gaunt against the darker sky of the east, but rose-colored in the lingering light of sunset, the bankhead of the colliery rose before them. They neared the corner with Ainslie silent and absorbed, and it was Margaret who saw the waiflike figure of Mollie MacNeil standing under the lamppost waiting for the tram. Camire, on seeing the approaching carriage, had drawn away from her, and Mollie seemed to be alone.

"Let's stop and drive her into town," Margaret said.

Without looking up, Ainslie said out of his thoughts, "Drive who into town?"

"Mollie MacNeil. She's such a nice girl and she's having such a hard time."

"What else did she expect when she married that blackguard?"

But when they reached the corner he suddenly pulled in the mare and called out, "Are you going into town?"

Mollie hesitated and Margaret saw her glance at the small, wiry figure of Camire. "Yes, I am going into town, Doctor."

"Then get in." Ainslie's hands were impatient on the reins. "Be quick about it. I'm on my way to the hospital."

Margaret moved nearer her husband, doubtful about Camire but seeing no sign from the Frenchman that he expected Mollie to remain with him.

"Come along, my dear," Margaret said. "We'd love to have you."

Still Mollie hesitated. "I would be in the way."

"If there wasn't room I wouldn't have stopped," Ainslie said.

If he had noticed Camire's presence, he gave no sign, and the authority in his voice decided Mollie. She climbed into the carriage and sat as far on the outside as she could, giving only one more quick glance in Camire's direction. The Frenchman's back was still turned. Ainslie flicked the reins and sent the mare around the corner on her trot into town. They passed the long wire fence enclosing the company's property, came to a short stretch of vacant land tilting eastward towards the cliffs and then passed the stark and ragged outlines of solitary wind-torn pines and thin cattle bending to the sparse grass.

Margaret said, "How is Alan? I haven't seen him lately."

Mollie glanced at the doctor's profile before answering. "Thank you, Mrs. Ainslie, but Alan is fine. We were on the shore all this afternoon."

"That must have been lovely."

"It was indeed."

"Don't you worry when you leave him alone at night?"

"It is not often, and Mrs. MacDonald has promised to drop in to see him, moreover. Alan never gets into trouble like other boys."

Margaret's manner showed the warmth of her interest. She knew all the miners' families and the private stories of most of them, for they all loved her and often the men hung about in the woods near the house waiting for the doctor to leave; when he did they promptly presented themselves at the door of the surgery to get their quotas of medicine from the Doctor's Missus. They liked the way she smiled when she talked to them about their families.

Ainslie, who had seemed lost in his own thoughts, broke into the conversation. "I suppose he'll soon be going to school?"

"Alan has been to school for two years now," Mollie answered. "He just finished his second grade."

Ainslie said, "Och! The school here is a disgrace."

"Indeed, Doctor, I and Archie have often worried over the school."

"Archie? I can imagine you worrying, but I can't see Archie fashing himself over his son's schooling." Ainslie let out the short laugh which Margaret had come to loathe, for it indicated anger as well as contempt. She understood it, but she was sure nobody else did. He wanted them all to be wonderful and gallant like the Highlanders of legend, and he was angry when they were not.

"Archie never got beyond second grade himself, I shouldn't think," he added.

"Oh, no, Doctor. Archie passed the seventh grade." She went on hastily. "I know he has been gone a long time, but he has not been lucky in the States, and he will come home when he can."

"Four years is pretty hard on you and the boy."

"Oh, but Doctor, it is harder on Archie himself. You should have seen him with Alan before he went away. He was so proud."

Ainslie said, "Och!" again, and then added, "So proud he became a prize fighter and hasn't come back once since he went away. I suppose it looked easier to him than the mines."

The carriage swayed down the rutted road towards town, a dog came out of some scrub to snap at the hocks of the mare and Ainslie flicked it off with his whip. Margaret decided to draw Mollie's attention from her husband's words by small talk.

"I noticed that our friend Angus the Barraman started in early tonight." "Oh, Mrs. Ainslie, isn't it a shame how Angus drinks these days?" "When Angus is sober, no man could be nicer." "But sometimes he gets the black feelings, and then it is only a drop and he is in liquor over his eyes." "Well, Mollie . . ." Margaret's musical laugh rang out. "You know what the Reverend MacAlistair says – first it's a thimbleful, then it's a glassful, then it's a bucketful and then it's too late!" "The night Red Willie MacIsaac beat Mick Casey he drank a bucket in MacGillivray's saloon." "Nonsense, Mollie, no one could drink a bucket of whiskey at one time and live. Red Willie's your neighbor, isn't he?"

The last color had drained out of the sky and the moon was growing bright. As they passed a cluster of miners walking together towards the town the men all tugged their caps and said good night to the Doctor and the Doctor's Missus.

Suddenly Ainslie's voice snapped out a question. "Who's that dark little fellow who was standing on the corner with you?"

"Do you mean Mr. Camire, Doctor?"

"Camire? What sort of a name is that?"

"He is a Frenchman from France."

"What's he do here?"

"He is now a timekeeper at Number Four."

"Dan," Margaret interrupted. "I told you about that young man. He was on the Italian ship that was wrecked and when the rest of the crew was taken back to Italy, he stayed here. Mother knows him. He was working in a store on Wellington Street for a time and she heard he could play the guitar and sing beautifully. She says he lived in Venice once."

"Oh, no," Mollie said. "Mr. Camire is a Frenchman even if he was on board an Italian ship. But he sings lovely songs."

They were on the outskirts of the town now and suddenly the glow of many street lights in the distance drowned the soft shadows of the twilight. Throughout every colliery surrounding Broughton, as well as in the heart of the town itself, the lights came on at the same moment, night after night.

"This Camire," Ainslie said. "He was in jail, wasn't he?"

Mollie's answer was quick. "For ten days he was in jail, Doctor, but it was a mistake."

"That's what people generally go to jail for, isn't it?"

"But it was the mistake of the magistrate."

Ainslie indicated his disbelief.

"But Doctor, it truly was not Mr. Camire's fault this time." Her eagerness to explain turned into a sudden bubble of laughter. "We all laughed at him when we heard. Poor Mr. Camire! But for him it was not funny at all. You see, he had no English then, and there he was in court and the rest of them were all so big and he was so small trying to stand up for himself without knowing a thing about what was going on. There was the magistrate with his red beard looking like Jehovah in the church window, and how could Mr. Camire know that behind the beard there was nothing at all but old MacKeegan?"

Ainslie said, "MacKeegan's a jackass, but he doesn't send a man to jail without cause."

"Let Mollie tell the story," Margaret interrupted. "You weren't there, so how do you know what happened?"

Mollie set out to explain and forgot her shyness in the telling. "It was one of those days, Doctor, when MacKeegan's courtroom was full to the doors, for it was the Monday after the biggest fight of all in MacDonald's Corner. Big Alec McCoubrie looks very fine in his brass buttons, and I know it is true he is strong enough to burst his uniform if he swells out his chest, but he can't see anything in the dark, Doctor, and he is not too smart in the daylight, either. Imagine Big Alec arresting Mr. Camire thinking he was Holy John MacEachern – but that is what he did; and on Monday morning there was Mr. Camire in court with the rest of them."

Mollie began to imitate the magistrate's accent as she continued to explain and Margaret smiled, hoping the story would not irritate her husband.

"'What are *you* up to?'" Mollie went on, her gentle voice suddenly as hoarse and broad as MacKeegan's. "'Wass it fightin' or wass it just tomcattin' around?' And of course," she continued in her natural voice, "not being able to understand the English, what could Mr. Camire do but stand there and shake his head? 'Now then, *you*,' said MacKeegan, 'you answer me – are you ghuilty or are you not ghuilty?' And Mr. Camire just stood there, not being able to understand. 'So the prisoner cannot speak English! Can you speak Gaelic?' And still Mr. Camire could not understand. 'The prisoner cannot speak Gaelic. Can you speak French?' And how could Mr. Camire know what old MacKeegan meant when he said it just like that? After MacKeegan said 'Can you speak Gherman,' that was all the languages he had ever heard of, so then he got mad and he grabbed his beard with both hands the way he does and he shouted out loud, 'I haff talked to this little bugger in four different languages and he hass not answered me in one. I say he iss as ghuilty as hell!'"

Margaret laughed in the hope of forestalling a comment from her husband, but the comment came.

"This town," Ainslie said flatly, "has far too many liars in it."

Mollie stiffened and her eagerness turned to a sudden dignity. "What I was telling was true, Doctor, and the language included. If you do not believe me you can ask Mr. Sutherland, the lawyer."

Ainslie let out a sigh of exasperation. "I wasn't calling *you* a liar. I was merely trying to suggest that you shouldn't believe everything you hear – whether you hear it from Mr. Sutherland or anybody else."

"I'm sorry, Doctor." She was still aloof in her dignity.

"There's nothing for you to be sorry for. I'm sorry for the – the general childishness of this whole place."

Margaret sighed inwardly. It was too frustrating to a mind like his to be constantly irritated by people he wanted to love and admire. She turned to Mollie. "Tell me some more about Alan. He's growing so fast. What would you like him to be when he grows up?"

They were well into the town now and the mare was taking the left turn towards the bridge over the inner harbor of Broughton.

"I would like for Alan to grow up to be a doctor, but it is not a thing I expect, Mrs. Ainslie. It would be bad for us to have too high ideas. Maybe Alan could be a minister. He's different, I know he is. And if his father is successful, Alan will have a fine education."

Mollie's answer seemed almost unbearably poignant to Margaret, for she knew that the boy *was* exceptional and she also knew that the odds were against any future for him but a life in the mines. Mollie herself came of worthy people; her father had been an elder in the church and it was said in the district that after her marriage he had never spoken to her again. When people began to talk about Archie as a fighter, she remembered Dr. Dougald saying that in spite of his family Archie wasn't too bad a boy. He had certainly been handsome and he had moved with the sure, reckless grace of a wild animal, but he had been restless and moody, and when he began to drink his eyes had flamed out of his face with the desperate look that was only too familiar in those of the young men who came to realize they had been trapped by the mines.

"You're living in a fool's paradise," she heard Dan saying, "if you think a man like Archie MacNeil is going to be any help towards that boy's bettering of himself."

Mollie stiffened as if he had struck her. "Archie is my husband, Doctor, and I am proud of him."

"Have you ever seen a professional boxing match?"

"Indeed I have not."

"Well, it's a brutal spectacle. Some people call it sport. If so, it's the only sport I know in which the objective is the injury of another man."

Mollie was trembling and Margaret said, "Dan, I don't think this is any of our business." To the girl she said, "The doctor didn't mean to be unkind."

"I know, Mrs. Ainslie. It is terrible, the life Archie is leading. They say he is getting too old to fight now, but he is only twenty-eight. Whenever he has a fight I feel so bad in here –" she pressed her hand against her stomach – "I can hardly eat my supper. I never thought he would fight for money, Mrs. Ainslie, but he was such a beautiful boxer they led him into it. And when he went away I thought, Well at least he will make money for Alan's education. But he has not even made money for anything."

The mare clopped over a bridge spanning a tongue-shaped inlet from the harbor. Fishing boats and potato schooners were moored at jetties farther out and a cluster of dories lay nearer the bridge. Three young men were leaning on the railing of the bridge engaged in a spitting contest with the closest dory as a target. "We should be haffing Big Alec McCoubrie here," Margaret heard one of them say in a melancholy lilt. She smelled the old familiar odor of drying fish and remembered her childhood when the harbor was more important than it was now, when Broughton was a small town with only a few collieries nosing their way into a back area, when all the land on the left-hand side of the bridge had been a field belonging to her father. In those days the bridge was on the edge of the town. Now the field had disappeared and the core of the business section had swallowed it. The mare entered a narrow main street with lighted store fronts close on either side, lampposts crooked and raw holding up incandescent lights which made the pavement look blue and naked, and narrow sidewalks between the stores and the street swarming with aimless people, as always on Saturday night. Among the many carriages on the street were a few motorcars.

Ainslie reined up before the motion picture theater where, so Margaret had heard, an audience could watch slapstick comedies, serials about cowboys, gypsies, cops and bathing beauties, and morality plays about nice young Americans who went hellward by way of drink and cards.

"I suppose this is what you came into town for?" he said.

"It is a change, Doctor, and it only costs ten cents."

When Mollie stepped from the carriage she looked at them both, and Margaret's eyes moved quickly from the girl's face to her husband's. She saw the strong, tense lines about his mouth relax and then tighten again, and she knew that he felt infinitely sorry for this girl.

Mollie looked up at him with the helpless dignity of a gentle person who has lost her way. "Doctor," she said, "I would like you to understand something because you have always been kind to us. I know many things here are bad for Alan, but I will not be talking to him against his father. It is not good for Archie to be away, but it would be worse for a boy not to be proud of his father."

Suddenly Margaret had the queer feeling that comes of having thought one was with two strangers, only to find out obliquely that they are friends. Her husband and this girl understood each other in a way she herself would never be able to understand either of them, because Daniel had been born in the same kind of poverty as Mollie had known. Margaret had not only never been poor, she was not even Scottish. Her family had been Loyalists with ancestors who had been prominent in Massachusetts before the Revolution. Her father had been born on the main peninsula of Nova Scotia, and though she had grown up in Broughton, Margaret had never been able to think of the Highlanders here as anything but strange.

But when Ainslie answered Mollie, Margaret lost her feeling of queerness. If he understood this girl – if he understood any woman who ever lived – he certainly knew how to disguise his knowledge.

"In my opinion there are some men who don't deserve to have sons at all," he said. "The fact of the matter is that Alan is your total responsibility. His future is up to you, and telling him fairy tales about what a fine man his father is won't help him in the least."

Margaret saw Mollie looking across her at her husband and she realized that the girl was not hurt. She seemed to understand that his words were not hostile. These Gaelic people, Margaret thought, had lived close together in small places for so long they could somehow communicate with each other in a way no one else could fathom. To Margaret, words meant exactly what they said. To her husband, words always meant either more or much less than they did to her.

"I have not told Alan his father fights for money," Mollie went on, still looking at Ainslie with the sad dignity in her large, dark eyes. "The men are always telling him how strong his father is, but that his father fights for money Alan does not know. And I hope he never will."

Margaret put her hand on her husband's knee and leaned away from him. "We'll say good night now, Mollie," she said, and then she smiled at the girl.

Mollie turned away and Ainslie started the mare up the street. Behind them a tram clanged its bell and Margaret glanced over her shoulder in time to see Camire join Mollie in front of the picture house. So they had been together after all! Why couldn't she have said so, instead of pretending to be alone?

The sound of the mare's hoofs echoed back from the store fronts as she clopped up Wellington Street. The mare's mouth felt Ainslie's tension as he jerked the left-hand rein and she tossed her head in protest before obeying and taking the turn into the street where Margaret's mother lived.

"Dan," she said. "It's doing you no good staying here year after year. Sometimes I think the only reason why you stay is because you're afraid to leave."

Ainslie's jaw hardened, but he made no reply until he had reined in the mare before the white house where Margaret's mother lived with her three daughters who were still unmarried. "They are probably all waiting for you," he said. His voice was cool, distant and courteous, and it frightened her, for she knew that the words she had said would continue to corrode deeply into his mind.

She put her hand on his knee again. "It's stupid for us to quarrel."

"Were we quarreling? I hadn't thought so."

"We can't go on forever like this. When there are only the two of us together it's dreadful if we can't understand each other."

He sat silently, holding the reins in his long fingers. Margaret knew she had hurt him and he was locking himself away in his pride.

"Please don't work too hard tonight," she said.

"That's not a matter of choice." He gave a slight shrug. "What is there to do but work?"

"Dan, do you know how cruel it is for you to say that to me?" But there was no expression of hurt on her face; experience had taught her to transform the frustration she felt to a look of cool serenity. She stepped from the carriage and was about to go up the path to the house when she turned and spoke again. "I won't see you until church tomorrow?"

"Probably not."

She went on up the path. She heard music and the stir of many feet on the polished floor of the big front parlor, and suddenly she was happy again. The door of her mother's house opened and her youngest sister was there to welcome her with a smile. Margaret forced herself not to look back at her husband, though she knew the carriage had not moved.

Four

WHEN THE DOOR CLOSED, Ainslie felt a smart of tears behind his eyes and the loneliness came down on him. He looked at the rambling house and he let himself feel angry about it because it was a thing he could consider objectively. Margaret's father, Noah Eldridge, had built the house and while he lived Ainslie had liked him, though he had never greatly respected the man. But Mrs. Eldridge, Margaret's mother, Ainslie disliked frankly and openly. She lived there like a queen bee, surrounded by a large and adoring family who worshiped her. To him, she had always seemed semialien, a selfish, superficial woman with no standards of education whatever. In his mind he always called her a Yankee, without any thought for the political significance of the word, because she stood for a state of mind opposed to everything his own emotions honored. Things came easily to people like the Eldridges and they were always ready to take the easy way out of a situation. Ainslie clucked at the mare and turned her about in the narrow street, then he leaned back and let the animal find her own way to the hospital.

The sadness, the sense of irreparable loss, persisted in him. As he sniffed the air he remembered an evening like this when he had been a boy of nineteen, earning money before the

mast during his summer vacation from college. He had put
out from North Sydney on the last of old Eldridge's barks and
the wind had been so right they had been able to set stuns'ls
before clearing Cranberry Head. The memory of that night
had lasted with him all these years. The westerly wind had
flattened the sea so that the keel was as firm as a dock, but the
wind had been strong and held the sails as hard as iron. All
that night at sea he had smelled forests, for the wind that blew
them to Newfoundland had previously traversed the length
of Nova Scotia and come to them laden with the pungent
scent of balsam. Those had been good days. The past had still
been honorable, unblighted by the mines. The whole world
had seemed too small to hold his future.

Now that future was the present, and what had it brought?
Only an end to seeing ahead. Not even posterity. Just the
moment of hard work. The memory of work endlessly hard.
The memory of striving, straining, heaving the huge rock up
the hill with the feeling that if he relaxed for a moment it
would become the rock of Sisyphus and roar down to the
valley bottom again. Was defiance all that remained?

The mare turned into Wellington Street and Ainslie's body
shifted position. His loneliness became a hungry desire. If
only Margaret had smiled at him he would have felt differently,
but she smiled at others so much more easily than she did for
him. He still thought she was the most beautiful woman he had
ever met, except for her eyes. There was no smoke in her eyes,
no mystery, nor any sense of it; instead there was a fearless
clarity that could look steadily at anything short of a Gaelic
ghost. Her white body was like a hill of snow under the moon.
It was tantalizingly lovely, it was unbelievably beautiful, yet he
had never seemed able to reach its inner warmth or to feel that
he had come home to her. Her body lived in its own right,
unconscious, never seeming a part of that mind of hers which
always appeared to be observing him coolly, thoughtfully, with

common sense always trying to improve him, never selfish, never demanding. And yet he knew she was lonely, too, and that he had made her so.

Into his thoughts came the face of Mollie MacNeil, the face of his own people. They were all lost here in the mines. They were inextricably lost in their own sea-deep feelings and crazy dreams. And Margaret had said he was unkind to the girl!

As the mare took her time pulling the carriage along the main street closer to MacDonald's Corner, the crowds thickened on the sidewalk, but Ainslie looked straight ahead and saw no one. The first fights had not yet begun, but they took part farther up the street in the vicinity of the saloons. The shops were now closed, the coal carts and slovens were off the streets, the tram had already traversed the length of the town and gone on its way, and for the moment Ainslie's was the only carriage in sight.

The Presbyterian minister stood under a lamppost with one hand scratching the small of his back and the other hooked by a thumb to his waistcoat pocket. He was brooding on the sermon he was going to preach tomorrow morning. He wondered if he should stop the doctor and ask him, as one scholar to another, if he thought it was going too far to warn the congregation against taking the promises of the New Testament too literally. For if God was love, what was to be done about Jehovah? But Ainslie passed the Reverend MacAlistair without turning his head.

Under the light of the next post was another man who wanted to speak to the doctor. He looked like a chubby walrus dressed in a bowler hat and a high white collar. Jimmie MacGillivray, the saloonkeeper, had a stomach-ache. He wanted to ask the doctor about an idea which had been scaring the wits out of him. Could a stomach-ache be sent as a punishment for sin? If it could be – and the Reverend MacAlistair said that was so – then there was no hope for the relief of Jimmie MacGillivray. For what more could a man do to keep the Sabbath holy than he was doing now? He made his daughters keep it, too. They cooked all the food for Sunday on the day before, put it on plates and the plates on the tables, and he even saw to it that they filled all the glasses in the house with water on Saturday night, so that not a tap was turned in the MacGillivray house on the Sabbath. But the stomach-ache was growing worse week by week, and the Reverend MacAlistair said that his sins would find him out. What more could he do? If only the doctor would look his way ... but the doctor passed, still staring at the rump of his mare, and Jimmie turned away with a small moan.

At the next corner a crowd was gathering and as the fringes of it spilled over the curb Ainslie had to guide the mare to the far side of the street to avoid running down some of the men. This maneuver interrupted his thoughts and he looked for the cause of the disturbance. He could hear the broad voice of Mr. Magistrate MacKeegan ... " 'And by Chesus,' I said to her, Big Annie McPhee, six foot two with the beam of a potato schooner moreoffer, 'you whould come into my court and swear that a man the size of the prissoner wass able to rape the likes of you! By Chesus,' I said to her, 'you whill get down on the floor and show me, or you whill get the hell owt of here and I whill haff you for perjury moreoffer.' And that ..." MacKeegan's voice tailed off as Ainslie passed ... "iss a hell of a lot more serious charge in my court than rapes iss, because perjury iss perssonal."

"Dear God," Ainslie muttered to himself. Now the crowds were so thick they spilled out into the street and he had to urge the mare on. Most of the men were miners who spent their days underground in the dark. He could tell at a glance how many years any one of these proud clansmen had spent in the pits. The young ones were defiant, cocky in the way they walked, and they pulled their rough caps down over their right ears like tam-o'-shanters. They were the ones who could be heard issuing a general challenge to a fight. The middle-aged ones were quieter, they moved slowly and talked little, seeming older than their age, and most of them were beginning to be plagued with sciatica and what they called the rheumatics. If a man had been in the pits beyond his fifty-fifth year, particularly in those mines with narrow seams, Ainslie's eye could measure fairly accurately how many more working years that man had before him. The young ones swaggered and the middle-aged ones could feel the break coming in their leg pains and their unspoken fears, but ultimately the mines would break them all. Those who survived accidents would become like the two white-haired men Ainslie passed near the corner, sitting side by side on the curb with sticks for support between their knees, their faces ennobled by the tremendous fact of survival, grave and white under the flickering arc light.

As the mare threaded her way through MacDonald's Corner, the T-shaped area of macadam which was the only social center most of the miners had ever known, the place where Archie MacNeil had got his start, several of the men touched their caps to the doctor as he passed, and he answered them with nods or an occasional word. The mare turned right and began to pull up the hill that led to the hospital, pushing with her hind legs so that her rump muscles bulged and glistened with sleek high lights whenever a lamppost was passed. Halfway up the hill they met the Salvation Army band marching down, instruments glinting brassily in the lights, only the bass drum booming to keep the men in step, and twelve women in black bonnets with red ribbons clapping their hands as they followed. Ainslie scarcely noticed them, for the Army always established itself in the middle of MacDonald's Corner on Saturday nights, timing its first hymns to coincide with the moment the first drunks staggered up from the rum shops in the lower part of the street.

The mare reached the top of the hill where the hospital stood like a lighthouse over the whole town. Ainslie tethered the horse in the yard behind the building, picked up his bag and walked briskly through the yard and around the front to the steps. When he opened the door and smelled the familiar odors of the building he felt a sensation of pleasure that began to relax the tense muscles of his back. Here was his own world where his skill had made him a master. He saw Miss MacKay rustling starchily down the corridor to meet him. His feeling of certainty grew and he began to smile.

Five

NIGHT FELL over the island and the moonlight picked out its shape like the claws of a lobster from the surrounding dark of the sea. The claws were ringed around by a faint line of white as groundswells crumbled against the shores, washed luminously and faded out. Inland the shadows turned with slow gravity in the hills as the moon went up the sky. The rivers and the windows of lonely farmhouses gleamed as the rays of light struck them. A soft breeze carried balsam-laden air into the packed area of Broughton, where the miners' rows looked desolate and the bankheads of the collieries loomed like monuments in a gigantic cemetery.

The moonlight came into the window of Alan MacNeil's bedroom, crept across the floor and reached his face. He woke to sounds on the other side of the common wall and knew that the father of the noisy family had come home. He heard Red Willie MacIsaac shouting and his wife telling him to be quiet, but Red Willie went on shouting and Alan could hear his words. He was saying he could whip any man in the collieries, he could whip any man in the world for all of that, and Alan smiled as he thought how small Red Willie would talk if he ever came face to face with his father.

He wondered where his father was and when he would come home. Some day his father would arrive and the people would see how strong he was. Perhaps he would even pick up an iron bar as Red Willie had once done and bend it so everybody could see. Alan heard the tearing noise of a tramcar wheel and wondered if it was the one bringing his mother home, but as the car passed he knew it was moving in the opposite direction. Then he heard a creak on the stairs and a moment later his door opened and he could see Mrs. MacDonald with the moonlight on her face.

"So here you are, all snug in bed! Haff you not been asleep yet at all?"

"Oh, yes, Mrs. MacDonald, I just woke up for a minute."

"That iss fine. Now then, go back to sleep and tomorrow I whill tell your mother what a good boy you haff been."

Her hand touched his forehead and he lay thinking how nice Mrs. MacDonald was. He knew it was because of Mrs. MacDonald that his mother could go out on Saturday nights and have a little pleasure and then tell him about it on Sunday mornings. The stairs creaked again as Mrs. MacDonald went away.

He lay awake listening, wondering what was happening on the other side of the wall where the bumps and shuffles of the MacIsaacs were still audible. After a time he reached under his pillow for the sea shell and held it against his ear. The noise was still there, singing in his ear as the shell remembered it, the oldest noise in the world. He wondered how long it would be before he grew up and had great muscles like the men said his father had, and he wondered what it would be like when he was a man. His mother wanted him to be the same as Dr. Ainslie, who worked sometimes all night. Alan had seen him coming home in his carriage in midmorning, asleep with the reins around his neck, tired out from curing people in the hospital. As Alan thought about him, the doctor seemed to be hardly a man at all. He was The Doctor, far above everyone else he knew.

Six

N O SUCH THOUGHT was in Ainslie's mind when the night superintendent turned and went back along the corridor with him, giving a meticulous report along the way. "I'm afraid your OB case will have to wait," she said. "A horrid accident has just been brought in and there's no other surgeon in the hospital. I telephoned Dr. Grant and Mrs. Grant said he'd come over at once."

Ainslie nodded. Angus Grant was his usual anesthetist. He kept on walking through the corridor with the nurse rustling beside him.

"It may not need operating."

"I'm afraid it will, Doctor."

"What's the damage?"

"It's a young Newfoundlander with his hands horribly crushed. I've ordered the OR prepared. I put him in that empty room next to the ward."

"Has he lost much blood?"

"A good deal, I'm afraid. They had tied some filthy rags around his wrists. Dr. Weir took them off and applied tourniquets. He hasn't lost consciousness."

"What about Mrs. Morton? Who's looking after her?"

"Dr. Weir's with her now. He says it may be a very long labor."

"Yes, I know. Is Weir the only houseman on duty tonight?"

"Yes, he is at the moment."

"All right. Let's take a look at this case. You may have to rouse out another houseman later."

When they reached the room next to the ward Ainslie saw a young, pain-drawn face staring up at him from white sheets. The boy's body was rigid from fright and dark stains were visible on the fresh bandages covering his wrists and hands. While the nurse stood at the foot of the bed, Ainslie drew up a chair, sat down and put his hand on the boy's forehead. It was covered with sweat and too cold for his liking.

Suddenly the doctor smiled and the pug-nosed face watched him. "Tell me something – how old are you?" Ainslie said.

"Twenty, zurr."

"And not long out of Newfoundland, eh?"

"No, zurr."

As Ainslie held the frightened eyes, all the strain faded from his own face. By an effort beyond the reach of words he tried to tell the boy that his fear was being absorbed and conquered. He said nothing for some minutes. Then, in a tone of voice that betrayed none of the considerations coursing through his mind, he said, "You've had a bit of bad luck, haven't you?"

"It's warse than bad luck, zurr."

"How do you know? You're not the doctor." He was still smiling and the boy made an effort to smile back. "Have you ever been in a hospital before?"

"No, zurr."

"Well, this is a place where people are made right again. We're going to take good care of you. You're in the best and safest place in the world."

The boy searched his face and Ainslie smiled back at him calmly. Then he rose and set quietly to work, checking the pulse, listening to the heart, looking at the chart of the blood pressure. He motioned to the nurse and she laid her hand on the boy's forehead, turning his head away while Ainslie removed the bandages from one of the hands. Weir had done a good job of packing them. The doctor pressed several places gently while he watched the boy's face for signs of pain, but the expression on the pug-nosed face did not alter and Ainslie replaced the outer bandages. When he examined the other hand the boy winced sharply.

"Good!" Ainslie said, and replaced this bandage, too.

After he had examined the boy's entire body and found only a livid, spreading bruise on the left side, with no internal injuries which could be detected, he replaced the blankets and smiled again.

"I don't know what happened to you, but it seems as hard as ever to kill a Newfoundlander."

The boy gave a twisted grin.

"I'm going to put you to sleep for a little while and you're not to be afraid. The stuff you have to breath will smell bad for a minute or two, but it won't smell half as bad as a beach after the catch is in and the fish have been gutted."

"There be beaches in Labrador," the boy said, speaking slowly through the narcotics that had been given him, "thet do stink 'orrible when the sun gits to 'em."

"Indeed they do. I've smelled some of them myself. Now you're going to sleep and when you wake up safe and sound you won't be feeling a thing."

The boy's eyes blurred with sudden tears and his Adam's apple moved up and down as he swallowed. Ainslie stood calmly smiling at him, a lock of dark hair loose over his forehead, and so he stayed until he sensed that he had reached through the boy's fear and found his courage.

Outside in the corridor he gave the nurse instructions in a quick, precise undertone and then hurried away to mount the stairs two at a time. He found Angus Grant waiting for him in the changing room, and as he made himself ready he answered the big, red-haired anesthetist's questions about the case.

"What I don't understand," Ainslie added after explaining the condition of the two hands, "is how such an accident could have happened. The pits and machine shops closed hours ago. It's damned odd."

"Well," said Grant, "I hope it won't take long. The *Strand* came today and I was halfway through the new Sherlock Holmes."

He laughed as Ainslie grunted his disapproval of such reading habits. The two men went to the operating room side by side, and by the time they reached it Ainslie's concentration was so intense he did not look at the patient on the table or bother to nod to the nurse and junior houseman in attendance. He stayed out of the Newfoundlander's sight until Grant set to work, and then he checked his instruments, articulated his fingers several times, and stood as though frozen until Grant gave him the signal. If he hesitated more than a fractured second in making his decisions while he worked, no one who watched was aware of it.

When the operation was finished and he stood back, his shoulders suddenly drooped. He took off his rubber gloves and handed them to a nurse. Then he nodded to Grant, squared his shoulders and walked briskly out of the operating room, down the corridor and down the stairs to the desk of Miss MacKay.

"Any news from Dr. Weir?" he said to her.

"No, Doctor. Are you going up there now?"

"Not unless Weir is in need of me. There's another matter I want to attend to first."

Miss MacKay pursed her lips. "I'm afraid Mr. Morton is getting very impatient to see you."

"He's not having the baby. Neither has he got a rheumatic heart. Let him cool his heels. He should have worried about his wife's heart nine months ago. I want to get to the bottom of this accident case."

"I'm sorry, Doctor," said Miss MacKay, "I tried to get Dr. McCuen, but he was out."

"What for? Oh – his colliery, was it? Well, you got me instead. That young Newfoundlander is probably illiterate and the loss of his hands is going to be a serious thing for him. I've saved four fingers out of ten and I was lucky to be able to do that much. Three was the best I'd bargained for. How did it happen? If he was on company property he's entitled to some compensation."

Miss MacKay made a gesture of helplessness. "The men who brought him in talked such a lingo I couldn't understand a word they said. You know what those outport Newfoundlanders are like when they all speak at once."

Ainslie was walking up and down in front of her desk. He stopped and looked at her. "Didn't you tell them to wait? Where did they go?"

"I ordered them to stay in the outpatients' waiting room. That's probably where they still are."

Ainslie was halfway down the corridor before she finished speaking. In the outpatients' room he found three young men, all with cowlicks in their hair and flat cloth caps in their hands, sitting on a varnished oak bench. They rose respectfully when he entered and watched him with the humble, fearful, protective expressions such people nearly always have in the presence of doctors. When he addressed them Ainslie's voice had lost its sharpness. He had always been fond of Newfoundlanders and he respected them as a man living in a hard country respects neighbors who live in a land even harder.

"Are you the men who brought in the boy with crushed hands?"

"Yes, zurr."

"Are you members of his family?"

"No, zurr."

"Where does he live?"

"Blow-Me-Down, zurr."

"I mean here, not in Newfoundland."

"Bill don't live no place 'ere, Doctor. But 'is old man and old woman and 'is brother Garge do live in Blow-Me-Down."

Ainslie's large eyes pinned their stares to his own. As he searched their expressions he saw no violence in them and knew the patient was not here as the result of a brawl. But he also knew they were trying to conceal something.

"Now see here," he said. "The first thing for you to understand is this – I'll put up with no lying."

"No, zurr."

"Very well. The second thing for you to understand is that I'm trying to help your friend. He's in need of help. I had to amputate."

They looked at him blankly.

"I've just cut off one of his hands and part of the other."

Ainslie knew they were moved, but their faces still showed nothing. One of them said, "I told 'e, Tom, they was squatten all abroad."

"Then you weren't with him at the time it happened?"

"Not us, zurr. But Tom, 'ere, 'e was with 'im."

Ainslie turned to a freckle-faced youth with sandy hair and a telltale line of coal dust circling his neck. After a series of sharp questions a story came together.

Tom and the injured boy had arrived in North Sydney the week before on a schooner from St. John's. There they had decided to leave their ship. Two days later they found a job breaking coal at the pithead of McCuen's colliery, and for the first time in their lives they encountered machinery more complicated than a motorboat engine. There was a steel cable in the engine house which fascinated them in particular. It seemed to come out of the floor very fast with a perpetual motion as though there were no end to it. Near the roof it disappeared into a wooden housing, then it appeared again about a foot and a half away and ran down again into the floor with what seemed to be the same perpetual motion. Tom was sure it was not just one cable but two, because one ran up and the other ran down. Bill thought it was a single cable. All week they argued about it, then Bill bet Tom a quarter that it was one cable and said he would prove it. Late this afternoon they had seen the foreman leave the engine house and both of them had sneaked in. They were alone inside and Bill was ready to win the quarter. He grabbed the upgoing cable to find out where it was bound for, and it swept him to the roof. Before he knew what was happening, his hands were crushed against the housing, and if Tom had not been underneath when he fell he might have killed himself. Tom tore off his shirt and bound up Bill's wrists as soon as he caught his breath and then he tried to wipe up the floor because they were afraid of getting into trouble with the foreman. But no one saw them and they had sneaked out the gate together and walked half a mile to the house of the two friends who were here with Tom. Everyone had taken some rum to help them think it over and then Bill fainted. So they finally carried him out to a coal cart and brought him to the hospital.

Except for questions now and then to keep the story from drifting off into aimless legend-making, Ainslie listened in grim silence. When he decided they had told him everything, he said shortly to the one called Tom, "Come with me."

The boy followed him down the corridor, his nostrils twitching with apprehension at the fear-inspiring smells of the hospital, and Ainslie turned him over to Miss MacKay with instructions to question him again and make out a report for the company.

After he had changed his gown and settled himself into his dark suit, Ainslie's tension began to ease. He went upstairs to see his OB case and then to pacify an anxious and indignant husband. When he returned to Mrs. Morton's room he found her in a state of manic talkativeness, so he sat down and forced himself to be calm in order to calm her. Dr. Weir went out and returned, and by the time Ainslie left, her fears had been submerged by her interest in the details of her own case as Ainslie had outlined them for her.

Once again Ainslie beat his way down the corridor, down the stairs and along another corridor to the doctors' common room.

Seven

THE ROOM WAS EMPTY when he closed the door behind him, for Grant had already gone home. It had the heavy smell of rooms where tired men relax and smoke their pipes. No curtains were at the windows and there were no pictures on the walls, but the floor was carpeted and two walls were covered by shelves of medical books and journals. A large oak table stood in the center of the room, a shaded lamp rested in the middle of it, two worn armchairs faced each other on either side of an empty hearth, and other chairs lurked in the shadows. The founder of the hospital had intended the room as a library. It still served that purpose, but few of the doctors ever found time to study a portion of the books on its shelves.

Ainslie dropped into one of the armchairs beside the hearth. He was still stiff with a tension that had become chronic. He heard through the open window the distant scream of tramcar wheels grinding around MacDonald's Corner. On the hat rack he recognized a battered felt with several fishing flies hooked to its ribbon and recognized it as the property of Big Collie McCuen, a man who might have found his professional level more easily in Nelson's fleet than on the staff of a hospital, Ainslie thought. In the corner behind the hat rack were a heavy blackthorn and a worn umbrella. Ordinarily Ainslie would have seen none of these things.

Tonight his eyes missed nothing. The blackthorn belonged to Jack Paterson, a man built as ponderously as McCuen, a heavy breather and a heavy eater, but a sound enough doctor so far as he went. His chief weakness was his incapacity for learning anything new and his resentment of those who did. It was Paterson who had dubbed Ainslie the Regius Professor. The umbrella belonged to Ronald Sutherland, a good surgeon but tied inexorably to the textbooks. Ainslie sighed and closed his eyes. The accouterments of his colleagues reminded him how few men there were in Broughton with whom he could talk.

Beyond the oak door the hospital was still. Ainslie began to feel some of the tension easing out of the muscles of his back and passing like a quivering presence down his legs and out his toes. He lay back in the half-darkness and tried to sleep, but his mind refused to blur. He thought about Margaret and the things she had said to him. Did they spring from something she had been thinking about for a long time or were they words of the moment only? It made no difference. They were one more symptom to add to the diagnosis. He was past forty, he had no children, he was in a treadmill which he could neither slow down nor escape by jumping off, and Margaret's unhappiness made him feel increasingly guilty day by day.

He heard the post office clock striking the hour, but he missed the count and could not trouble to take out his watch to check the time. When had he got to sleep last night? He couldn't remember. As his mind began to blur at last he saw the curve of a woman's hip as golden as a harvest moon, but when he reached out to caress it, the color changed to white and it was Margaret. The doctor's hands went loose on the arms of his chair, his head dropped to one side and his dark hair became tousled over his forehead. The lines of his face smoothed perceptibly as his consciousness disappeared like a ship into a fog.

Dr. Dougald MacKenzie was standing over him when Ainslie's eyes opened, and for an instant Ainslie thought he was looking up at the picture of the founder of the hospital that hung over the mantel of the fireplace, rather than at the man himself. But he came out of sleep with a doctor's trained rapidity. He rubbed his forehead and looked with undenied pleasure at his old friend, the only person in the whole of Cape Breton whom he honored totally and without question.

"Sorry, Dan. I should have left you to rest."

"I wasn't really asleep." Ainslie sat up. "What time is it, anyway?"

Dr. MacKenzie took a gold hunter from his pocket and snapped open the cover. "Twenty past eleven. What keeps you here so late tonight?"

"A confinement. It's Morton's wife. I thought it was best to bring her in here because she's got a bad heart and I don't like the look of it."

MacKenzie sat down in the other armchair across the hearth, jerked it forward and lifted his long legs until his heels rested on the edge of the low mantel. His heels had been scraping that mantel ever since it had been built, but this was MacKenzie's favorite posture at home and he saw no reason to change it here.

Ainslie felt some of the weight leave his mind as he looked at the old man. Dougald MacKenzie was now seventy-six, he was still active and all his life he had been equal to whatever he had tried to do. In the early days of his practice he had ranged over the whole of Cape Breton, and it was said with truth that he had once known every family in the island. The story of his three-year assault on the smallpox had already become a legend. He had traveled by carriage, by horseback and by boat until he had visited every village and outpost to vaccinate the children, and it had taken all his force, all his volume of character, to persuade some of the parents to let him do so. His physical size had helped him. MacKenzie was six feet four and broad in proportion. His feet were so big his boots were made to order, and now, with the whole length and breadth of them exposed on the mantel, the toes wide, boxed and glistening with polish, they looked to Ainslie like a pair of bear cubs winking down at him in the light.

"Tired?" MacKenzie said, looking sideways at Ainslie.

"Not particularly."

"Why not admit once in a while that you're human? It would do you good."

"I'm human enough. Did Miss MacKay tell you about the amputation I did tonight?"

"She did, indeed!"

"That upset me. They're such fools!"

"Of course they are." MacKenzie's strong white teeth showed in a smile as he took a pouch of tobacco from his pocket. "At that, it's better than it was in the old days when we were a novelty to them. I well remember an old farmer near Cape North who never forgave me for telling him that the only reason why he was plagued with boils was that he ate nothing but porridge and pork and beans. He lived all alone with his Bible and he was convinced he was the Chosen of the Lord. The boils made him a latter-day Job." MacKenzie chuckled. "Man's trouble isn't what he does or doesn't do, it's what he dreams. That old fellow was dead in a few months without a boil on his body. I changed his diet and I probably killed him by telling him the truth."

Ainslie watched MacKenzie's large, lined thumb pressing the tobacco into the bowl of his pipe, and he wondered as he had often wondered before how a man with such huge hands had been able to perform thousands of careful, precise operations. He saw the long mustache, drooping at the ends, making its white splash against the ruddy cheeks, and thought about the change in MacKenzie's personality in recent years. When Ainslie had first met him, Dr. MacKenzie had been consciously the chief, a silent, earnest listener who was so absorbed in medicine he never seemed able to give a moment's thought to anything else. After giving up practice in the colliery to which he had been attached, he had remained as chief surgeon and director of the hospital which owed its existence to his energy and determination. At one time or another all the doctors in Cape Breton had come under his influence. But now he lived alone, and in his partial retirement he had taken to reading with the same quiet thoroughness he had once given to his work. It was the reading that had made him more talkative and self-revealing, less clinical and more given to speculation. There had been a time when Ainslie had believed MacKenzie to be a genius, but he knew now that the old man's mind was one which understood, rather than discovered.

"I suppose I ought to be going home," MacKenzie said without moving from his chair. "Since Janet died and the children went away that house of mine gets on my nerves. Some day you'll know what it's like to be afraid of going home in the dark."

MacKenzie's rich bass voice broke into a laugh and Ainslie watched the tobacco smoke rising in clouds over his stiff white hair. It was the head of an old Highland chief, but it was also the face of a man who had worked with Lister in the Old Country and against Lister's advice had deliberately chosen to return to his isolated island. That choice, and the hard years since he had made it, were all marked in the expression of his deep blue eyes. Ainslie knew himself to be grateful to MacKenzie for many things which would never be told, but perhaps for nothing more than the sense he had given him of belonging to the great world of international medicine.

"It's the unnecessary nonsense that I grow weary of," he heard himself saying. "About a third of the work I do is unnecessary. Last night it was a hysterical old woman with indigestion. The night before I was had out by a blackguard who'd gotten into a brawl and wanted me to patch his eye. Och, I could brain them!"

"Why don't you?" MacKenzie smiled. "You can put a stop to that sort of thing any time you want to, and when you stop feeling sorry for yourself, you'll do it."

Ainslie flushed. "How? By barricading my surgery door?"

"No. There are other ways. The turning point in my life was that flash explosion fifteen years ago in my colliery. Do you remember it?"

"Yes, I remember." The flush began to recede.

"Since that time I've saved myself a total of about three years of sleep. I'd been on my feet fifty-eight hours by the clock after that explosion and I'd just managed to get to bed when the surgery bell rang. I went down in my nightgown and there was Jumping Rorie MacNair with nothing worse than a cracked septum and a black eye. 'It took two of them to fix me, Doctor, honest to God' – that was how he introduced himself." MacKenzie paused. "Didn't I ever tell you that story?"

"No."

"I should have. I hauled Rorie inside by the scruff of the neck – I could do it in those days – and I said, 'It's only going to take one man to fix you now.' And I made him stand in my surgery and begin to count the bottles with the Jolly Roger on them. When he got to twenty I said, 'Do you know what the skull and crossbones mean?' 'Indeed, Doctor, yes I do.' 'Do you know who signs death certificates when men die?' He knew that, too. 'Well, Rorie,' I said, 'think this over. The doctor is a very busy man. The doctor gets tired and needs sleep just like other people. And when the doctor gets wakened up by a rogue at three in the morning, only God Himself has the slightest idea what he might think of doing. Wouldn't it be an awful thing, Rorie, the next time you came in here like this for nothing, if you died knowing that the man who would sign your certificate was going to be me?'"

MacKenzie's right eyebrow cocked as he looked at Ainslie, his blue eyes twinkling. "It fixed him, Dan. What's more, it fixed the whole lot of them in my colliery. I never got so much respect in my life as I got after that."

Ainslie pulled himself to his feet, stretched and then began to laugh grudgingly, more at the old man's remembered pleasure than at the implications of the story, for any sense of fun had to rest in his mind for a while before it began to amuse him.

"It's time for me to have another look at Mrs. Morton," he said as he left the room.

The hospital was dark and silent as he walked through it. In Mrs. Morton's room the nurse in charge was timing the pains and Mrs. Morton was half asleep as she waited for the next one. Ainslie looked at the nurse's chart, made a mental estimate and went away again. In the ward he discovered that the Newfoundland boy had vomited twice on coming out of the anesthetic, but now was resting. After glancing at the charts of several patients on whom he had operated earlier in the week, Ainslie retraced his steps. On his way he saw that Mrs. Morton's husband was with her and he did not go in.

Dr. MacKenzie was still in the common room, hunched over the table reading. Ainslie took off his shoes, hung up his jacket and stretched out in the chair he had left, flexing and unflexing his toes.

MacKenzie closed his book and pushed it aside. "It's nearly midnight," he said. "Why don't you go to sleep? Weir's on duty, isn't he?"

"I don't feel like sleeping." Ainslie stretched. "If I'd remembered to bring my Homer I might have got through a hundred lines."

MacKenzie turned away from the table and looked into the empty hearth, and as the minutes passed and he made no further move Ainslie had the unmistakable impression that the old man was gathering his forces.

"Margaret's right," MacKenzie said finally. "Your tension's not caused by your work. It's rather a new thing they're calling

hypertension." He smiled. "But then, you're rather a new type
of man."

Ainslie ignored the last comment. He said sharply,
"Margaret? What's she been seeing you about?"

"Friendship, you might say. After all, I was the first person
in this world to make her acquaintance." MacKenzie's voice
became the persuasive voice of a doctor confronted by a recalcitrant patient. "Dan, you're the best man we ever had here."
The old man spoke gently. "But for the past three years you've
been getting so irritable there's no knowing what to do with
you. What's causing it? Don't tell me it's your work, because
it isn't."

Ainslie crossed and uncrossed his legs. He saw the old
man's kindly smile and he knew it was prompted by a deep
understanding, but he felt himself rigidly on the defensive.

"Whenever a man courts unnecessary work – and believe
me, you've been doing it – it's not natural," MacKenzie went
on. "You don't really want to read Homer tonight. Why do you
flog yourself into doing things like that?"

"Benjamin Jowett could read Greek as easily as he could
read English."

"Could he also remove an appendix?" The blue eyes were
studying Ainslie closely. "You're forty-two years old, and
you're going into a pretty hard time of life. A man in middle
age is like a ship on fire at sea with a gale driving her."

Ainslie looked away from the searching eyes. "You were
talking about Margaret," he said.

MacKenzie cleared his throat. "Don't be proud with me,
Dan. The last thing I want to do is intrude, but you mean a
good deal to me and so does Margaret." He swung his long
legs up until his heels once more rested on the mantel. "Let
me talk and maybe it will help all of us. It does sometimes."
He paused and Ainslie said nothing, so he went on. "As a man
gets older his life narrows down to two things – his work and

his family. In your case there's no family – there's just Margaret. You are trying to substitute work for – for what you lack between you. But no man can deliberately exclude his wife from the center of his life and hope to escape the hounds."

Ainslie flushed a slow deep red. "So!" he said. His face was that of a man caught naked in his dreams.

"She's a lovely woman, Dan, and a sensible one, too. Even if she can't read Latin and Greek."

After that Ainslie found himself confronted by the old man's silence. It was not a judging silence; it was warm and kind. If he could let himself go he would sink into it and be absorbed by it, but something within him fought it fiercely, as though to yield to peace would be to yield to destruction.

Finally MacKenzie said, "It would be easier for Margaret if she had had children."

Ainslie's mouth became a straight line.

"Never mind, Dan. I'm sorry I said that. Why you didn't want to have children when you were first married is your own business. Margaret says you want them now very much. Only now it's too late."

Ainslie's anger exploded. "God damn her!" he said in a harsh whisper. "Why did she have to go to you, of all people?"

"Why not say – God damn me?"

Ainslie fought to keep the tears out of his eyes. He swallowed and then he looked up at the old man. "Dr. Dougald," he said, "you examined her, of course. That operation five years ago was a medical necessity. If you had been here then I would have sent her to you and your decision would have been the same as mine. But that happened to be the winter you spent in Barbados." He had gained control of himself and his voice fell back to normal. "I didn't believe there was any point in confirming my judgment by asking the advice of Collie McCuen or Ronnie Sutherland. You'll say it was my pride, I suppose. Anyhow, I performed the operation myself, and if Margaret told you I did it because I wanted to sterilize her, I say to you it was a deliberate lie."

It was the turn of the old man to flush. His huge, steady hand reached out and closed over Ainslie's fretful one.

"Oh, Dan," he said. "This is too bad! This comes from deep underneath and it's too bad. It's my fault, not Margaret's. The poor girl loves you more than she does herself."

Ainslie withdrew his hand. "How could she say things like that to you? How could she? It's the . . ." By an effort of will he controlled himself and became silent. His eyes looked like those of a wounded animal, but the lines about his mouth were tight.

"I tell you this is my fault, not hers," the old man repeated. "Words are the real trouble-makers. I never was any good at using them."

"It seems to me you presented the case very well. After all these years Margaret went to you to find out if her husband is the kind of man who would deliberately mutilate his wife." It was a moment before his pride would let the question come out. "Well, what did you tell her?"

"I told her the same thing you'd tell any patient under the circumstances. At this date, and with the evidence available, it was impossible for me to say whether the operation performed five years ago could have been avoided or not." He raised his hand against Ainslie's expression. "I also told her," his voice deepened and he measured his words, "that I could assure her absolutely – not as a physician but as a man – that the operation had been necessary to save her life because you had said it was."

There was no sound and no movement in the room. Ainslie sat quite still. Finally he said quietly, "And what did she say to that?"

"She said, 'Thank you, Dr. Dougald, I knew that was so.'"

"And she did know, too." Then Ainslie added, softly and with precision, "But in spite of knowing, she still had to go to you! She still had to make sure!"

"Dan," MacKenzie said quietly, "not everyone in the world is a Highland Scot. To most other people, life is more important than these niceties about loyalty. To Margaret this was a question of life. I know – and she knows too – that Collie McCuen's opinion is medically worthless compared to yours, but I still think she was entitled to have it. Your hope of children disappeared forever in that operation. And yet you probably never told her how disappointed that fact made you. Dan, boy, can't you imagine some of the questions a defeated woman can ask herself in the nights?"

Ainslie's eyes burned in a face which had become pale. "Did it never cross her mind that there are some questions people don't ask? Why did she wait all this time – why did she nurse her feelings – and then go to you?"

"Why don't you ask her that question yourself? At any rate, if she ever did have any doubts, she has none now. She has accepted things, and you must accept them, too."

Ainslie said between barely opened lips, "People trust each other, or they don't."

MacKenzie glanced at him sharply, then his expression changed to that of the commanding officer and his voice thundered, "That's enough, Dan! I was clumsy – I was worse than that, I was stupid. But I won't permit your pigheaded pride to make this a cause of grievance against a fine woman. You love Margaret and she loves you. You both have your faults and so have we all, and you're not alone in that. But you are alone in life with each other, and if you seek for grievances, you'll find it only too easy to discover them. If we were all perfect, Dan, there would be no need of love in this world."

When Ainslie made no reply, his voice dropped and he measured his words. "I'm an old man and things have been easy for me. I haven't your ability and never did have it, but nobody has ever accused me of being unobservant. So listen to me, Dan – ninety-nine times out of a hundred, when a man and a woman hurt each other, they don't know why they do it. They don't know what it is that impels them to wound each other. They don't realize it's the flaw within themselves. Each of us has a flaw, and when two people love each other, each seems to expect the other to cure his flaw." MacKenzie paused, and added in a quieter voice, "As long as you've been married to Margaret, you've resented her because she hasn't been able to wash away your sense of sin."

"What on earth are you talking about?"

The old man smiled at his own thoughts. "Dan, you haven't forgotten a single word you've ever heard from the pulpit or from your own Presbyterian father. You may think you've rejected religion with your mind, but your personality has no more rejected it than dyed cloth rejects its original color." MacKenzie's voice became sonorous with irony as he tried to remember Calvin: "Man, having through Adam's fall lost communion with God, abideth evermore under His wrath and curse except such as He hath, out of His infinite loving-kindness and tender mercy, elected to eternal life through Jesus Christ – I'm a Christian, Dan, but Calvin wasn't one and neither was your father. It may sound ridiculous to say, in cold words, that you feel guilty merely because you are alive, but that's what you were taught to believe until you grew up. I've met New Englanders whose families had stopped going to church in their grandfathers' day, but every man jack of them felt guilty notwithstanding."

Before MacKenzie had finished speaking, Ainslie left his chair and crossed to the window. With his fingers on the ledge, he leaned out and found himself staring into total darkness. His sin? All the quiet reasonableness of the old man's sentences had withered away under the power of that word. His burden of guilt? Did MacKenzie, in spite of what he had said earlier, still believe that he had committed the appalling sin of sterilizing Margaret deliberately? No, that was ridiculous. He and MacKenzie were both medical men and as medical men they understood each other perfectly. Of course the old man knew him guiltless of such a crime. So MacKenzie must have meant something else. But why must he, Daniel Ainslie, forever feel guilty before he could reason away any cause for guilt? What MacKenzie had meant had been no more than what he had said in plain words. MacKenzie had told him that although he might be an intellectual agnostic, he was an emotional child in thrall to his barbarous Presbyterian past. As he thought this, he felt guilty again. But why? Was there no end to the circle of Original Sin? Could a man never grow up and be free? It was deeper than theory and more personal. There was Margaret – he felt guilty before her, guilty in his soul. Why again? Merely because, when he had married her, he had been so swayed by sexual desire? As he thought this he saw her anew, as he had seen her the first time, that wonderful, white, firm body so eager for pleasure with him, himself desperate for the joy in her, yet at the same time half afraid and half ashamed. Why again? What was wrong with desire except that within himself it was overpowering and he feared it? Why did he fear it, since she had always been able to satisfy it? Because he had been taught to fear it. Because it led hellwards. But he was a physician, a learned man of forty-two years, and he no longer believed in hell and damnation. No, but he did believe, and believed because it was true, that he had permitted the fables of his childhood to destroy much of Margaret's happiness. So the circle was complete again. Any way he regarded himself, he was guilty, and there was no way out.

He stared into the dark and longed for the sight of something distinct. He wanted to see something, anything. A row of hills against the sky or the furry lines of a tree cool in the night, a forest into which a man could disappear and lose himself. He wanted to go off and lose himself in the forest and find there a woman with Margaret's body and the eyes – good God, the eyes of that girl Mollie MacNeil – who would hold his head and tell him that for all his worthlessness she loved him and for all his confusion she understood him. He sniffed like a dog and smelled salt in the air. Then he turned and spoke casually.

"This confounded climate! We were set for a spell of good weather and now you can practically smell Newfoundland." As he crossed to his chair, he added, "I suppose I ought to call an orderly and tell him to unhitch the mare and stable her for the night. I'm becoming forgetful and incompetent. I'd completely forgotten the poor beast was still out there."

He sat down and looked at the ceiling. MacKenzie was silent on the other side of the hearth. Ainslie became aware that his whole body from the neck down through the diaphragm felt sore, aching and lacerated. His doctor's intelligence awoke, and as it began to function the curse of his ancestors seemed farther away. Why did a man like himself have no migraine headaches and no stomach ulcers? Why, instead, did he have frequent spasms in the muscles of his back which he knew were caused by nervous tension? Could it be possible that all emotional processes reacted physiologically in one of these three different ways with various individuals? Could emotional stress reflect itself physiologically in the brain tissues of one individual, in the stomach lining of another, in the back muscles of a third, so that a hypertense patient might have one of these ailments at some time of his life, but never two or all three of them? His mind began to race, then stopped short. It was a theory, no more. It was a theory that could not possibly be proved until more was known of neurology than was known today. Suddenly Ainslie wished himself away from here, in Boston working with Cushing. Cushing was already moving into mysteries.

But when he finally spoke to MacKenzie, Ainslie revealed none of these thoughts. "I hear that Miss MacKay has been offered a post in the Montreal General. If she leaves, we'll not have another nurse in Broughton capable of running this place at night."

MacKenzie gave a quiet laugh. "Don't be silly, Dan. You believe that no more than I do. You can always find someone to run a hospital."

Ainslie took his pipe from his pocket and filled it. By the time it was burning, his nerves were quieter. The beast no longer growled and he was able to look up and meet MacKenzie's eyes and talk naturally.

"Dr. Dougald," he said, "I'm thoroughly ashamed of myself. There was no sense in my saying those things I did about Margaret, because I love her very much. Surely you know that."

"Of course I do. So does she."

"It's simply that – well, Margaret had an easy time of it when she was young. It's the truth her family was lazy and easygoing. She has no notion of the pressure our people live under. There's something cold about those New England Loyalists. Something – I don't know myself what it is."

"I do, Dan." MacKenzie smiled. "They don't see ghosts. And after all, can you name any type in history more ridiculous than a Scotch Presbyterian? If you can't laugh at him, you'll be tempted to murder him."

Ainslie bridled. "What do you call yourself?"

"A Scotch Presbyterian." MacKenzie was still laughing, but he checked himself. "Our people were poets once, before the damned Lowlanders got to us with their religion. The old Celts knew as well as Christ did that only the sinner can become the saint because only the sinner can understand the need and the allness of love. Then the Lowlanders with their Calvinism made us ashamed of living. The way it's made you ashamed."

MacKenzie leaned back in his chair and studied his own feet on the mantel. His huge body lay in the shape of a half-opened jackknife as he tapped the edges of his soles together. Ainslie continued to stare into the hearth.

"It's time for you to leave us, Dan," the old man said. "You've been saving money for years against that trip to London and Vienna. Use it and go now."

When Ainslie gave no indication of having heard him, MacKenzie rubbed the bowl of his pipe against the side of his nose, then slowly filled it again, pressing the tobacco with his huge thumb. "I've often wondered how you managed to stay here so long."

"This is where I belong," Ainslie muttered. "Why should I take what I can from the island and then go off with it?"

"You have no duty that holds you here. The work isn't easy, but it doesn't require a medical genius to perform it. Other men who are less able and high-strung can manage it. Your work belongs to a bigger world."

Ainslie went on puffing in silence. Much of the tension had drained out of him, leaving him exhausted.

"For a man with your imagination Broughton was never the place, Dan. I'm convinced that God Himself can never lick the mines. It's a kind of blasphemy, I know – fighting clans going into the blackness of the earth to dig coal. But *you* can't solve the problem. At least not here." MacKenzie waited a few moments in the silence, then he went on. "Why don't you go down to Boston and work with Cushing? Or go to the Old Country if you're not happy in the States?"

"There's more to Cape Breton than the mines," Ainslie said at last. "You know that, Dr. Dougald. They're only a – a corruption."

"Yes, there's more here in Cape Breton than that. And each year the best of the island emigrates. We're a dispersed people doomed to fight for lost causes."

Ainslie wanted nothing now but sleep. The hospital was a silent organism in a silent town. Cold foggy air from the sea began to move softly through the darkness to engulf the island so secretly that not even a leaf rustled to its progress.

"With hands like yours," MacKenzie's voice was quiet and strong with authority, "with the flair you have, you could become one of the great surgeons of the world. But you need wider experience. You need to measure yourself against bigger men. I'd like to write to Pyke about you. I had a letter from him only last week. I wrote him when he was knighted. His work at Golden Cross may not be quite as advanced as Cushing's, but it's pretty close to it." MacKenzie smiled. "Did I ever tell you that Sir Wystan Pyke was my junior once?"

He looked at Ainslie, knocked out his pipe and pulled his feet from the mantel. "Man," he said, "you're dead to the world. And no wonder." At the door he paused, so tall and broad and solid he filled most of the opening. "If I've said anything tonight that was ill-considered, forgive me. I've probably become an interfering old man since my boys went away."

Eight

N ow once more Ainslie's brain dimmed and for three hours he was out of the world. His sleep was so profound that it took him longer than usual to come out of it; he kept clinging to the borderline of consciousness because he felt so cool and peaceful he hated to return. He was home in the Margaree Valley where he had been born, it was the Queen's Birthday and he was a boy of fifteen walking down the slope of the hill from his father's house through John MacGregor's field to the river bottom. The meadow at the foot of the hills was stately with lone elms, the fans of their upper branches distinct in the first light, their trunks dim. The tall grass was heavy with dew and he felt the cold wetness come through his trouser legs as he walked through it. As he neared the stream a deer came out of an alder clump and bounded into the field ahead of him, stopped to stare and paw the ground with head held high, feeling safe because it was spring when no guns were fired. The deer's hide was wet with dew and there was a scar on his right shoulder from combat in a past rutting season. The sky lightened, and before the boy reached the river it was gray bright over the hill lines; then the whole landscape began to open up and now he could see the full sweep of the hills coming splendidly down the flanks of the valley to their final bend a mile below him where the river straightened and ran smoothly between meadows to the sea. The boy reached a spit of shingle from which the freshet had receded, walked out on it past a dead hawk with its eyes pecked out and found a washed-up spruce at the place where he wanted to fish. The spruce had been years in the river and its branches were worn as smooth as old bones. He dragged it away from the point and stood in its place with the mainstream at his feet, the water narrowed by the spit so that it poured deep without a ripple and ink-dark in the first light. He secured a homemade fly to his leader and the sound of his reel tore brassily across the monotone of the stream as he made the first trial casts to lengthen his line. The smooth stones of the spit grew white as daylight increased, and by the time he had his second trout, red clouds were splintering out of the east in advance of the rising sun. He remembered Homer's line about the rosy-fingered dawn and was proud of the Margaree, for here as in the ancient Troad the dawn was exactly as Homer had described it. The moist air was fragrant with alder, the cleanest, most innocent smell in the world, and when his rod bent double and the line screamed out for the third time he knew he had a grilse instead of a trout. The grilse broke water once so far down the pool it seemed to have no connection with him at all. The deer returned and stepped noiselessly over the white stones about twenty yards to windward and drank. The reel clacked as the boy wound it in, sang out again, clacked and sang. Then its noise disappeared as the entire valley opened up, the hills rolling back like the Red Sea before the Children of Israel into a light-flooded plain loud with the movement of men in armies, and Dr. Daniel Ainslie opened his eyes.

"I'm sorry, Doctor."

He was back in the hospital again and the air was not cool with alder but stuffy with the smell of the tobacco he and

MacKenzie had smoked, compounded with a sharp stink of carbolic sneaking in the open door. The voice of a nurse, so Gaelicky it made two syllables out of every one, actually did sound sorry. A voice like hers sounded sorry all the time.

"I did not want to trouble you, Doctor, with you so tired, but Dr. Weir says the patient is getting too much for him to handle."

Ainslie jumped to his feet. "Confound it, why wasn't I wakened earlier?"

"Och, Doctor, but it iss not the OB case at all, it iss the young Newfoundlander. I think he iss going crazy."

"Is he bleeding?"

"He tried to tear off the bandages, but without hands he could do little harm to himself. Another patient called out, and when I went into the ward, there he wass with his teeth into the gauze. Now he hass the whole ward awake."

"You say Dr. Weir is with him?"

"Yes, Doctor."

Ainslie sat down, scuffed off his slippers and reached for his shoes. "He's probably a little drunk from the ether. However, I'd better take a look at him. People like that with high thresholds of pain sometimes get beside themselves when they panic. Is everything else quiet?"

"There hass been nothing to bother *you* with, Doctor, but of course it iss Saturday night."

Ainslie grunted as he worked his toes into his shoes. The Margaree was still close to him and he hated to leave it.

"Dr. MacMillan hass been busy," the nurse went on. "He iss new and not used to it, and he wass very nice to them, I must say."

"They're lucky they had him to deal with instead of me."

"Indeed, Doctor, that iss just what I said to Red Whillie MacIsaac when he came into the outpatients."

"So he was at it again, was he?"

The nurse was relieved because the doctor she feared more than any of the others seemed to be so congenial tonight.

"Indeed he wass, him and Mick Casey again. They started in front of Jimmie MacGillivray's and before it wass over it spread all the way up to MacDonald's Corner. Everybody it seems got in on it tonight." She failed to notice that the doctor had begun to frown as he tied the laces of his shoes. "It wass real disgraceful, Doctor. They say Magistrate MacKeegan talked them into it. They were so drunk they were ready to kiss each other, but MacKeegan said loudly why should he spend two dollars to see Archie MacNeil in the ring when he could see Casey and MacIsaac fighting in MacDonald's Corner for nothing, and after a while MacKeegan himself would have been in it only Big Alec McCoubrie reminded him of his position. We had two broken noses, one broken jaw and compound fractures of two ribs altogether. But everything is quiet now."

"Everything?" Ainslie said dryly and walked past her out the door.

He could hear the boy's cries before he reached the open door of the ward. When he entered he saw the heads and shoulders of patients sitting upright in their beds. Only the night lights were burning and the ward was a forest of shadows. Young Weir's white jacket rose from a bedside and approached him with a what-have-you shrug of the shoulders, but he cut the houseman short before he could speak.

"You'd better rest, Weir. I'll take over."

He sat on the side of the Newfoundlander's bed and with quiet strength forced the boy to lower his right wrist. Then he felt the pulse with his finger high on the forearm. It was fast but steady, though the boy's whole body was shaking so violently the bed shook with him. Ainslie put his hand on the forehead and felt the sweat.

"It's not easy, is it, lad?"

The boy sobbed again and his body gave a convulsive twist. "You can't go on like this, you know."

The boy started up wildly, his chest bursting Ainslie's hands away. "Only a week ago I was 'ome in Newfoundland and look at me now since I come 'ere! I want to go 'ome." He lifted his bandaged stumps and shook them at the doctor. "What kin I do with these?"

"You can lay them on the bed and rest them." Ainslie's hand returned to the sweating forehead and remained there. His fingers felt the trembling nerves begin to relax. Suddenly he smiled. "What's your name?"

The boy swallowed before he spoke. "Bill Blackett." Then for nearly half a minute he lay still, his mind roaming through fear, shock, the lingering delusions produced by the ether and the cloudy effect of the sedatives he had been given.

"With a fine name like that," Ainslie said, "you're going to be famous."

The boy gave a twisted grin. "Blackett ain't so much, but 'ome in Blow-Me-Down they do call me Billy Foreskin."

"What did you do to earn that?"

"Nuthin I done, zurr, but I got a long 'un."

Ainslie smiled. The quivering in the boy's nerves was less noticeable now. "Can you read and write, Bill?" he said.

"No, zurr, I ain't smart."

"Ever been to school?"

"I were out in the dories when I were eight."

"How do you know you aren't smart," the doctor said, smiling, "if you never went to school?"

"I were none too smart in the dory, thet were what my old man said."

"Don't believe what he said. Believe in yourself, Bill."

"With thim squatten 'ands?"

Ainslie bent forward. "Listen, my boy – you aren't too badly off at all. I've saved four fingers, and on your right hand, too. Did you think I'd turn you loose with no hands?" In the night light the doctor's face became lined and concentrated as once again he merged himself with the patient and moved forward towards the boy's need. "Those four fingers – you think about them. Tonight they became the most important four fingers in the world." He paused as he saw the stare of wonder flicker upward towards hope, and then he continued in a voice so low the man in the next bed could hear nothing but a murmur. "Before you get out of hospital, you're going to begin to learn how to read and write. All you need for reading is your eyes – and you've got fine eyes, much better than mine. For writing all you need is two fingers of the four you've still got. The day will come when you'll think this accident was the luckiest thing that ever happened to you."

Blackett looked up, then shook his head. "Doctor, I were a fool about them cables with Tom, but I ain't a fool enough to call these squatten 'ands lucky."

"That's just where you're wrong. This accident is going to compel you to get an education. So long as you had your hands, there was nothing in front of your bows but coal heaving or the dories. But now, Bill, you're going to be a man of brains because you've got to be."

It took a while for the shocked mind to grasp even a partial meaning in the doctor's words. Ainslie watched the boy's face quietly and at last he saw the lips part in a slow smile.

"My old man can't read or write neether."

Ainslie smiled back at him.

"My brother Garge knows 'ow to run a motorboat, but last election 'e made 'is mark, same's me." The smile turned into a wide grin. "Doctor, you ought to know Garge, for he's real smart. Last election 'e got two dollars out of the Liberals for voting five times, and seventy-five cents from the Tories for voting twice."

"There couldn't have been many votes left in Blow-Me-Down after that."

"It weren't in Blow-Me-Down Garge done thet, Doctor, it were in Port-aux-Basques."

"Forget about Garge," Ainslie said. "Think about what you can do yourself for a change. Garge is going to envy you some day."

Ainslie sat by the bedside for another five minutes, speaking occasionally. His quest with the patient had taken his mind out of Cape Breton to a dark gray coast so clean and pure that men, whose crops must rise out of corruption, could grow scarcely a vegetable on it. He saw the outport villages of Newfoundland perched on stilts in nooks of the granite cliffs, square gray huts under a gray sky with sudden blinks of green and yellow emergent over the ocean. He heard the dragging surge of water in Bonavista Bay. He remembered his first glimpse of yellow dories lifting and disappearing in the shelving Banks' roll under a cold mist of rain and the mate of the bark pointing at them, shouting over the scream of a sticky halyard block that those men fished all winter long with bare hands, adding that they couldn't navigate but smelled their way through the fog like seals. He remembered the Newfoundland doctor whose entire practice depended on a motorboat because there were no roads in the district, a thick-set man with bowlegs and wind-burned cheeks telling him there was less fuss in taking the leg off an outport Newfoundlander without anesthetic than in removing the tonsils of a city man with all the innovations of a modern operating room.

"I saw your home once," Ainslie said.

"You seed Blow-Me-Down, zurr?"

"A long time ago. I was younger than you are now. I only saw it from the sea." Ainslie got to his feet, wondering if the place he remembered really had been Blow-Me-Down. "Now turn over and go to sleep. And when you wake up, remember – you're going to learn to read and write."

The ward was silent as Ainslie left it. This time he did not trouble to remove his shoes when he reached the common room, but stretched out in the chair, expecting to be called within the hour. He was wrong. He slept until eight o'clock and then he was wakened by a smiling nurse who was bearing his breakfast on a tray.

Nine

MARGARET lay drowsily between sturdy sheets in the bed where she had slept as a child. It was in the old part of the house which had been constructed from timbers salvaged from the last brig her grandfather had built. Over her head was a porthole instead of a window. Even in her childhood that porthole had been a reminder of brave days that were gone forever. She had heard so often of the great fire in the shipyard, of how her father and grandfather had fought it for two nights and a day, that she could hardly believe, even now, that she had not seen the fire herself. Her father and mother were scarcely a year married at the time, and since the foundation of their house was already laid, they had used the few undamaged sections of the brig from sentiment as much as from thrift. The timbers built into the wall by Margaret's bed had come from the ship's deckhouse.

She heard a creak of boards in the narrow corridor outside her room as one of her sisters went to the bathroom. A door closed and there was a faint rumble of water filling a tub. She smiled to herself, remembering what a rush there had been for that single bathroom in the days while her father was still alive, before her second-nearest sister had married and gone to live in Upper Canada and her two brothers had left for the States.

She stretched luxuriously and eased the muscles of her throat, wondering if she had sung too much the night before to have any voice left for her solo in church this morning. Everyone in the house had gone through passages from "The Messiah," parts of which had been sung by the church choir at regular intervals for the past eighteen years. They had also eaten sandwiches and drunk coffee and sung light opera until eleven o'clock, and afterwards they had danced in the hall until the advent of the Sabbath put an end to the party. No matter how many of the Eldridges married and moved away, there were always young men in the house on Saturday nights.

Margaret yawned. It was good to be back now and then in a place where laziness was a normal state of being. There had never been any tension in this family. After the loss of the shipyard her father had lived quietly for years as the town's postmaster, while her mother reigned in the house like a queen. Mrs. Eldridge possessed the female kind of ambition which concentrates on being rather than doing. It was still hard for Margaret to accept as natural the inexorable inner drive of her husband, just as it was difficult for her to believe that a man's judgment could ever be as final as the judgment of a woman. Her own father had never stood up against her mother, and all the young men who thronged the house had come to sue for favor from its female inmates. It was a house that had always been quick with changing female moods, and until her father's death there had generally been a baby on the way, a baby just arrived, or an older girl falling in love.

Margaret stirred lazily in the sheets and began to think of her husband with increasing fondness. She wondered if he had spent the whole night on his feet and would be too tired to enjoy her later in the day. A cat smile appeared on her lips. She loved having Dan enjoy her; it was her secret belief that she was very good at making love and she wished Dan would give himself more time to enjoy her properly. Under her closed eyes the smile lingered while she stirred languorously. All her annoyance of the night before had disappeared. She had sung it away in Handel's arias, and this morning she wanted to tell Dan how sorry she was for having hurt him.

Some minutes later she opened her eyes to see her youngest sister, Ruth, sitting on the edge of her bed. Ruth was in a flannel dressing gown and her cheeks were shining with soap and water. At sixteen her mouth was so generous that most of her smiles resembled grins; at thirty she would probably still have the face of a gamin.

"Wake up," Ruth said, "even if you are old and married. You've got to sing 'O Rest in the Lord' this morning."

"Your hair looks nice the way you've put it up," Margaret said and yawned.

"I know it does, but you might tell Mother so. You can have the bathroom next. Norah's in the tub now. And Sheila's getting breakfast." Ruth made a wry face. "It won't be any good, either, because she burns the pancakes on purpose whenever it's her turn. She always thinks that's the way to get out of her day in the kitchen, but it never works."

"Annie used to do the same thing." Margaret stretched her toes. "I wonder what she's like in her own kitchen now."

Ruth made another face. She knew she was Margaret's favorite sister. "You were mad at Dan last night, weren't you?"

"Did it show?"

"All over you. I thought maybe you'd decided to give him up for good."

"Oh, he's not as bad as all that." Margaret stretched her creamy arms and smiled broadly. "The poor man just happens to be a genius, but he doesn't know it."

Ruth's face showed alarm. "But suppose – I mean – if Dan really *is* as good as that you shouldn't say so, should you?"

"Why not? Dr. Dougald says it."

"But you're tempting Providence."

"Do you really think Providence has nothing better to do than to put His foot down and squash people when they get too bold?"

Ruth frowned. "Well, Mr. Toast in the bank said that no genius could possibly live in Broughton. That was when I told him I was going to be an opera singer. And Mother says there's no such thing as genius anyway. It's just making up your mind what you want and sticking to it."

"You know, my dear, your brother-in-law is a far more remarkable doctor than Mother could possibly guess. She mocks him for being impractical and taking himself so seriously, but that's only because he's a Highlander and she feels superior because her ancestors were Loyalists from New England."

Ruth was puzzled. "I don't see what difference it makes. But anyhow, I find him simply *terrifying*."

"So do I – sometimes."

"But you do like him, don't you? Mother says you just go on standing him because you have a noble character."

"I don't like Dan at all," Margaret said. "In fact, there are moments when I dislike him intensely. But I love him, and that's something quite different, as you may possibly discover for yourself some day."

Ruth put her hands to her temples and strained the hair back from her face. "*I* don't intend to get married at all," she said. "I'm going to sacrifice myself for music. I'm going to be a star at Covent Garden or the Metropolitan, though I expect Covent Garden would be more patriotic, but Mr. Toast says there are so many Italians in New York I'd be more appreciated there."

"Who is this man with the strange name?"

"Oh, he's the new teller in the Royal Bank and people are unfair. A person can't help his name and Mr. Toast can't help his voice, either."

"What's the matter with his voice?"

"Nothing, really. He says everybody in Ontario sounds the same way he does. You should hear him say 'tomato.' It's even worse than the Yankees. But he's very nice, you know. He said a wonderful thing when I said I was going to be another Lillian Nordica."

Ruth waited for Margaret to probe further, but Margaret seemed to be thinking about something else.

"He told me if I didn't live in Broughton people would think I had a glorious voice even now, but he thinks everyone in Broughton is stupid and ignorant, or almost, and can't tell the difference between good and bad." She seized Margaret's arms and tried to pull her upright. "You've been lazy long enough. If you don't get up, Mother will put on her persecuted look and tell us how much she suffered bringing us all into the world, and then you can go home to Dan but we'll have to stay right here and stand it."

Margaret put her feet to the floor, ruffled her sister's hair and stood up. "Run along then," she said. "I'll be down soon. And I want to meet Mr. Toast."

An hour later the whole family was in the street, bound for the choir of the Presbyterian Church. They walked in step like a file on parade: first Mrs. Eldridge and Margaret, then Norah and Sheila, then Ruth bringing up the rear like a lance corporal. But everyone went to church in Broughton, even those who had been brawling the night before. Red Willie MacIsaac and Mick Casey met at the holy water font barely eight hours after their fight and anointed their swollen eyes before hearing Mass. In recent years the Catholics had been carrying on the major share of the fighting in town, but it was by no means unusual to see a young Presbyterian with a black eye sitting dolefully in his pew with his head turned to one side.

Mrs. Eldridge and her daughters joined the rest of the choir in the vestry, as they did every Sunday morning, put on gowns and mortarboards and waited for the organ to change key. Then they entered the loft at the front of the church with

Mrs. Eldridge leading. Margaret took her place at the head of the alto section, sat down and bowed for a brief prayer with the others, sat up and looked at the congregation. It was the usual attendance, the only conspicuously empty pew being their own. She saw Jimmie MacGillivray bent forward praying hard, and Mr. Magistrate MacKeegan, impeccable in a black suit and stiff white collar, bearded chin held high in his usual fashion, staring with appreciation at a young woman on the far side of the church.

Margaret followed his glance and saw Mollie MacNeil with Alan beside her; Alan in an Eton collar and water-flattened hair which had dried unevenly, sticking up in spikes here and there. Margaret stood with the rest of the choir as Sandy MacAlistair mounted his pulpit and the whole congregation rose for the Doxology. Just as they were sitting down, she saw a flutter among the elders at the back and Dan himself came striding down the aisle to their pew. From the state of his clothes she knew he had slept in them at least part of the night, yet his large dark eyes looked very tired. He sat down, bowed his head briefly and cleared his throat in embarrassment when she smiled at him, but as she studied his face she knew he was over his annoyance of the night before.

The service proceeded in the usual way. After the plates were passed, Margaret rose to sing her solo, as she did every fifth week, and while the organ went through the introductory bars she smiled at her husband openly. She found herself in good voice and let herself go into the music. When she sat down again with studied grace she raised her head and this time she winked at him. He lowered his eyes and raised them again, and a sheepish smile was starting on his face when her mother spoiled the mood Margaret had evoked between them by leaning across the aisle from the soprano section to congratulate her on her solo in a loud whisper.

During the whole fifty-seven minutes of Sandy MacAlistair's extremely pessimistic sermon Margaret sat watching her husband while he read his copy of the Greek Testament which rested throughout the week in their hymnal rack. Now and then he put down the Greek text and picked up the King James Version to find the meaning of an unfamiliar word. Towards the end of the sermon Margaret felt a tug on her sleeve and looked to the left to see her mother leaning across the aisle again.

"Dan should be ashamed – reading a book with Mr. MacAlistair trying so hard!"

"It's the Bible, Mother," she whispered.

"It doesn't matter what it is, he's not listening to the sermon."

"Neither are you."

Margaret tried to catch Dan's eye once more, but he went straight out the main door after the benediction and she guessed he was bound for the hospital again. When she saw his shoulders disappear she settled back on the bench, resigned to a dull day. An entirely new service was about to begin in Gaelic, with new psalms, new prayers and a whole new sermon in Gaelic by Sandy MacAlistair. The choir had no separate part in this service but it was expected to remain.

Ten

WHEN AINSLIE reached the hospital he discovered that an emergency appendicitis case had been brought in and they were waiting for him to operate at once. In the late afternoon he had high tea in the hospital, but he had to leave the table when an orderly appeared with a message from young Weir that the OB case had been taken to the room they had set aside for the delivery. It was a long time before it was over and Mrs. Morton's heart caused Ainslie grave concern. At the end he had been forced to ease up on the anesthetic and at the same time allay the fear that grew in the patient when she realized his reason for doing so. His shoulders sagged and his shirt dripped with sweat when he finally left the baby to the nurses and the exhausted patient to Dr. Weir.

He knew the day had gone without a count of the hours, but he was amazed to see that it was already after eight. For a while he sat in the common room, smoking his pipe while he waited for a nurse-in-training to bring him a cup of beef tea. It was an hour of the evening when thirty minutes can pass like five. He was loose with fatigue, and the long talk with MacKenzie of the night before seemed years away in the past. He heard a rustle of starched linen as the nurse came into the room with his tea, but he did not even lift his head to speak to her. She set it down on the table at his side and left quietly.

Ainslie picked up the cup after a time and sipped the brown liquid. It felt hot all the way down to his stomach and from there its warmth fanned out. He looked at his watch and wondered how it could be so much later than when he had looked at it last. He pulled himself to his feet and went out into the hall. Evening visitors had gone and overhead lights were turned off, leaving long shadows to merge between the dim night lights which burned at infrequent intervals along the walls.

Even for Ainslie, who tried so hard to shut all emotion out of his work, a hospital at this hour seemed to have a mysterious beauty. Life was never so vivid as when it was in danger, nor was a human being ever so vitally himself as when he had passed through pain and emerged on the other side of it.

In the ward a nurse was preparing the last of the patients for sleep when he reached the bedside of the young Newfoundlander. The boy had slept most of the day and looked up at him now with a sheepish smile. Ainslie smiled back, touched the boy's temples with his fingers and passed on to the appendicitis case of that afternoon. The patient was over his nausea and was sleeping, and after a glance at the chart Ainslie said good night to the nurse in charge and left the ward. He stopped at Mrs. Morton's room and found her too tired to look up when he stood beside her bed. He took Weir's stethoscope and listened and then beckoned Weir to follow him into the corridor.

"Sometimes the textbooks get in the way, don't they?" he said. "According to the books, no woman with a heart like that should ever get pregnant, but she took the risk and . . ." He shrugged and the quiet smile returned.

"Her husband said he never knew the heart was so bad," Weir said. "He kept repeating it over and over."

"Perhaps he didn't, but I have a pretty good idea that she knew. Women are far more courageous than we are, Weir." He touched the houseman lightly on the shoulder. "You must get some rest."

Ainslie found his mare in the hospital yard with a feed bag over her nose where the boy from the livery stable had left her. As he walked across the yard he could see the shadows cast by the beast and the carriage, long and pulled out on the naked ground. The weather had cleared again and the moon was low in the sky. A cat shot across the yard, belly to the ground, sprang onto the wooden fence at the back, darted along its edge, stopped to stare at the doctor, twitched, turned and jumped down on the far side. Ainslie took the feed bag off the mare and rubbed her nose. Then he tossed the bag into the carriage and climbed in, turned the mare around and put the reins about his neck. His eyes were closed as the mare went down the hill. She took the right-hand turn through MacDonald's Corner and trotted down the empty main street with her hoof strokes banging back from the empty store fronts. The hoof notes deepened on the timber of the bridge, sharpened on a short stretch of concrete beyond it, then thudded all the way down to the heart of the earth on the dirt road beyond. There was a whiff of salt water and of sulphur from a colliery. Somewhere a dog was howling, but the doctor's senses were dimming so fast the howl whirled down in a diminishing spiral until it buzzed like a pin point at the base of his brain. Then there was a smell of grass and the delicate scent of alder wet with dew. Ainslie slowly opened his eyes.

There it was, the ultimate solitude. A scent remembered from childhood told a man how lonely he was in middle age. Ainslie looked up and the stars taunted him because he had watched them as a boy and found them beautiful. His hands twitched on the reins. The face of his father flashed before his eyes. How could he ever hope to win the kind of struggle such a father had bred into his son? The old Calvinist had preached that life was a constant struggle against evil, and his son had believed him. At the same time he had preached that failure was a sin. Now the man who had been the boy must ask, How could a successful man be sinless, or a sinless man successful?

Ainslie's body swayed as the wheels hit a rut. He wished he had a son. To work as he did now was senseless. To work for a son's future would give purpose to the universe. He wanted a son who would grow into a learned man and a daughter who would be gentle and admiring of him.

The wistful face of Mollie MacNeil floated across his memory and he recalled suddenly that he had seen her boy and had marked him out. The boy really was remarkable, as remarkable as Mollie herself was good. This could only mean that goodness was insufficient, for the mines were going to get that boy as sure as fate. Slowly Ainslie's thoughts faded into the hum of the carriage wheels. When he fell asleep, his sleep was profound.

It was profound, but short. The mare reared and the doctor jerked upright, opened his eyes and saw a rough young face in the light of the left-hand carriage lamp.

"What's the matter? Who's sick now?"

At the sound of the doctor's voice, the face jerked back into the darkness and Ainslie heard the muttering of several men. Anger rose in him so hard he felt the blood pound in his forehead.

"Come back here!" he snapped. "I saw you, Gillies, come back here!"

There was silence. Then a soft, lilting voice broke out of the darkness. "Doctor, we did not think it wass you!"

The absurdity of the remark, the childlike surprise in the voice, were too familiar to seem funny to Ainslie in his present mood.

"Step up," he said, "the lot of you."

Three young men edged sheepishly forward into the light of the lamp. Gillies looked rough, but the other two had finely cut features with simple, wide-open eyes.

"Doctor," another of them said, "honest to God now, we did not know it wass you!"

Ainslie regarded them and they stood still, two of them with their caps in their hands, Gillies with his hands in his pockets and his cap pulled down over one ear.

"What were you up to?" Ainslie snapped at them. "You say you didn't know it was me – if it had been somebody else, what would you have done?"

The men looked from one to the other in the light. Then the third one spoke.

"Doctor, only the good God knows what we would haff done if it had not been you."

Ainslie took a deep breath and released it audibly. Their voices were as soft as Hebridean mists, but a man would be a fool to judge them by the sweetness of those tones. They had obviously been looking for a fight.

"Since when have you started brawling on the Sabbath?" he said.

"But Doctor, it iss not the Sabbath any more. It iss now half-past twelve."

He sighed and picked up the reins. "Go home and go to bed. And God help you if I catch you bothering people on the roads again."

"Yes, Doctor, we whill remember. And if Mrs. Doctor iss awake, would you say good night to her for us?"

The mare trotted off and left the three young men standing by the roadside, but Ainslie was wide awake now, awake with anger and a kind of despair at the endless accumulation of evidence that MacKenzie was right and that the time had come for him to leave this place. The horse passed the colliery, turned right and trotted down the coal-colored road past the darkened row of miners' cottages. Even in the cool night air, Ainslie felt he could almost smell their dusty, dark interiors, the rooms where they lived crowded together, the kitchens steamy from dishwater and the perpetually boiling kettle, the diapers of the babies and the sweaty underwear of the men, the high odor given off by heavy muscles. As he passed the MacNeil house, he remembered that Mollie's continued presence in it was evidence that this colliery was going downhill. Archie had not worked in the pits for five years, but the company let Mollie keep the house because otherwise it would have been empty. There were less miners in this colliery than there had been ten years ago because the seam was beginning to run out. The mare went down the slope, crossed the bridge and entered the doctor's grounds.

Ten minutes later Ainslie was in bed, having undressed so silently that Margaret did not even stir. He heard her quiet breathing, felt her warm presence beside him as he lay tense and reflecting. What MacKenzie had said to him, what he had said to MacKenzie, now seemed far away. He loved Margaret and wished she were awake so he could hold her in his arms. The knowledge of what they might have been to each other was huge in the darkness, but he did not touch her and his own effort to lie still only tightened his nerves the more and kept him awake.

He dozed, still tense, and when he opened his eyes he seemed not to have slept at all. Light was in the room and he saw that Margaret had forgotten to draw the blinds. He thought of getting up to draw them now but did not want to wake her by his movements, so he lay on his back and looked out the window at the dawn. It was geometrical, he decided, framed by the window with the tops of the birches softening the lines on the right. He counted twenty-three separate bars of color made by the dawn, each ruler-straight and of differing width, mauve at the bottom, then pale lavender, dark pink, scarlet and chrome in varying shades up to a green so unearthly pure he knew he had seen its like only once before, and remembered it was the blue-green of Lake Louise. Above the dawn's geometry was the faded blue of heaven. He saw a moving speck and recognized the ponderous wing-beats of a crow. The bird flew on a long, mounting diagonal across the bars of the dawn, black and solitary until it lost itself in the upper blue. As he watched it disappear Ainslie felt an emotion so unbearably intense he breathed out heavily and murmured aloud. Margaret stirred, saw him beside her and smiled.

"How long have you been here?"

"A couple of hours, I should think."

"And you haven't been asleep?"

"I dozed for a time."

Her arms came about him. He felt her soft, firm resilience warm and full of life against his tense, lean body. Resistance broke within him and with a half-sob he pressed his lips over hers.

"Oh, Margaret, I love you so much!"

He held her as she lay warm, satisfied and relaxed as a cat, and he was still holding her when she fell asleep. He took his arms away gently and lay on his back, loving her and wishing he had given her a son. He thought of all the children who played and brawled in the colliery rows while his own house was empty. He thought of young Alan MacNeil and of McCuen, who followed all the sports, saying in the hospital that Alan's father was on the way downhill but was soon going to have a crucial fight with some American light-heavyweight in some New Jersey town. The town's name came to him, Trenton, and he knew he had seen it years ago from a train window on the route from New York to Philadelphia. It was an old place, but it had as much smoke and iron-oxide red as Broughton and it ought to be one place in America where a broken-down Highlander like Archie MacNeil could feel at home.

Eleven

ARCHIE MACNEIL felt at home nowhere any more, so
Trenton seemed as good and as bad a place to be as any
other. He thought of nothing but the fight with Packy Miller
that was coming up a week from Friday. Even after the many
beatings he had taken, fighting was still all he wanted to do.
Now he was in Mooney's gymnasium training hard.

It was a small gymnasium which had once been a livery
stable. The stalls had been cleaned out and a large central space
had been cleared, but dried manure which had seeped under
the flooring was still there, so the place smelled of the manure
in addition to sodden boxing gloves, sweaty training suits, lin-
iment, steam from the showers and the cigars smoked by the
trainers and hangers-on. A skylight over the ring and a row
of windows just under the roof gave the boxers all the light
they ever had for their work.

This afternoon the semi-pros and preliminary boys, all of
them wearing black combination training suits, had stopped
skipping rope and pounding the light bags along the left wall
to watch Archie stalk his sparring partner, Ed Wagner, in the
ring. A sense of excitement had been building up during
the past hour, for the day was going as all the other days of
Archie's training had gone before. He had been picked as a
trial horse for Trenton's native son, Packy Miller, and now for

five days he had battered his partners with such expert savagery that the original odds on Miller had dropped considerably. More loafers than usual had paid ten cents apiece to watch the fighters train and the gym smelled of their sweat and sounded with the steady shuffling of their shoes on the bare floor. The only seats in the place, besides the stools provided for the boxers in the ring, were occupied by two men with a professional interest in Archie, one as fat as the other was thin.

The fat man was Sam Downey, who had traveled quite a distance in the four years since he had appeared in Cape Breton with his tongue hanging out for any kind of meal ticket. He now had five other boxers on his string beside Archie MacNeil; it was thought that he was getting steadily closer to the big promoters in New York. Laughin' Sam, the sports writers called him, because he had a nervous tick that gave him a falsetto laugh. In a profession where mutilation of features is taken for granted, Downey's face was still remarkable. At some point in his career his nose had been bitten off, and as his face was now fat and pale, that smudge of a nose with the scar of someone's incisor in the healed flesh gave him an appearance extreme enough to frighten children. Perhaps to offset the face, he dressed invariably in light-colored worsteds and large cravats with high stiff collars. He wore a large gray hat squarely on the top of his head, and while it stayed in place, which it did through all the hours of the day, he smoked cigars neatly without chewing their ends.

The thin man who sat hunched over next to Downey was the trainer, Charley Moss, a one-time lightweight contender who had abandoned his dreams of glory fifteen years before. It was believed around the gymnasiums that the stop watch he held in his hand remained there even in his sleep. As a trainer, he had converted his old razor-edge intensity into a churlish sullenness which made his boys think he hated them as well as every aspect of the boxing business.

He nodded towards the ring. "Eight days to go, and look at the son of a bitch. He's going to take Miller before the fifth."

Downey's left hand stroked his paunch, which bulged in pale gray worsted between his legs. "Hell," he said, "what can you tell about how good he is with nuttin better than Wagner to work on? That Dutchman's been fighting too long. Most of the time he don't even know where he is."

Moss kept his eyes on the ring. "Wagner threatened to quit this morning," he said.

"Yeh? Does he think he can eat better some place else?"

"He's had hell beat out of him all week." Charley's forehead wrinkled as he saw Wagner's head snap back from a left. He was glad that Archie's right cross that followed was a graze, for had it landed it would have knocked the Dutchman cold. He turned back to Downey. "This don't make sense. You want me to stop it?"

Downey shook his head while his left hand continued to stroke the gray worsted. "No. I want to see some more of Archie." A moment later his voice piped an octave higher, "I've seen him look good like this before."

"Sure you did. And you saw him win his fights, too."

"So what if he's got one win more? He's been through for two years. One win more, what difference will it make? The stupid bastard. He's through."

Moss gave Downey a quick look and a jerk of wrinkles appeared on his forehead as he took in the meaning of Downey's words. He wasn't surprised. No one surprised Charley Moss. If Archie were the only fighter Downey had, the fat man would be chortling about how wonderful his boy from Cape Breton was. But with five other fighters, Downey was a businessman now.

Moss went over to the ring apron with his watch in his hand, pulled back the striker of the gong and let it slam even though his watch said there were twenty-two seconds left in the round. Suddenly he was angry at everybody – at Archie for turning a training bout into a grudge fight, at Downey for being Downey, at himself for continuing to work for such a man. As the boxers moved into their corners he vaulted into the ring and crossed to Archie's corner.

"Take it easy and quit showing off," he snarled.

Then he ducked through the ropes and jumped to the floor, landing lightly on his toes. In spite of his opinion of his own profession, his heart was still in the canvas-covered rings where arguments could always be settled and a man needed more than a fast tongue to survive – if the promoters would let things take their course.

"That boy of yours is sure rough on his partners," said a voice behind him. Charley's forehead jumped into the crease of angry wrinkles again. He turned and recognized the speaker as a sports writer who worked for one of the Newark papers. He was the first out-of-town reporter to have a look at Archie before this fight.

"What's your boy trying to do, Charley – leave all his fight in the gym?"

Charley's reply was drowned in a thunder of noise as the men in black training suits began pounding the bags on the far wall. He sat down again next to Downey and the reporter sauntered after him. Downey leaned close and began to talk to Moss with his hand cupped against Charley's ear. As Moss listened against the thunder of the drumming bags his face grew sullen as well as angry. He looked at his watch, got up again and went towards the ring, and the roar of the bags stopped abruptly as the men in black turned to watch.

The voice of the reporter came through the silence. "MacNeil's a hell of a lot better than you fellows have been giving out about him. I wouldn't give Miller even money to go the distance."

Moss rang the gong and looked up at the ring. If this fellow printed what he thought, the odds on Miller would drop.

Everyone read the Newark paper in Trenton. Downey wouldn't mind, but what bothered Moss was that he minded himself. He didn't like MacNeil as a man, but when he was good he loved him as a fighter. When he had first begun to train Archie he had been sure he had a coming champion. Archie was too open in those days, he took more punches than he needed to take, but he was fast and he had that rippling strength that made him deadly when his timing was on. In the early days he had known too little about boxing, but Moss had corrected most of his early faults. He had trained balance into him and taught him to move in one piece. He had taught him how to bob and weave and had let his natural instinct strictly alone. MacNeil's natural instinct was to go in and finish it as quickly as possible, no clubbing or gouging, but fast, lancing blows. In his early days, Archie's terrible eagerness to fight had reminded Moss of Terry McGovern, the boy Moss still honored as the darling of them all.

Charley stood by the apron with his right hand rubbing abrasively at his blue jaw, studying Wagner impassively. Wagner was the bull type of fighter and he had been selected as a partner for Archie because he was short and strong and was supposed to resemble Packy Miller. He was muscle-bound, his hair grew so low on his forehead it was only two inches over his eyebrows, and his expression was so stupid a man could doubt legitimately whether he was even capable of feeling pain. Downey was right when he said the Dutchman was no good. Archie belonged to the cat family and even a third-rate tiger couldn't help looking pretty good against a bull.

Up in the ring, his red hair bristling, his jutting jaw held low, moving smoothly and in one piece, Archie was setting Wagner for the right cross. Around Archie's eyes was the redness that always showed when he was angry. Wagner must have said something or done something today to have made Archie hate him so much. Wagner was dirty in his habits and there was a queer fastidiousness about MacNeil. Anyway,

Moss thought, it never took much to make Archie feel that he had been insulted. He watched impassively as a left knocked Wagner's head back and Archie flashed in with a volley of punches which seemed to bounce off the Dutchman's head as he covered up. A right to the body made a bang that echoed from the back wall of the gym, and Moss turned away from the ring, knowing Wagner wouldn't last the round.

"Listen, Charley –" Again Downey was leaning over to talk into Moss's ear. "All it needs is a graze to open those eyes, and Miller's a crowder. By the fourth Archie's sure to be blinded, so what's the use?"

Moss brushed away the fat hand next to his ear. "Listen, Mr. Downey. Let's get this straight. Packy Miller's nuttin but a roundhouse slugger. Your boy up there's worth two of him, even now."

Downey ignored the anger in Charley's voice. "I never said Miller was good. I said he was young and he's still got his legs. I said he was the kind the crowd goes for."

Moss gave the fat man a long stare of angry contempt and when Downey let out his falsetto laugh he turned away to watch the ring.

"Okay," he said, without expression. "You're the boss. Only don't expect me to talk him into throwing it because that dumb bastard wouldn't throw a fight even to keep out of jail."

When Moss got up and walked around to the far side of the ring, the reporter was at his elbow again.

"I want to do a story on MacNeil. What was Archie like when you first got hold of him?"

"Not too smart," Moss said, and the words came from the depths of his experience and resentments. Not too smart. And yet before he got hurt he had had everything else. Everything but the calculation that makes the real killers, the coldness under the surface of the nice guys like Gentleman Jim Corbett and the mean ones like Kid McCoy.

"He comes from some place up in Canada, doesn't he?" the reporter said. "Irish, isn't he?"

"MacNeil's Scotch."

"That's too bad. The Scotch never seem to get anywhere in this game. The Irish, the Jews, the Negroes, the Italians – sometimes even the Poles. Miller's Polish, you know. Some day I'm going to do a piece about the racial origins of boxers."

Moss looked at him coldly. "You don't say."

Then his eyes went up to the ring. Wagner had been retreating and protecting his jaw and Moss knew from his stance that his legs had gone rubbery and he had reached the point of not caring. It was stupid – a grudge fight in training eight days before the main go. But what difference did it make? Downey was going to fix MacNeil.

"It looks like he's got him now," the reporter said, but Moss was not listening.

His eyes were on the ring in critical appraisal. On his toes within range, all of a piece and swaying, Archie waited for Wagner to make the first move. The Dutchman obliged. He lowered his left for a hook and lurched forward. A current of force shot up through Archie's calves, thighs and buttocks, gathered power through his swinging lumbar muscles, merged itself into the enormous leverage of his forward-driving shoulder and transmitted the full weight of his 172 pounds into the ram of his arm. It came out solid with a flick of the wrist, beating Wagner's hook by at least six inches. The crack of Archie's glove on Wagner's jaw was like a bat hitting a baseball and Wagner was unconscious before the back of his head hit the floor.

Moss grinned broadly. The sweet, lovely son of a bitch! He wondered how Downey liked it. It was going to take a good deal of fixing to keep Archie from finishing this Trenton Polack that Downey had his eye on, even if it was the one good fight left in Archie's system. Moss jumped into the ring and gave Archie a slap across the back and then bent down over Wagner. The Dutchman's eyes were already beginning to open and it occurred to Moss that they looked no more glassy now than they did normally.

"Okay, MacNeil," Charley said. "You're through for today."

Archie put a towel around his shoulders and jumped down to the floor. He paid no attention to Wagner; it was an aspect of his nature that Moss had always respected. Archie didn't like Wagner and when he didn't like a man he never pretended that he did. It wasn't smart, Moss knew, to have this kind of integrity in the boxing game because crowds were alienated by it. Fight crowds were not only cruel, they were also sentimental, and it gave them a pleasant feeling to see a fighter cut a man to pieces and then embrace him afterwards. Take the O'Leary fight, for instance. Archie had liked Tim O'Leary and after knocking him out he had helped bring him around. But when he had no respect for an opponent and knocked him out, he walked off and left him lying.

As Archie went to his dressing room the Newark reporter stopped him and began asking questions. Some of the loafers crowded around to shake his hand, but Archie pushed through them and went on to his shower. Moss turned back to Wagner, who was now on his feet, standing like an ox and saying he was through. Charley left him to fend for himself and jumped down from the ring. The gymnasium was a roar of noise again. Downey beckoned him to follow and led the way towards the office in one of the corners of the former stable. When Downey sat down in the swivel chair behind the littered desk and lit a cigar, Moss shut the door and waited.

"What I say still goes, Charley."

Moss shrugged his shoulders. "He's your property."

"He's got eight days to go." Downey leaned back, his cigar working in his mouth, and stroked his paunch. "Eight days can seem a mighty long time to a boy with an edge like he's got."

Moss waited.

"Is Wagner quitting? You told Archie to go easy on him, didn't you?"

"You heard me tell him."

"Well, I'm sick of Archie. Who does he think he is? Look what I've done for him."

"All he's got to do," Moss said, "is look in the mirror to see what you done for him."

Downey took out his wallet and opened it. "Here, give him this dough and then leave him strictly alone. Eight days can seem a *mighty* long time to a boy like him. Tonight you and me're going to New York. I got a new boy I want you to start working with tomorrow."

Moss leafed through the bills and put them into his right-hand pocket. "This is one Archie wants to win," he said. "Don't be surprised if he does, is all I got to say about this deal. If you got any money on the line you're taking a chance."

"I'll take it." Sam Downey pushed himself back from the desk.

"Will I tell him to come up to New York with us?"

"You can tell him to go to California if he feels like it, so long as he shows up here for the fight."

Moss went out through the gym to the dressing rooms. Archie was in the shower and the reporter was on a bench making notes in a small brown notebook.

"It's always a good story," the Newark man said, "when a fighter makes a come-back."

Moss could hear Archie splashing and singing under the shower. He went out again and found the Dutchman in the dressing room next door sitting in a stupor with the sweat cold on his naked body and his ring shoes still on his feet. Wagner looked up without expression when Moss spoke to him and Moss tossed him a towel. He caught it and draped it slowly around his shoulders. Moss shrugged and left him, and when he returned to Archie's room he saw him standing naked rubbing himself vigorously while he answered the questions the reporter shot at him with his usual childlike seriousness. It took another while before the reporter had all the notes he wanted and got up to leave. He shook Archie's hand and saluted Moss as he went out the door. Archie had his shirt and trousers on now and Moss went over to him and held out Downey's hundred dollars.

"The boss told me to give you this dough."

Archie sat down on the bench and reached for his socks. "I wass going so good today all I need is another partner. Wagner iss no better than an ox."

"He's quit," Moss said. "Do you know what that means? It means you've knocked yourself clean out of partners. It means from now on you're strictly on your own."

Archie looked up. "What the hell are you saying?"

Under the scar tissue was the sadness, the fighter's sadness, in Archie's eyes. Nearly all of them got it if they stayed in the game long enough. Even an imbecile like Ed Wagner showed that look sometimes. Again Moss thought of animals. Even ferocious animals had that look in their eyes when they were sick.

"I can beat the hell owt of Miller." Archie's voice had the incredulous, protesting tones of a child refusing to believe. "You said so yourself."

"After Miller, who else do you think you can beat?"

"If I stay good, I can beat anybody."

"I told you to go easy on Wagner," Moss said. "And look what you did to him. Wagner's a punch-drunk stumblebum and look how you fought him. Okay. Now Downey's disgusted. He figured on just so much for your training expenses. Wagner came cheap and now he's quit. So there's the picture."

Archie bent down and pulled on a shoe. With great deliberation he tied the lace. Then he put on his other shoe and tied the lace of that one and then he got to his feet and faced the trainer. Moss held the roll of bills on the palm of his outstretched hand while Archie stared at him.

"Downey's taking me to New York," Moss said. "He told me to give you this dough to look after yourself with till the fight."

Archie picked the money off Charley's palm and put it into his pocket. "I whill take this because Downey owes it to me," he said. "He owes me more than this, too."

Skinny in his turtle-necked sweater, his forehead creased with wrinkles, Moss said, "You won't do yourself any good if you shoot your mouth off to that newspaper guy, either. If you do, Downey will say why aren't you at Nick's in New York."

"All right. I whill go to Nick's."

"And when you get there Nick won't have any space for you. Any more than Mooney will have any space here. Take my advice. Live quiet and go out on the roads every day. Downey thinks he has you figured out. Take my advice. Fool Downey and go out on the roads. That's something he's not figuring on."

Archie stared at him, his eyes beginning to show red around the rims. Then his right hand shot out and caught Moss by the front of his sweater. He twisted the wool into a knot until he had a firm grip on the collar, his knuckles pressing hard on the thin man's windpipe. Lightly he began to knock Charley's head against the wall.

"Now you little bugger, you will lissen to me. I haff been keeping my mouth shut while I wass bad, but now I am good again and I whill tell you something. Downey iss a son of a whore and you are worse than that. By Chesus, the both of you! You thought I did not know what you wass up to." The soft Gaelic voice issued from a grim, red-eyed face as Archie continued to emphasize his points by tapping Charley's head against the plaster. "You little bugger. You are too small for me to be hitting, and Downey iss so fat I would lose my fist in his guts. But by Chesus, I am showing you what I think about you. You can go back to Downey and tell him I whill beat the hell owt of Miller next Friday night. You can tell him the reporter from Newark saw how good I wass and he iss going to put it in hiss paper. After I beat Miller the both of you can go to hell."

He released the collar of the sweater and Charley was jaw down and fists up, but Archie stood off on the balls of his feet, watching.

"You God damn fool," Moss said finally, and turned away.

Twelve

IT WAS SEVERAL HOURS before Archie felt the beginnings of the long loneliness he knew would grow into the final loneliness of the moment before the first gong rang when his seconds would leave the ring and he would be under the lights facing Miller. He moved through the dingy streets of Trenton walking fast on the balls of his feet, occasionally weaving and dancing, so sharp was his edge. He was still intoxicated by the knowledge of how good he had been today and he could think of nothing else. Nothing else mattered beside the great fact that he was good again. The thing was back inside him, the thing that had ridden with him that great night in Providence when he had knocked out Tim O'Leary in three rounds and O'Leary had not once laid a glove on him. This lovely, wonderful thing that enters an athlete occasionally and does his thinking for him, gives him the sweet moment of leisure before every move that makes the move perfect. It was there again.

He rubbed his clenched right fist into the palm of his left hand and wished to God he were fighting Miller tonight instead of a week from tomorrow. He saw Miller there in front of him – young, swarthy, black-haired, overconfident, a round-house slugger made to order for a clean left. As easy to hit as a two-hundred-pound bag. Archie began to laugh aloud.

He turned a corner into another slum street. The sweat oozing through his pores had already saturated his shirt. He pulled his cloth cap down over his right ear with a remembered gesture of truculence. Since coming to the States he had tried to be what Downey called a dresser, but today he had left his felt hat in the hotel and put on the old cloth workman's cap that had come with him from Cape Breton. From now on he was going to do things his way.

Then he remembered his eyes. His fingers probed at the scar tissue on his lower forehead and felt the hard, lacerated scar over his left eye. After Chip had done that to him Archie had apologized to Downey for not winning. By Chesus! And Downey had sent him in against Chip only ten days after the fight when Ryan had opened the cut for the first time. Why? He knew why now. Because Downey was playing with the promoters, and when the promoters had wanted a substitute for a highly advertised fight in Baltimore, Downey had obliged with the eyes of his own fighter. By Chesus, he said again to himself.

Then he remembered that he was all alone. They thought he was stupid. They knew this was his last chance and he would have to make the most of it. They knew he couldn't complain or prove to anyone that he was getting a raw deal. He stopped on a corner and gave a twitch to his cap, hoping it made him look tough, but his blue serge suit was too well pressed and there was something too Highland about his features to classify him easily with the middle-European and Sicilian laborers who lived in this district of Trenton.

Again Packy Miller jumped into his mind's eye. Miller had shoulders. He had a banging hook, he bulled his way in close and already he had a reputation for being a dirty fighter. Archie grinned. He wasn't afraid of Miller. It was only a dancer with a fast jab he was afraid of now, not a slugger. His watch showed five o'clock and it was still eight days and maybe five hours before he would actually face Miller. Suddenly he felt frightened. This was one thing they had never done to him before. They had never left him all alone, telling the local gym that he would finish his training in New York and telling him to stay where he was.

He wondered if he ought to go to New York. If he did, what was to keep them from offering him a new partner and then fixing it for the partner to butt his eyes open before the Miller fight? Archie shook his head. He was unaccustomed to thinking. All he wanted to do was to fight. He decided to stay in Trenton and do what Moss had said. He would go out on the roads every morning. He would keep in condition by shadow-boxing and skipping rope all alone, and his wind and legs would be so good for Miller he would surprise them.

But the loneliness flooded into him. As he passed the shutter door of a saloon he stopped to look over the top of it. He saw the hats of the men inside and smelled malt and whiskey spills and tobacco smoke and remembered when he had been sent out after supper with the enamel pitcher in his hand to bring home the rum to his father. He remembered his mother dying in the back room of the one-story house, crying over and over to herself, "Och – och – och ay!" because she would never get better and her husband was no good and had shamed her all her life before the neighbors. Archie pulled at his cap and walked away from the saloon. He remembered how he had handled Ed Wagner that morning and his spirits rose. He felt his whole heart lift up and swim on the sudden glow of good feeling and he wanted to share it with somebody.

"I will haff a little one," he said to himself as he turned back. "The good God knows how bad I need it."

At the bar, clutching his whiskey glass and looking up at the picture of the naked woman hanging over the mirror, Archie told himself they would be proud of him in Broughton when they got the news of the fight. He stood very still, gripping his glass in a huge hand. After a while he reached inside his coat and took from his pocket a worn piece of paper with ruled lines and a message written in pencil. He spread it out on the bar and hunched over it, guarding it with his hands as he read it again.

ARCHIE DEAR, the men are all talking about the fight and I hope you win. Alan and I are all alone here and it has been a long time. There is not much money left. Will you come home soon, Archie, for we want you.

Your wife, MOLLIE

He kept trying to think and after a time he folded the letter and put it back in his pocket. Then he reached for the glass, saw it was empty and asked the barman for another one. The redness had left his eyes now and he merely looked sad. "She iss too good for the likes of the bitches I know here," he muttered into the whiskey. He tried to think of her and felt ashamed. Then he thought of her some more. "Oh Chesus, but when she loves a man he knows it!" She wass not a bitch, she wass a lady, she wass his wife, but oh Chesus, when she had loved him!

He finished the second drink and his face became more Highland and sadder than ever, and now he began to feel truculent. It wass the boy wass the trouble with her, it wass the boy she would never leave. She would always be thinking first of the boy.

He ordered still another drink and put down half of it. "What does she know about it?" he muttered to the whiskey. "It" was everything he had undergone since leaving home. "It" was Downey and Moss and the gravel-voiced men. "It" was the loneliness. "It" was the crowd roaring for the other man, the man they had bet on to knock him out, and "it" was the answering roar in his own brain saying that if only the good God would clear the blood out of his eyes he would show the crowd what he could do, but always the blood kept blinding him and when he could see again in the dressing room there was nothing better to look at than the sour face of Charley Moss.

Charley Moss? Maybe he wass wrong in pitching him around today? Charley wass under Downey too. It wass Downey wass the big bastard.

He looked up and there was the naked woman in the picture smiling especially for him. All naked and smiling down. He began to smile back. "By Chesus!" he said aloud. He studied her thighs. They were half again as large as the slim thighs that curved down from Mollie's hips. He nudged the man standing nearby and pointed upward with his glass. "That iss a bitch," he said. He remembered the first time he had seen Mollie. It was the evening after he had first fought and beaten a grown man and she was the daughter of old Rorie MacIntosh who thought so much of himself he would never speak to Archie because Archie's father was Sandy Long-Hair and no MacIntosh thought any of the Long-Hairs had ever been any good. But that night he had seen Rorie's daughter for the first time.

He looked up at the picture again. "There iss other women," he said.

The man next to him had moved away and someone else had taken his place. Archie felt that he was being watched sharply, so he turned around to find out who was staring, and then the new man next to him said, "Archie MacNeil, for the love of God. I thought it wass you. *Ciamar ha she?*"

Archie answered in Gaelic and the sound of the words made him feel warm, but he still didn't know who the other man was. He was medium-sized with high Scottish cheekbones, good color in his face and a graying mustache. He looked old-fashioned and proper among the Polish and Italian workmen who were drinking at the bar. Then he said his name was MacLeod – John George MacLeod from Big Bras d'Or and he had worked in the steel plant in Sydney for seven years before coming down to the States for the money.

It was four years since Archie had listened to a Gaelic accent, and its likeness to his own made him feel suddenly shy. The other Cape Bretoner beckoned to the barman for two more drinks. When they arrived he set one up in front of Archie with an air of some formality.

"I hope it iss all right, Archie MacNeil, for you to be drinking before a fight?" he said.

Archie picked up his glass and downed the brown stuff. "I always take a little one when things iss going good." As he began to smile the grimness left his face and he looked like a boy. "It makes me feel fine."

"And what would be the harm in one little drink when you know when to stop? Look at John L. Sullivan, now, what he did, and he neffer knew when to stop at all." MacLeod turned his back on a hulking Pole who seemed eager to get into the conversation. "There wass a man from Cape Breton knocked out John L. once – did you know that, Archie?"

"There wass no man in Cape Breton I could not beat, and I am telling you –" Archie shook his head for emphasis. "I would not haff the weight for John L. John L. could knock a silver dollar into a mahogany bar without brass knuckles, even."

"No, it iss true, what I am telling you. And you can go home and ask Magistrate MacKeegan and he will say I am right. Hootie MacDonald from Whycogamagh knocked out John L. Sullivan one night in Boston. He iss Dr. Hootie now, but then he wass a young man and he wass in a place where John L. was boasting he could whip anyone in the world, and that wass too much for Hootie. So he stood up to him. Right there. And when it wass over, it wass John L. wass on the floor."

"Och!" said Archie. And a moment later, as MacLeod still looked at him with open eyes waiting to be believed, "Maybe he did and maybe he did not. And maybe John L. wass as drunk as Paddy's pig. John L. used to say a man wass not drunk when he fell to the floor. He wass only drunk when he began to hold onto it."

Archie turned his attention back to the picture of the naked woman. By Chesus, but that wass a fine pair of legs. That wass the woman he wanted, and he wass what a woman like her deserved to have.

MacLeod's voice lilted in his ear again. "The Yankees haff their money on Miller for Friday night and I haff to laugh. Two days ago I bet on you because I come from Cape Breton and I know what you can do. And look now!" He took a rolled copy of the Newark evening paper from his pocket and pointed to a small paragraph on the sports page. "Look here what it says, and it iss their own paper, too. It says you are so good it iss crazy to give Miller better than even money. On Friday night next week, my glory, but there will be a time!"

Archie felt the beginning of an annoyance against MacLeod. What did he know about it? It was easy to talk with money. All MacLeod wanted was to boast to the foreigners in his factory that he was from Cape Breton, too.

"There iss something else you will want to hear," MacLeod went on, unconcerned with the change in Archie's mood. "I haff been down here three months only. So I can tell you that one day before I left Sydney I wass in Broughton and I wass in the store. I saw your wife there, Archie, with the little boy. She wass fitting him to a new pair of shoes."

Archie's fingers tightened on his glass. "What did she look like?" he said.

"She looked pretty good to me."

"And the boy?"

"He iss getting to be quite a big little bugger, and my glory, but your wife iss proud of him! People ask when you will be coming home to see for yourself."

Archie turned on him. "And what business is it of theirs if I come home or not?"

"It iss none, but they would all like to see you."

"By Chesus, nobody can make me go into the mine again!"

MacLeod picked up his own glass, at last sensing Archie's rising mood of anger.

"They can say what they God damn well please," Archie said hoarsely, "but I whill not go into the mine again. That iss what *she* wanted and she iss one of those that know how to make you ashamed of yourself. For the sake of the boy she would make an ox out of me, but I saw what she wass after. She iss one of those that will haff their way by being nice no matter what the hell you do, but by Chesus, it will take more than her, or you either, to get me back to the mine."

He picked up his glass, saw that it was empty, and shoved it out of reach on the bar. "They can say what they like. And she can think what she likes. And the little boy can grow as high as the wheels on top of Dominion Number Two, but I whill not go back to the mine again."

MacLeod made haste to call for another drink, and when the barman had filled their glasses he again moved one before Archie with careful formality.

"It wass not the mine I wass talking about," he said humbly. "I wass not even thinking about the mine."

"There are some that whill live their whole lives like oxes and cows," Archie muttered. "I am not one of them."

"I wass only meaning if maybe you could haff a fight in Sydney now," MacLeod put in tentatively. "If you could beat a big Yankee in Sydney – why, there would not be enough tramcars in the whole of Cape Breton to take the men from Broughton to see it, and from Reserve and Glace Bay and Port Morien and New Waterford, moreoffer."

Archie's anger disappeared as suddenly as it had come. "That iss different," he said gravely.

"It would be a great day. In Sydney it is hard telling who would make the purse big enough to get a Yankee worth knocking out, but it would be a great day just the same. They think it an awful shame for you to waste your fighting on those that can't appreciate it down here."

Archie raised his glass and poured down the drink in a single gulp. Then he felt the haze spread through him and knew he had taken too much, for he was feeling the beginnings of the sadness even though it was still daylight. It was not unhappiness such as city people know. It was concerned with no one thing in particular, for it was the primitive sadness of his whole race. He began to hum a song, and as MacLeod recognized the tune he joined him, singing the words in a melancholy cadence. *Horo ma Nighean Donn Bhoideach, Hiri mo Nighean Donn Bhoideach, mo Chaileag Laglach Bhoideach . . .*

MacLeod stopped singing in the middle of a bar as he saw Archie's face rough with the growing redness about his eyes.

"I whill go home when I am the champion," said Archie. "I could beat efferybody in Canada, the heavyweights too, and what difference would that make? I could go up to Montreal and knock out that bugger Masson if he would step into the ring with me, and what would the Canadian title be? They think they are better than the Yankees, but I – tell – you . . ." his fist pounded the bar . . . "it does not matter how good a man iss up there in Canada, the Yankees haff got to say so before anybody in Canada will believe it. And that iss why I am going to beat the hell owt of Miller. And after Miller I will beat the hell owt of them all, and I will do it my own way." He was shouting hoarsely now, his face dark with rage. "Then in Broughton they will not be able to say I am no good and why didn't I come home sooner."

He dropped a bill on the bar and walked out of the saloon without waiting for change, leaving MacLeod with a flush on his face and a sensation of shame as he pulled on his mustache and wondered what he had said to anger his hero.

Thirteen

THE FIRST THING Archie did when he reached his room in the hotel was to clear the desk of soiled clothes and old newspapers. He sat down and placed his hand on the rough green blotter and looked at the ink marks left by someone else's pen. Even the thought of writing a letter took more out of him than an hour's hard work in the gym, so he got up and went downstairs and ate a large meal. In the dining room it was easier to think about what he wanted to say to Mollie. The words formed themselves carefully in his head. But after dinner, when he reached the desk in his room again, the pieces of white hotel stationery daunted him. Finally he thought about Mollie's neat, lithe legs and before he could grow afraid of the paper again he began to scratch some words to her.

He said he wanted her to leave Broughton right away and come down and meet him in Trenton. Right away. He was going to beat Miller and she would be proud to see him do it. After that he would go on to be the champion and they could both go home together. He said nothing about Alan because right now he was lonely for Mollie and it was hard for him to think what Alan was like after four years. His childish handwriting crawled to the end of the page, where he signed his full name as it always appeared in the papers – *Archie MacNeil from Cape Breton*. After he had folded the letter and put it in an envelope he felt better.

By Tuesday of the following week he had become tired of getting up early and skipping rope on the roads and no answer had come from Mollie. It was hot and the humid air of New Jersey had taken the starch out of his legs. He was tired and sick of being alone. So he stopped skipping rope since there was no one to time him and urge him on. Instead, he walked the streets of Trenton and the rage and sadness boiled in him. When he didn't want a woman, he wanted to fight somebody. He felt himself to be in a trap with the gate blocked by the grinning face of Packy Miller. He saw the hulking, pork-barrel body with the muscular forearms jerking up to guard the head and catch the attacker's wrists with the arm bones. Miller would come in low and try to butt, he would gouge and thumb and the fight would be as loose and dirty as the promoters thought the crowd would endure, and since this was Miller's home town the crowd would let anything go provided it was Miller who was getting away with it. With a neck like that one it would take half a dozen punches to rock him and as many more to put him to sleep, and he wondered how long he could keep Miller away from his eyes.

When thoughts like these made Archie forget where he was, he stopped and breathed three times deeply and let the air sigh out between his lips. Then he became calculating as again he saw clearly the essential thing. Miller would not do much at a distance. He would have to come in solid, and like all hookers he would be easy to hit. Maybe it would be Miller's eyes that would take the beating on Friday?

So Archie went on walking. He wanted to talk to somebody who knew what he was feeling and what he was up against. He wanted an experienced man – not a fool like MacLeod – to tell him he had been just as good on his last afternoon in the gym as he had thought he was, for if he was as good as he thought he was he would have Miller rocking before the first round was over. He narrowed his eyes and continued to see everything coldly. It was going to be all or nothing in the first five rounds. The time was when he had entered the ring feeling easy because he had known the clock was on his side, but George Chip's left jabs and cutting rights had ended that time forever. He would have to hit Miller early.

An hour later he was still walking and by now he was another man again. The few drinks he had taken somewhere on the way to lighten the approach of the sunset had depressed him. He had never been left alone like this before a fight. He had never been turned loose with a roll of money that could mean only one thing. His own manager and trainer wanted him to lose.

Archie stopped in front of another saloon, but this time he decided not to go in. He leaned against a lamppost in front of it and for something to do to show his nonchalance he began to pick his teeth with a match. Men in work clothes lounged down the street or sat on nearby doorsteps talking in foreign tongues.

He looked at the broad shoulders of one of them with a fighter's appraisal of a possible enemy. Then he tossed the match away with a gesture of contempt. If a man was a fighter he would not be sitting on a doorstep in a street like this.

On the next corner he bought a newspaper and opened it at the sports page. It was a Trenton paper and they were beginning to build up publicity for the fight on Friday. He saw Miller's picture and also his own. There was no mention of the peculiar fact that he was no longer training in Mooney's gym. He was supposed to be with Sam Downey somewhere in New York.

It began to dawn on Archie by a method of reasoning he could scarcely have understood that this was not considered an important fight. Apart from the man who worked for a Newark paper – the one who had talked to him last week –

nobody was interested in him any more. Miller was the comer and MacNeil was already finished. They wrote about Miller because he had a future. About himself there was nothing but a few noncommittal words. They said he was tough and could take it. They added that Downey had reported him in good condition and that Downey admitted Miller was good but expected Archie would beat him.

Archie tore the paper in two and watched the parts of the separate halves flutter to the brick gutter. Then he thrust his hands deep in his pockets and walked more slowly now for another half hour. He wondered if he went to New York if he could find Charley Moss and tell him he was sorry he had man-handled him. He wanted Charley to be his friend in the corner on Friday night. But New York was a big place and probably as empty as a little place like Trenton. He lowered his head and walked on, a Highlander lost in the lowlands of the shrewd men. His battered features and huge hands frightened the old lady whom he bumped into as he turned a corner, but he was unconscious of her feelings and failed to notice her surprise at the gentle lilt in his voice when he touched his cap and told her he was sorry.

The space between now and Friday night closed abruptly. He no longer cared. Nothing existed for him any more but the necessity of escaping from the emptiness. Mollie was far away. She had always been far away. Far, far away ever since Alan was born. What did she know about it? What did she know about anything?

He found the woman he was looking for after a while, because there is always a woman in every emptiness who can sense the value to herself of a big man who is lonely and afraid. So for a time Archie forgot what he knew without knowing it.

Fourteen

T HE STORY about Archie MacNeil in the Newark paper
was picked up by Canadian Press and one of the Halifax
papers reprinted it in full several days later. That was where
Angus the Barraman saw it when he pushed his cup of tea to
one side of the kitchen table and opened the paper at the
sports page. The kitchen, hot from the stove and steamy with
dish water, was noisy with clattering dishes and an argument
going on between three of his four children.

"Get owt of here," Angus said to the boys, "before I whill
be angry. Your father hass something important to think
abowt."

As soon as they had gone outside, he turned back to the
paper and brooded with slow joy over the paragraph in which
an American ring expert predicted victory for Archie MacNeil
over Packy Miller in Trenton next Friday night. Angus read
the paragraph twice, then looked up at the picture of the
Sacred Heart over the table. Being a Barra MacNeil, he was a
good Catholic and he took a long look at the picture for luck.
Then he closed his eyes and let his mind dwell on the scene
he hoped would be enacted in Trenton, and finally he could
hold his excitement no longer.

"It looks good for Archie," he said carefully.

His wife paid no attention as she kept on washing the dishes in the sink. Angus scratched his head and his voice became melancholy.

"The trouble iss, you neffer can tell for sure. God knows how it iss, but the Yankees always seem to win. That iss something I do not understand, for I haff seen a Yankee once and he wass not so much." He continued to scratch his head and his voice became more melancholy still. "I wonder whill there be dirhty tricks in Trenton next Friday night?"

Still his wife paid no attention to him.

"All the same," Angus the Barraman went on, "Archie iss good, and by this time he should be knowing plenty of dirhty tricks hiss ownself, for there iss no doubt abowt it, he hass the cleverness." He shook his head judiciously, as he had once seen Magistrate MacKeegan do when giving him a suspended sentence for being drunk and disorderly. "Look what Archie did to the champion of the Boston States that night in Jehovah!" He scratched his head again and looked puzzled. "Or wass it Jehovah, now? Where in hell wass the place where Archie knocked the hell owt of him?" He began to show relief. "Och yes indeed, I remember now. It wass Providence, and that iss the same thing whateffer. Look what Archie did that night to the champion of the Boston States!"

He stopped hopefully, and this time his wife decided to pay heed to him.

"You and Archie MacNeil! If you would think as much abowt getting to the pit on time as you do abowt him and hiss fights, we whould be haffing money in the drawer, mayhbe."

"Hold your tongue, God dahmn you, for my legs iss hurting me! What would you be knowing abowt Archie, for God's sake now? When he iss good, he iss the best light-heavyweight in the world."

"And what iss that, except something to be ashamed of? Your own sons haff to hear you talk all day about that good-for-nothing bruiser, and what iss the sense in me hoping some of them whill get the education, with you around?"

Angus looked at her square back and went on scratching. Then he got up and mumbled that he was going for a walk, and soon he was picking his way behind the houses to Mollie MacNeil's. He knocked on the scullery door and was admitted by Mollie herself. When he saw Alan in the kitchen, he winked at him solemnly and said that his elders had a matter of important business to discuss in the front room. Mollie showed him into the parlor and closed the door, and then Angus the Barraman took the paper from his pocket and spread it out on the table.

"There iss news," he said solemnly.

Mollie read the paragraph without expression. Then she reread it very slowly as if committing it to memory, while Angus watched her face with the look of an Aberdeen terrier inspecting a marrowbone.

"Thank you for showing it to me, Mr. MacNeil." She handed the paper back and forced a smile. "But he has not won yet."

"Och, but hassn't he as good as whon?" Angus shifted from one foot to the other. "Look at the Yankees their ownselves admitting he iss going to?"

Again she smiled and walked with him to the door, knowing that Mrs. Angus would make trouble if she discovered he was here alone. Angus the Barraman shuffled out and went farther up the row looking for someone else to talk to. His initial optimism had now degenerated into a superstitious fear that he might have done Archie a bad turn by accepting the newspaper story at its face value, and he wished he had kept his mouth shut and not told Mollie her husband was sure to win. Three houses along the row he came upon Neilly MacKay on his doorstep and sat down beside him. After the two men had chewed tobacco for a while, Angus showed the paper to Neilly and Neilly read it with care. He said "Whell now!" and chewed some more, and at last the two men began to talk. The more they agreed that Archie was the finest light-heavyweight in the world, the harder they worked at telling each other he was going to lose on Friday night. Something was going to happen, of that there was no doubt whatever. The sun had set before Angus felt he had been gloomy enough to appease the gods, and he shuffled homewards feeling more comfortable.

Back in her own parlor Mollie pulled a large oblong frame into the middle of the room and settled herself to work on the rug she had mounted on it. She was following a new pattern that Mrs. Ainslie had given her and she thought it was very beautiful. Mrs. Ainslie had shown her how to blend her colors in new ways. The design had been in a book belonging to the doctor and Mrs. Ainslie had explained that the pattern came from Persia where the most beautiful rugs in the world were made. The other Scotswomen in the row who had come in to look at it decided that Mollie was putting on airs. Who would walk on a thing as fancy as that, they had said. But the rug was more than half finished now and Mollie still liked it.

Tonight, however, she kept dropping the hook and every time she reached down to pick it up she felt the flutter in her stomach that always appeared whenever Archie was facing an important battle. It was a long time since she had felt it like this, but that was probably because she had received a letter from Archie at last, after all these months. And he wanted her to go to him. He loved her after all. She smiled quietly and the smile brightened her face. She was still smiling when the door creaked and Alan stood on the threshold in his nightgown and bare feet.

"Mummy, what did Mr. MacNeil want?"

"He had news of your father. Good news, too."

Alan's face brightened. "Was Father's name in the paper again?"

"Indeed it was!"

"Let me see?"

"It was Mr. MacNeil's paper and he has taken it away with him."

"Then I'll ask Mr. MacNeil tomorrow."

"No, Alan, you must not do that."

"Why?"

"Remember what I said – you are too young to be reading the newspaper."

His face fell. "Then tell me what the paper said about Father."

"Well, there wasn't much about him, but it said how well he is doing in the States."

"Did it say when he was coming home?"

"Oh no, the paper would never say that. But we knew he was not coming home right away, didn't we?"

Alan moved towards her and began to stroke the edge of the finished part of the rug. "Mummy – what does a prize fighter do?"

She took in her breath with a little gasp and then she reached once more for the hook that had fallen to the floor.

"How did you ever hear a word like that?"

"Danny MacIsaac says they are men that fight in front of big crowds and the people in the crowds pay lots of money to watch them."

She gave a nervous laugh. "What does little Danny MacIsaac know?"

Her fingers talked for her as she stroked his tousled hair. If only she could tell him that his father was a man with a profession like a doctor or a lawyer, or even a storekeeper, or even a foreman in one of the mines. She wanted her son to have everything, but most of all she wanted him to have a father he could be proud of, not a prize fighter to be ashamed of! If only Archie had not had so much of the wildness in him! But he loved her still. He had said so in the letter, and now as she thought about him her body ached with longing. Meanwhile, Alan was waiting for an answer.

And suddenly she had an answer. If Archie ever did come home his fighting days would be over. So what was the harm in telling a small lie for Alan's sake? He always believed her.

She turned the boy around to face her. "You know your father is a very strong man and I have told you when he was young he knew how to fight. But so do all the boys in Broughton. Now you can hardly imagine your father doing anything rough or dishonest or shameful, can you now?"

"No." He turned away again to finger the rug.

"The work your father is doing in the States is so special he couldn't do it here and that is why he has to go away. Lots of boys who grow up in Broughton go to the States to do their work. But he loves us very much. Wherever he is, that is what he is thinking about. And we couldn't ask for more than that, could we now?"

She was smiling again now, for the sound of her own words had convinced her that they were the essential truth. It was only when Alan turned to look at her with round eyes that told her nothing of his thoughts that she began to feel uneasy.

"But, Mummy, why can't you tell me what kind of work he does?"

She became flustered. "Well, it's – it's sort of a secret. But when he comes home he will tell us all about it himself."

From the expression on Alan's face she knew he was going to ask her no more questions that day. She smiled with relief and pulled him towards her, balancing his weight against her thigh.

"Now – what really matters most to your father is what you work at yourself. You must grow up and finish school and get the education so you can become an important man. That is why I do not mind about your father being away for such a long time. When he is successful he will come home and then he will have the money for us so we can do all those nice things we talk about."

"Yes, Mummy," Alan said.

"Now I'll tell you about the surprise I have for you." She shifted her position and Alan slid to the floor and they laughed together at his awkward posture before he got to his feet.

"On Friday if it's fine we will go on another picnic, and this time we will get up early and go into Broughton and take the train for Mira and we will be away all day. Now then – what do you think of that?"

He leaned against her again. "A picnic when it's not even Saturday?"

"Yes. Friday is a sort of special day too, sometimes." She got up and guided him towards the stairs with her hand on his shoulder. "Your father would like us to enjoy ourselves because he is such a great one to enjoy himself. Did I ever tell you about one time when he was still in the mines, he came home at the end of the day and got washed like all the other men in the row, then he put on his second best suit and got on the streetcar and went into Broughton after supper for a boxing match. He was very good, you know, and he loved it. He won his match and then he turned around and came home and washed again and changed into his other suit and I put on my best dress and we went back to Broughton to a dance. We danced all night long until five in the morning and by then I was so tired I could hardly stand up. But your father was not tired at all. The next day he went back to the mine as if he had slept all night."

Alan tried to remember what his father was like. It was as hard as trying to remember how he had been born. His mother had told him about when he was born. She said she had wakened up one night and found him in bed beside her. He was very small, but the first thing he did was to reach up and rub her nose with his fist. He thought he could remember rubbing her nose but he was not sure. His memory of his father was clearer than that. A red-haired man of great size with a wonderful laugh had carried Alan on his shoulder, and that was the way Alan always thought of him. But this story about the boxing and the dancing must have happened before he was born, because he could not remember his mother and his father doing anything like that.

He went upstairs ahead of her and climbed into his cot while she rubbed his chilled feet before pulling the covers over them. Then he lay back and looked up at her with round eyes as he thought about the picnic they would have on Friday.

"Mira is where the river is – isn't it, Mummy?"

"Yes, and it's one of the prettiest rivers in the world."

"Is it as big as Dr. Ainslie's river?"

"Dr. Ainslie has only a brook. The Mira is so big it belongs to the government."

"How can the government have a river? The government is in Ottawa."

"Don't ask any more questions and close your eyes and we'll talk about it some more when we get there."

He was asleep before she left the room.

Fifteen

ON THURSDAY EVENING Daniel Ainslie received a telephone call from an old friend in Louisburg, an Acadian doctor called Fernand Doucette, who wanted him to perform a major operation on the following day. The patient was a longshoreman who had fallen down the hold of a vessel and fractured his skull and Doucette believed a fragment of broken bone had penetrated the brain and damaged some of the tissues so badly they would have to be removed. The patient would probably die, he said, but it should be a lovely case. If the man lived it would be the first time a Nova Scotian surgeon had ever succeeded in such an operation.

While Dr. Doucette talked, Ainslie studied his engagement pad and decided that the work in Broughton could wait on his return from Louisburg. He promised Doucette that he would arrive on the morning train, and after telephoning the hospital to say he would not be in until after the train returned from Louisburg in the early evening, he went into his surgery and pored over his medical books for three hours.

He went to bed at midnight excited by the challenge of the operation, feeling almost superstitiously confident of his own powers even though he had never in his life performed an operation in which there were so many unknown quantities.

It was just before seven the next morning when Ainslie reached the railway station in Broughton. The waiting train was a composite local of three box cars, four coal cars, a dozen empty flats, two wooden passenger coaches and a caboose. The coach Ainslie entered was empty and he sat down on one of the red plush seats at the back and opened his medical bag. After taking out a school edition of the Sixth Book of the *Odyssey* he settled himself to study it. More passengers entered the coach and found seats, but he paid no attention to anything but the lines before him, turning to the vocabulary in the back of the book whenever he required the meaning of a word.

The train started with a violent jerk and then it pulled out through the streets, passed a colliery and dragged off into a stretch of open country. After finishing five lines Ainslie put the book down and stroked his eyelids. His continued consciousness of the coming operation made him too tense to concentrate on Homer, but he blamed himself for laziness and flogged himself on through another five lines until he came upon three words which were unfamiliar. He stopped and counted the lines left in the book and saw that he had still a hundred and eighty to go.

"I'll never finish it at this rate," he said under his breath. He marked the completed line with a pencil, closed the book and looked about. Halfway down the car he saw Mollie MacNeil and a small boy, Mollie with a picnic basket on the seat beside her and the boy on the red plush opposite with his nose pressed against the windowpane. There were several other passengers in the seats between them, but nobody he knew, so he got up and walked along to their seats.

"Where are you two going?" he said, and wondered why Mollie flushed when she looked up and saw him.

"Alan and I are on our way to Mira."

"What are you going there for?"

"It is just a picnic, Doctor." She brushed back a wisp of hair and smiled at Alan, who had stopped pressing his face against the window and was sitting neatly on the plush-covered seat with his knees together and his feet dangling. "This is Dr. Ainslie speaking to us," she said.

Ainslie saw the boy look up with his eyes large and eager.

"Mummy said the river in Mira is lots bigger than yours," Alan said.

"Did she, now? Well, so it is."

He saw the boy smiling at him with the happy composure of a child who thinks everyone is his friend. Nobody in all of Daniel Ainslie's memory had ever looked at him with such an unquestioning welcome in his face. Ainslie smiled back, and the tight lines about his mouth relaxed.

"You're the boy I've heard so much about." He moved the picnic basket and sat down on the seat beside Mollie. "So you know my brook?"

"Oh, yes."

"Well, you mustn't drink any of the water in it. Some chemicals are seeping into it from the mine and it's not fit to drink. What are you going to do in Mira besides eat all the food in this basket?"

"I'm going to find more sea shells." Alan's voice grew confidential. He took from his pocket the white shell he had picked up in the cove and handed it to the doctor. "Mummy says the noise in this one is the oldest noise in the world. Did you know that?"

"I certainly didn't." Ainslie gave Mollie a startled glance.

He saw a look of uncertainty pass across Alan's face, and the flush return to Mollie's cheeks.

"Mummy says," Alan told him gravely, "that the oldest things in the world are on the bottom of the sea, and she says the shell remembers the sounds they make."

Before Ainslie could answer the boy, Mollie interjected, "It was just something I told him for fun."

"And you weren't so far wrong, at that," he said. "But what gave you the idea?"

"It is what I read."

Ainslie took out his pipe and stuffed it carefully, and although there was a sign at the end of the car forbidding smoking, he lit the pipe and began to blow smoke steadily before him. When the conductor opened the forward door of the coach Mollie looked up at the sign, and then she saw him begin to punch the tickets of other passengers, so she started to search the picnic basket for her purse. By the time the conductor reached them, Ainslie's wallet was in his hand.

"Three return tickets to Louisburg," he said.

Mollie leaned across him, holding out some coins. "We are only going to Mira," she said. "We were too late to get our tickets in the station."

"Louisburg," Ainslie repeated to the conductor, who recognized him and disregarded the pipe because he was the doctor.

Mollie was too embarrassed to say anything more until the conductor had moved beyond them up the aisle and Ainslie had handed her two tickets, after slipping one into his wallet.

"But Doctor, we *wanted* to go to Mira."

"There's nothing in Mira but the river, and Alan can see that when we cross the bridge. In Louisburg there's a lot he can learn." Ainslie smiled cheerfully at the boy. "You'd like to see Louisburg, wouldn't you?"

"Yes."

"Then that settles it. Louisburg was once the strongest fortress in the world, and the Highland regiments had a part in capturing it. I have to operate on a man in Louisburg. It won't take too long. After I've had my lunch, I'll go down to the museum and meet you there about half past two. Do you know anything about Louisburg, Alan?"

"Mr. Boudreau in the third house from us comes from there."

"Yes, so he does. I doubt if he knows much about the old town, though. The old town was built by French kings more than two hundred years ago and the British drove the Frenchmen out. That's why Cape Breton is British country now." He turned to Mollie. "You won't really mind, will you? You can have your picnic there just as well as on Mira beach." As he got up, he took a two-dollar bill from his pocket and handed it to her. "You'll need this to take you from the station to the old town. As nearly as I remember, the old town is a couple of miles away."

Again her face flushed. "Doctor, we will pay our own way, and for the train tickets, too."

He dropped the bill on the seat. "You'll do nothing of the kind," he said, and walked back to his own seat at the rear of the coach, humming to himself.

He sat down, looked out the window and marveled. Suddenly the whole world was fresh, exciting and beautiful. A sense of well-being had risen in him like a rill of fresh water in the spring, and as he picked up his Homer, he knew past any reason or logic that today he was going to perform a great operation.

He did perform a great operation. For three and a quarter hours his fingers seemed endowed with the power of thought, while Doucette beside him assisted flawlessly, administering only a touch of anesthetic at the beginning, stopping it when the instruments entered the cerebral areas where pain does not exist, resuming again at the finish when Ainslie replaced the broken fragments of bone, fitted them together and sealed them. If total concentration on a healing task is a form of holiness, the two doctors were saints during that period. For the first time in his life, Ainslie worked successfully below the cortex of the brain. Operating from intuition as much as from exact knowledge, he performed a work of such art that Doucette's eyes glowed with excitement. When all the slow, meticulous work was finished, Ainslie knew that the man would almost certainly live, and might in time recover the full use of his limbs.

When the operation was over and the patient in his own bed, the two doctors, both moist with sweat, washed their hands at the kitchen sink and went out to sit on the doorstep and breathe the fresh air. It was now past one in the afternoon.

"Well, Dan!" Doucette said, and smiled.

In spite of himself, Ainslie smiled back at him. Doucette was a little man with liquid eyes and a dark skin which he attributed to the root-stained water he had drunk as a child. Everyone else called it Indian blood, but not to his face, for Doucette was proud of his French ancestry. He and Ainslie had known each other for years and showed their mutual affection by interminable arguments and criticisms of one another's character.

They lit their pipes and rested. The house stood on the crest of a low hill just outside the modern village and they could look across a scattering of houses and the flat land beyond to the glint of sunshine on the ocean. Behind them in the kitchen the patient's Acadian wife was on her knees before a crucifix, a rosary in her hands.

"Listen to her!" said Doucette. "Thanking God when she ought to be thanking us!"

"A fine Catholic you've turned out to be!"

Doucette grinned. "When I saw through the sham I was finished with it – which is more than you can say."

"And when you get your first coronary you'll call the priest just like the rest of them."

Doucette grinned. He put his hand on Ainslie's knee and squeezed it affectionately. "Tell me something – when you've finished a good job, do you feel you deserve a new woman?"

"Och!" said Ainslie.

"So you do!" He let a few seconds elapse. Then he said, "How's Margaret?"

"She's the same as ever."

"You don't deserve her." As Doucette got to his feet he gave off an aroma of ether and chloroform. He looked into the kitchen and made a face. "She's still at it. If that husband of hers was worth anything, or if we lived in Montreal or Boston, this morning's work would bring us two thousand dollars apiece." Doucette's liquid eyes smiled affectionately. "You're a stuffed shirt, Dan, but oh, you're a lovely surgeon!"

"Rot!" said Ainslie. "Cushing does this sort of thing every day. So does Pyke in London."

"On kitchen tables? I'm serious. You can go home and tell that tribal god named Dougald MacKenzie that this operation was better than anything he ever dreamed of doing. Whenever I think of the ability you have, I get angry. You hold a full house and you play it like a man with two small pairs. If I had half what you have, I'd be in New York making fifty thousand a year."

Ainslie sat with an impassive face, smoking his pipe and staring across the sloping land to the sea. He was filled with a sensation of peaceful excitement, for today he had fulfilled himself and justified himself, and he knew it. After a time he uncrossed his legs and took his pipe from his mouth.

"Old Dougald's right about you, Doucette. He always did say you'd be a rogue if you had the chance, but he's wrong about one thing – he doesn't appreciate what you can do in diagnosis. It's wasted here. I mean, it's wasted for someone like you. Why don't you go to New York yourself?"

"Perhaps I will, Dan, perhaps I will." After a moment he added with a note of amused pleasure in his voice, "So old Dougald thinks I'm a rogue, does he?"

"I wouldn't be surprised."

The nurse Doucette had brought over from a neighboring parish came to the door to say she had cleaned and packed Ainslie's instruments. He rose and stretched, knocked out his pipe and returned to look at the patient once more. The man lay as though dead, but Ainslie felt sure he would not die for many years to come. Not of that particular wound, at any rate. The two doctors gave the nurse her final instructions, accepted the tearful gratitude of the man's wife, and for the first time caught a glimpse of the rest of the family. A grandmother and eleven children of graduated sizes, beginning with a two-year-old and ending with a lank girl of seventeen, were crowding through the kitchen door to stare at them as though the two doctors were visitors sent by the saints. Ainslie gave them a reassuring smile and followed Doucette out to the carriage. Again Doucette rubbed his hands and said what a lovely case it had been.

"What do you think, Dan – if you'd cut away more tissue, would he have lived?"

"How would I know?"

"You needn't pretend to me you didn't know what you were doing."

"It was mostly luck and guesswork. Medically speaking, this case has no significance."

"Luck and guesswork – what else is medicine anyway?" Doucette's large eyes became speculative. "All the same, it doesn't have to be that. The Viennese have the right idea. I'm told there are men in Vienna who experiment every day on those Balkan peasants who come to their clinics. We ought to do the same here." He grinned, and watched Ainslie's face as he added, "I couldn't do it, but you could. All these Scotchmen trust you."

Ainslie grunted and refused to rise to the bait. The horse had descended the hill and entered the village. Ainslie looked at the cluster of mean brown houses that was modern Louisburg and then at the chutes for dumping coal from the trains into the ships that carried it around Cape Breton, through the Gulf of St. Lawrence and up the river to Quebec and Montreal. From this raw modern village a winding grass-covered track went off into an empty nowhere at the harbor mouth where the famous and historic Louisburg once had stood.

"Your ancestors might just as well have stayed home," Ainslie said, "for all the good they've done themselves here."

The carriage creaked over the uneven road and Ainslie saw Doucette's house come into sight around the slope of a hill.

"If you don't mind, Fern," he said suddenly, "you can leave me here. I'm going to take a walk over to the old town and get some of the knots inside me untied."

Doucette reined in the horse and turned to look at Ainslie. "You're not serious?"

"Yes, of course I am. I've ordered a carriage to pick me up in time for the afternoon train."

"But Monique's expecting you for lunch! She's even made the children put on their Sunday clothes."

Ainslie shifted uncomfortably. "I can't eat so soon after an operation like that."

"Well, then, come in and have a drink."

"You know I don't drink."

Doucette looked at his stubborn profile. "You're fifty miles from home, Dan, and nobody around here is going to stick out his nose to smell your breath." He put his hand on Ainslie's knee and grinned like a brown monkey. "Have you ever been drunk in your life?"

"Yes, of course."

"I don't believe it."

Ainslie laughed shortly and stared down the empty land towards the sea. "I'd better be on my way."

"You mean you're really going down there?"

"I've always wanted time to study the place."

"Good God, what for? Graves of dead nuns are down there. Sometimes a mad dog howls around them. He's probably after their bones."

"Probably." With a quick movement Ainslie picked up his bag and put one foot on the step of the carriage. "I'm sorry I don't feel up to going home with you this time, Fern. You know how much I always count on seeing you whenever I come down here. But another time . . ."

Doucette's eyebrows rose. "What have you been doing that makes you so ashamed of yourself?"

"Och!" Ainslie said in reply, cursing his friend inwardly for his lack of reserve.

"I know. You Scotchmen are all crazy and the whole lot of you have corrupt consciences. A crazy Highlander nearly broke down my door the other night hammering to get in. It was a long way past midnight and when I let him in do you know what he said?"

"Whatever it was, it wasn't what you're going to tell me."

"He was a big fellow about six feet four with black hair like yours. He began to shout at me, 'Doctor for the luff of God the whole sky iss full of them.' 'Full of what?' I said. 'Full of women and effery one of them iss my wife and they are after me.'" Doucette gave Ainslie a winning smile. "You see what I mean?"

Ainslie jumped out of the carriage. "Give my regrets to Monique," he said. "Yes, I see what you mean." The tone of his voice was noncommittal. "The fact is, I'm very tired."

"So tired you want to take a two-mile walk." Doucette shrugged. "What you're lying about I don't know, but for God's sake, Dan, don't feel guilty about it afterwards. I hope you enjoy yourself in the old town. There's nothing there but grass."

Ainslie turned without answering and set off down the side road, his medical bag swinging in his left hand. He heard Doucette call to the horse and then the squeak of springs as the carriage went on.

Sixteen

H E FOUND THEM on the old battlefield on the edge of the
sea. As he walked down the rutted, grass-grown track
towards the gray stone museum, he saw their tiny figures sil-
houetted against the sky as they watched the sea from the top
of the only ruin which protruded above the grass. It was the
bomb shelter which appeared in all the pictures of the fortress
and which he believed, though he was not sure, had been
part of the great Dauphin Bastion. It was shaped like three
beehives laid side by side, and like everything else here it was
covered with grass. Grass grew over what had been streets and
foundations, it almost obscured the rusted cannon and car-
ronades which had been fished up from the harbor bottom
by the coal company and deposited on the ground outside the
museum. Nothing but grass, as Doucette had said, but it had
conquered everything.

Ainslie stopped and watched them. The operation sank
below the surface of his mind as he began to think about
these two as human beings and see clearly what was involved
in their lives. The boy was all she had. That boy had a world
to win, but he was all she had and she knew nothing about
the world and the winning of it.

They turned as though his thoughts had called and saw
him standing there. Mollie smiled shyly and Alan waved

boldly. When Ainslie saw the welcome on Alan's face, something turned over inside him and he waved back. He felt an ache of longing in his chest which confirmed the flaring thought that it had not been an accident which had caused Doucette to call him to Louisburg that day.

"Oh Doctor," Mollie said, when he reached the bastion and stood below them. "Thank you for making us come here. It is a wonderful place!"

He looked up and Alan was smiling down at him. Then the boy went to his knees on the edge of the gray stone wall and spoke confidentially from his height. "We saved one sandwich for you."

"Have you been through the museum?"

"No, Doctor, not yet," Mollie answered. "We thought you might explain it when you came."

"All right. If you can get down from there, let's go inside."

He reached up and caught Alan as he clambered down. Mollie found it harder to get down gracefully, but he was too reserved to help her as he had helped the boy, so he turned his back while her skirts were pulled awry and then he heard her land on the grass. Alan laughed, so he knew she had fallen, but she was laughing too as he turned to help her up. He accepted without a word the sandwich they offered. When he had finished it he said it had tasted very good, and they left the picnic basket where it was.

There was no one else inside the museum and not even the curator was in sight. It was a nearly empty building in this empty place where a battle had been fought which was almost as important as Marathon, but Ainslie filled it with word pictures for them. He explained the old maps and the history of the period they represented, and for a long time they studied the drawings of the original city and the old paintings of British ships fighting close against the forts. Alan learned what Louis XV looked like, and the difference in the faces of Admiral Boscawen and General Wolfe and General

Townsend. By the time they came out it was already after four.

"That's enough history for one day," Ainslie said to Alan. "Why don't you go down to the shore to play for a while?"

As they made their way back to the picnic basket Alan darted off. Ainslie watched him with an appraising eye. The boy was frail, his skeleton was light and he would never be strong compared to the rugged youngsters who would be his companions as he grew up. He probably had a sound enough constitution, but he was the type whose strength would come from will and nerves. He would succeed by his brain and his imagination or he would fail utterly.

Ainslie sat down on the turf and stared across the humpy, grass-covered ground towards the harbor. Mollie, still shy, still conscious that he was the doctor while she was merely a miner's daughter, not understanding why the doctor was showing such special interest in Alan and herself, sat down shyly some distance away, her calves tucked under her thighs.

For nearly five minutes neither of them spoke. They understood each other insofar as two Highlanders always understand each other. Each, within limits, could trust the other, but the limits were absolute.

When Ainslie finally turned to her, he said, "How old is Alan now?"

"He is eight and a half, Doctor."

"A boy of fourteen wouldn't have asked questions as intelligent as his this afternoon."

She flushed with pride. "I am very glad you think so, Doctor."

"It would be a crime for a boy like that to go into the pits."

The flush turned to a sudden pallor, but she did not reply.

"I understand his father is fighting some American boxer in an important match tonight. Is that so?"

"Yes, he is. I came down here today because I hoped I would not be able to think about it. Indeed, I had almost forgotten."

"Forgetting a thing doesn't rule it out of existence."

He looked away to the harbor again. He knew it was unethical for him to talk to her as he was doing. He was a doctor, not a priest, and the private lives of the people in his care were none of his business, except as their bodies were affected. Yet he could not leave the thing alone. The realization began to grow within him that if he had a son like Alan MacNeil he would be content to live and work anywhere, even in Broughton. But as soon as the idea was fully formed and he began to inspect its implications, he discarded it. Again something seemed to turn over within his chest and he was afraid of the feeling. Habit came to his rescue and he forced himself to think as a doctor. He told himself that it was a crime for a boy such as Alan to be raised with no future but the mines. Any man with a simple sense of humanity would do what he could to prevent such a boy from being sent into the pits. It was only his plain duty to do what he could.

He turned to Mollie again. "If Archie wins tonight, will he come home?"

"I don't know. I have never known what he would do. There has always been the wildness in Archie."

"Have you heard from him lately?"

He could see that his question troubled her, so he began to study her as he would study a patient. He saw a face with small features and a short Celtic nose so straight it was almost Grecian. He saw her frail body with a certain wistful grace and he saw that her eyes had the eager loving-kindness of a deer's eyes. He knew, as one Highlander always knows when he sees it in another, that she had quality. She was incomparably superior to her husband; therefore her marriage proved that she was excessively malleable. When he came to this final conclusion he felt ashamed and knew why, for he realized that if he wished to influence her, he could do so.

"Doctor, I got a letter from Archie only a few days ago. He wants me to take Alan and go to the States."

There was a silence before he answered. "Do you tell me this because you want my opinion in the matter?"

She hesitated. "You know so much more than I do, Doctor. What do you think I ought to do?"

"Absolutely don't go. You'd be taking Alan into a kind of life down there with Archie that would be ten times worse than what's in front of him here."

She looked away and Ainslie's eyes sought the boy.

"I'm afraid if I do not go he will never come home."

"For Alan – as I've said before – it will be better if he never does."

"It is bad for a boy not to have a father."

"Yes," Ainslie said, "it is. But it's better not to have a father than to have one who . . ."

The expression in her eyes unmanned him, and he refrained from finishing the sentence. A woman like that, he thought, can make any man feel helpless. Again he turned his mind sharply away from the ideas which were forming in it. As he got up from the grass he felt more strongly than ever that he had been unethical and incorrect, that he should never have forced such a conversation. Then he saw Alan clamber down from the bastion and start running towards him and he thought, let the devil take the rules. The future of a first-class human being is worth more than all the rules in the world.

"The fog is coming!" Alan was crying. "The fog is coming!"

As he ran up to them Ainslie bent over and caught him.

"Where does the fog come from? Mummy says it comes from the sea, but why does it come from the sea? What makes it?"

"That's an easy one," Ainslie said. "Let's go down to the shore and take a look at this fog."

Less than a mile away was an incoming gray wall, dark below and fluffy with light where it reached into the sky.

"Why does it always come towards us like that?"

Ainslie looked down at the eager face. "Let's find a bit of sand and I'll draw you a map."

They went down to the shore together and Ainslie picked up a stick. He sketched in the continental coast and added circles for Greenland, Newfoundland and Iceland.

"Here is where we are now," he said, pointing with his stick at the easterly corner of what he called Cape Breton. "Out there in the sea, a little way up to the nor'east, is a great meeting place." His stick pointed north of Newfoundland and came down in a sweeping curve. "There are rivers in the ocean and this is one of them. It's called the Labrador Current and it comes down icy from the polar sea. If it weren't for that, it would be warm enough in Cape Breton to grow grapes."

The stick dropped down to the Gulf of Mexico. "Here is the greatest of all the ocean rivers – the Gulf Stream. It comes warm out of the tropics and just off here –" again the stick moved – "it collides with the Labrador Current over the Grand Banks of Newfoundland. The warm water meets the cold water and that produces moisture in the air that's about the same as the hot steam from your kettle in the kitchen. That's what we call fog. The fog blows into the land on an easterly wind and it gets so thick and heavy it makes rain. The rain makes the grass grow, cattle and sheep eat the grass and we eat the cattle and sheep, and that's how we stay alive."

Alan was listening to him intently, watching his face; and Mollie was watching both of them with her mouth slightly open and her eyes eager. Ainslie felt his spirit rise like a bird in the sky. Suddenly he felt young and joyous.

"Oh, but it's a fine thing to grow up on an island! Here we are at the beginning of so many different things. You can learn about the land and the sea at the same time. How many inland people even stop to think what it means – all life originally comes out of the sea! If all life died – all of it – the sea in its own good time would fill the world with life once more."

Even as he said this, Alan's attention wandered, and Ainslie realized that he did not yet know how to talk to a small boy. Alan was far more interested in the sea itself than in words about it. The boy was staring across the harbor mouth to the little flatiron island which once had been fortified. A moment ago it had been flecked white with roosting gulls, and more gulls circled and cried above it in the sky. Now the whole flock rose and began diving, and Ainslie watched them, too.

"A school of herring has just come into the harbor," he explained. "That's what the gulls are after."

Alan turned back to him. "Will the gulls eat the herring?"

"If they can catch them."

"Does every alive thing eat other alive things?"

"Most of them do."

The atmosphere had become somberly dramatic. Already the first wisps of fog were blowing over the gulls' island like gray smoke, yet as the three watched it come in, the backs of their necks were warm from the sun. Ainslie turned around. Westward the sky was cobalt over the dark green of spruce and the shining green of sun-swept grass, but under the overhang of the fog the water looked as coldly dark as the back of a haddock. Then the fog, as soundless as it was swift, began to enclose them. The sun became a pallid disk and disappeared and the whole landscape was as gray and cold as a wet dawn.

"It's time to be going," Ainslie said. He looked at his watch. "Did you tell the carriage to come back for you at five o'clock?"

"Yes, Doctor."

"Well, it's five now. We'd better start for the road." He turned to Alan. "How would you like to ride on my shoulder?"

"The way Ronnie rides on his father's shoulder?" He looked skeptical. "But I'm lots bigger than he is."

"Let's see how heavy you are."

As Ainslie bent and caught Alan by the waist and lifted him up with both hands he thought the boy winced. "Did I hurt you?" he said.

"I never get hurt," Alan replied, as he shifted himself on the doctor's shoulders and prodded his heels against Ainslie's chest.

The boy was even lighter than the doctor had expected. "Here," he said. "Suppose you carry my bag for me."

So they returned to the museum, where Mollie retrieved the picnic basket, and then they set off on the grass-covered road, Alan jogging up and down on the doctor's shoulders and Mollie walking silently beside them.

"We'd better not go too far," the doctor said. "The fog's getting thicker and they might not find us."

He bent his knees and let Alan slip off, the medical bag still clutched proudly in one hand. As they returned to the museum in the mist Ainslie suddenly felt that everything was all right. Nothing was visible in the fog. And his happiness grew. The fog thickened and circled over the stone monuments to the dead nuns and the mounds of the ruined bastions. Moisture dissolving on the slate roof made a whispering sound as it fell from the eaves, gulls screamed far away over the water and there was a rattle of wings and a scrape of claws as one of the birds came to rest on the stone.

"Listening to them," Ainslie said, "you'd think they were the ghosts of drowned Newfoundlanders."

"Mummy sees ghosts sometimes."

"There are no such things as ghosts," Ainslie said, aware that he had taken Alan by the hand. "But we all see them sometimes."

Then they heard the thud of hoofs on the grass and the squeaking of a rusty spring. A shadow emerged out of the mists and turned into a horse and carriage and a small man in a bowler hat. They climbed into the carriage without a word and the small man turned it around and started for the station. No one said a thing. Ainslie could feel the boy pressing against him.

In the silence, the ideas which the doctor had been forcing beneath the surface of his mind all afternoon rose again and this time he looked them in the face. The boy must be given a chance. It seemed the most important thing Daniel Ainslie had ever wanted to do. Alan must be given an education, freed from the pits, made safe from everything in his background that would try to hold him down. Ainslie wasn't sure what steps he would have to take, but he knew his purpose. As yet, he thought only in terms of the boy's future and what he might be able to do for such a lad. For the moment Mollie was forgotten.

When the buildings of the town came blurring through the fog and the station emerged before them Ainslie spoke at last. "I think I may have some books." His voice was once more noncommittal. "A boy can learn a great deal from reading. When I was Alan's age I lived in the Margaree and there were very few books for anyone, but the ones I did read were the most important in my life."

Seventeen

IN THE STREETS of Trenton, the temperature was still ninety-two and the air was like cotton wool that had been dipped in hot dish water. The arena where the Miller-MacNeil fight was being held had a flat roof and the sun had been baking it for days. In an improvised dressing room Archie lay naked on a rubbing table. He usually tried to fall asleep on the table during the preliminary bouts, but in this heat he could only lie naked and sweat into the horse blanket that covered the raw boards beneath him. They said it was a hundred and ten in the ring under the overhead lights.

For a measureless span of time he lay and felt the sweat ooze out of him and felt angry because the only seconds he could look forward to were a pair of moth-eaten, bald-headed fellows provided by the arena for the preliminaries. He thought about Charley Moss and wondered what it would be like without him there in the corner. The door opened and closed as people looked in and went out again. Archie had no idea who they were and he didn't care. He wished there were a sheet between him and the horse blanket. He felt sure that Miller had been given a sheet. The door opened once more. When he waited for the sound of its closing and there was no sound he opened his eyes. For a moment he thought Charley

151

had come back. He was straddling a wooden chair in his turtle-necked sweater and a towel was draped over his right shoulder. A cigarette was pasted into the left corner of his mouth and his forehead was dry and wrinkled. Archie closed his eyes again, but the next time he opened them Charley was still there.

"If it iss *you*," Archie said, "I can say I am sorry."

Moss took the cigarette from his lips and threw it on the floor. A fragment of torn paper adhered to his lower lip and he rubbed it off as he scowled in irritation.

"It wass Downey I wass sore at," Archie said, a note of pleading in his voice.

"Maybe. But it was me you took it out on."

"I said I wass sorry."

"I heard you the first time." The harsh voice went on. "Maybe I hate your guts, but no boy I ever trained is going to let himself get stopped by that Polack. I told Downey tonight I was through with him." He scowled at Archie. "A hell of a lot I got you to thank for!"

Archie squinted at the door as he heard the noise of rhythmic clapping from the crowd. This was the second preliminary the crowd had booed. By the time he got up there under the lights the crowd would be in a bad mood.

"What kind of shape are you in?" said Moss.

"This heat iss terrible."

"It's the same for Miller as it is for you."

"He iss used to it. My legs iss like putty already."

"They were good enough a week ago." Moss looked him over with narrow eyes. "You bastard! I bet you couldn't leave the women alone."

"I wass all by myself for a week."

Moss lifted his lip. "Just like Downey figured it! You got anything left, or did you leave it where you left your brains?"

"It iss not that. I want my wife to come here, but she hass not answered my letter."

"She's a smart girl."

"It iss four years since I haff seen her."

"All right. Forget her." Moss got to his feet and his thin little body became tense and alert. "Now you listen. Tonight you get it into your head you got nuttin to lose. You're so low down right now no matter what happens to you, you lose nuttin. Do you know how big that crowd is out there? Less than two thousand people. That's how low you are. They don't think you're even good enough to give their boy a workout." Moss stood over Archie. "Okay – hate them!" He put the palm of his hand on the lower part of Archie's face and rubbed it up so roughly that Archie sat up and the angry redness showed in his eyes. "All you got to do now is listen," Moss added as he watched Archie closely. "No boy I train is going to be taken by that Polack."

Archie was still staring at him as Moss opened the palm of his left hand where the stop watch usually rested. Now it held a pearl-handled penknife. He opened it and the blade he pulled out was less than an inch long, slim and tapered to a needle point. He held it flat on the palm of his hand.

"Tonight you're going to do what you're told. You're going to keep that left of yours pumping into his puss till I tell you to cut loose with the right. When he comes into you, you're going to move away from him. If you step in and mix it right away –" Moss jabbed the knife in sharp thrusts towards Archie's groin – "I'll stick this into your ass the minute you come back to the stool. You're going to box and keep out of clinches and watch for his thumbs. In this crowd Miller could chew your ears off and they'd love it. To hell with the heat. You got a left and he hasn't. Any fool with a left like yours can crucify a roundhouse slugger if he keeps his head, and you don't even have to do that. All you got to do is what I tell you. Now lie back and rest."

Archie closed his eyes. After the loneliness it felt good to know there was someone who was looking after him. Charley

Moss was his friend after all and tonight he would make Charley proud of him. The horse blanket chafed his back and he turned restlessly. Then he sat up and slid off the table and poised himself on the balls of his feet, snapping punches into the air in an effort to build up his tensions. Moss eyed him critically and his forehead wrinkled.

"Okay," he said. "Save it. You don't have to work up a sweat tonight."

"It iss too hot to lie down."

Archie crossed the room to a row of hooks and fumbled in the pocket of a jacket hanging from one of them. He came back with a snapshot in his hand and held it out to Moss.

"That iss the boy," he said.

Moss squinted at the picture through the smoke of his cigarette. "Yeh. He's a nice looking kid."

"He iss why my wife will not come to me."

Moss handed the snapshot back and shrugged. "Women are only good for one thing. It's something to remember." He turned to the table. "Come here under the light. It's time for the bandages."

Archie held out his right hand and Moss wound the bandage over the knuckles and wrists with expert care. Then he bandaged the left and Archie clenched his fists and knocked the bandages solid until they seemed like parts of his hands. The door opened with a creak of rusty hinges and one of the semifinal boys came in, followed by the bald-headed seconds supplied by the arena. The fighter's right eye had a mouse under it and his nose was bleeding, but he was pleased because he had won the decision.

Moss picked up a faded green dressing gown with ARCHIE MacNEIL in a flourish of white letters on the back, and Archie put it on.

"Okay," Moss said, "let's go."

"I whill do my best, Charley."

"You better had. It's all you got left."

As they went out and down the sloping concrete aisle the circus roar of the crowd pounded against the steamy walls of the arena. The crowd was in darkness and suddenly the familiar roar came out of it savagely. But it was not for them; it was for Packy Miller, who had entered the ring from the other side and was dancing about, caparisoned in a shiny black silk dressing gown, shaking hands with himself and showing his grin. Archie looked at this exhibition with scorn. He crawled through the ropes and went straight to his corner, and his back was turned when Miller cavorted over to give him some more of his grin and slap his shoulders with his bandaged hand.

"Get back where you belong," Moss snarled at him, "before I paste you one myself."

Miller's theatrical grin changed to an equally theatrical scowl and Moss turned back to Archie, well pleased. "That'll bring the bastard out fast," he muttered.

Archie sat down and let Moss massage his legs. Under the lights it was even hotter than he had expected and he hoped he would not have long to wait. At the same time he found it was easy to sit down. Across the ring Miller was dancing and scuffing his toes in the resin, snapping punches at the air and jumping backwards into the ropes and coming off them with his chin down and his arms driving. Archie opened his mouth wide and yawned to fill his lungs. He felt old. Once he had danced around like that before a fight but now he felt none of the old tension. He wanted to knock Miller out and go home. He wanted to sleep in cool air. He realized that an announcer with a voice like a hog caller's was baying his name, weight and birthplace, and he got up and bowed curtly. The only applause he got was the sound of shuffling feet, but he was used to being unpopular and did not care. It was fully two years since he had fought with a crowd behind him. When Miller's name was bayed, the mob roared.

Archie got up and stood erect, then walked to the center of the ring with Moss beside him to listen to the automatic instructions of the referee. Before they turned back to their corners Moss needled Miller once again and Miller made a rush at him which was blocked by the referee. Then Archie was alone in his corner waiting for the gong, with Charley's salt-and-pepper hair sticking up over the apron at his feet and Charley's voice snarling at him to keep his left going. In the opposite corner Miller was acting as though he needed all his will power to keep from exploding.

Suddenly Archie felt better. Miller was going to come out fast and he would nail him. He was going to win this for Charley Moss. He loved Charley Moss, by Chesus, he did. Looking sideways he saw Sam Downey's pale noseless face for the first time that night. Downey was in the middle of the front row with a cigar in his hand. Archie stared at him and licked the back of his right glove, then the gong rang and he slid forward, saw Miller rushing with his chin down and drove his left into the swarthy face, followed it with a short right to the body that spun Miller halfway around, knocked him back with another left, danced, feinted and split Miller's lips with a left as straight as a piston. He saw the whole face as exposed as a full moon, heard Charley's scream behind him and let go with the right. It smashed in solid and the next thing he saw was Miller on his haunches with a line of blood trickling out of the corner of his open mouth.

He stepped back and felt the ropes chafe his spine. By Chesus, it couldn't be as easy as that!

Then he saw Miller on one knee holding his right glove down on the canvas and he knew he was coming up and was still strong. He saw Miller's grin indicating to the crowd that he was all right and remembered the measurement of his neck. But in spite of that size-eighteen neck, Miller took a count of nine before he got up and Archie saw, as he slid forward, that the Pole's eyes were none too steady. He snapped a left into his face and liked the feel of its impact, but immediately Miller went into a crouch with nothing showing but arms, elbows, gloves and the top of his head. Archie crossed his right and felt a stab of pain and wondered if he had broken a knuckle on Miller's skull. He slammed another right into the pork-barrel body and felt pain again, but he did not believe he had broken any bones in his hand. He decided to work over Miller methodically, but the pork-barrel body exploded against him and his head snapped back in a cloud of stars as Miller butted his jaw in the clinch. Archie felt ashamed to be caught by a butt in the first round, shook loose and went after Miller in a rage. He found nothing but arms and elbows and he seemed to have been punching for hours before the gong ended the round.

"You crazy bastard" – Moss was snarling into his ear – "quit slugging and box him!"

"Work on my legs," Archie muttered. "They feel like they wass nothing in them."

He felt Charley's skillful fingers kneading his calves, but there was no sign of returning life. By Chesus, wass this the time they all waited for, the time the legs went? He told himself he must be careful, but in the next round he let himself be lured into another flurry which ended with Miller wrestling him hard against the ropes. He kept snapping his left into the face in the third round and in the fourth Miller missed such a theatrical swing that he fell down with the momentum of his own blow. By the end of the fourth Archie was well ahead on points and Miller had failed to land a single solid punch. But Archie came back to his corner shaking his head.

"He iss still strong."

"Keep your left going," Moss muttered. "That's all you got to do."

"By Chesus, I feel like there iss nothing inside of me whateffer."

"Maybe there ain't, but there's enough for tonight. This bum is worse than I thought he was." Moss looked down at Downey in the front row and jerked his thumb towards

Miller's corner. "How do you like him?" he snarled, so loudly that men three rows behind Downey heard him.

Through a haze of sweat Archie saw the pork-barrel body opposite and could almost feel its strength across the ring. There were six rounds left and he was so tired his loose legs were quivering. That neck on Miller, by Chesus it wass not a neck at all. His head grew out of his shoulders like a gorilla's.

Archie was thinking about the neck when Miller got into a series of clinches in the next round and he had to keep his head off his chin. It was a bad round of boxing without a single clean punch, but when Archie came back to his corner he told himself desperately that the fight was half over and he was still ahead. He felt water splash over his face and shoulders and gulped for air, but the harder he fought for it the less air there seemed to be. Suddenly Charley's face was right there in front of his eyes and Charley was telling him to go in and finish it this round. The gong rang and he did not move. He felt a stab of pain in his left buttock and sprang up from the prod of Charley's penknife and for a moment his head cleared.

Miller was in front of him, chin down as usual, forehead wrinkled, black curly hair sodden with sweat. Archie's left shot out and cut Miller's eye. Another and another left, and Miller staggered back with Archie feline and lethal after him. There was a surge from the crowd, a surge like the noise of water when the tide turns, and Archie knew that support was coming to him at last. Miller heard it too, and in one single lucid moment Archie had time to think what a fool this boy was, for though he had just been shaken, Miller picked this moment to charge. Archie's left flashed out and landed solid. With Miller rushing, that shot would have been decisive if there had been any real snap behind the glove. As it was, it stopped Miller upright and glassy-eyed and the right fol-lowed with all Archie had left flickering up through his legs and shoulders and coming out with a bang on Miller's jaw. Archie stepped back with trembling knees and a white coldness clamping his forehead and knew he was through. Miller rolled heavily on the floor and got his elbows under his chest. The referee was counting as slowly as he could and get away with it. Miller tottered up, turned his back on Archie and grabbed the ropes with both hands. Archie went after him and for several seconds stood there, his brain clouded, not knowing what to do, no reflexes working as he found himself confronted by Miller's back. He swung his right and it landed feebly on Miller's hulking shoulders. Then Miller bent down like a crab, lurched around, grabbed Archie by the waist and hung on. By the time the clinch was broken, he was at least as fresh as Archie was. The round petered out in fumbles and clinches and Archie's legs were weaving when he went back to his corner.

"My luck iss run out on me!" he gasped to Charley Moss and began rolling his head for air.

It was two rounds later before Miller was sufficiently recovered to make a fight of it, two rounds in which the men had lurched around the ring while the crowd booed them. Now Miller was strong again. He wrestled Archie against the ropes and got in four slugging body slams. As Archie staggered, Miller kept after his body, clinched again and savaged the scar tissue over Archie's eyes with the palm of his glove. If Miller was in front of him now, Archie did not know it. The roar of the crowd was something he remembered having heard a long time ago. He saw nothing but the red haze which kept renewing itself in front of his eyes and he felt hardly any pain from the reverberating shocks pounding against his ribs and stomach and the sides of his head. Even now Miller was unable to land a clean punch, but the pounding told. When Archie went down he seemed to be taking an endless time about it. As he lay on a heaving sea he heard a voice screaming that he was yellow. He crawled up out of the tumbling waters and a renewed reverberation told him he was on his feet again, but everything faded out quickly this time. A round later, when he foundered finally into the red thunder inside his own head, he had no knowledge of the fact that he had gone to the floor seven times and come up seven times before he fell for the eighth and last time.

In the front row under the lights, in the heat, smell and roar of noise, Sam Downey stared up at Charley Moss with his little mouth making a circle like a baby's as he sucked on his cigar. Three seats down the row a red-faced reporter leaned towards him and yelled, "What did you bastards do – dope him?"

Downey turned his noseless face and lifted his pudgy hands in a gesture of resigned disappointment. He took the cigar from his mouth and pointed it at the glaring lights over the ring.

"It's hot in here," he piped. "Archie comes from a cold country. He never could fight in heat like this."

Eighteen

NEXT MORNING in the Broughton hospital Ainslie remembered to look at the sports page of the paper. He read the brief account of the fight before Collie McCuen came into the common room and began to rage about what a sordid spectacle it had been, adding that if Archie had been properly handled he could have beaten Jack Dillon.

Ainslie had no idea who Jack Dillon was. He tossed the paper onto the table and put on a fresh gown as he wondered why it mattered to anyone but speculators who won a prize fight. In the operating room he forgot about Archie MacNeil and about everything else but the condition of the gall bladder from which he was removing three stones.

In the rest of Broughton men talked over the fight on their way down in the cages and behind counters. None of them could understand how a man could be so superior to his opponent and still be beaten like that. They felt the luck must have been against him, a superstition which more or less satisfied them all. It made them feel at one with Archie because they knew that luck was certainly working against themselves.

Breakfast was scarcely over before Alan discovered that something was wrong. Mrs. MacDonald came in from next door and spoke to his mother in the parlor and they talked in voices so low he could not hear what they said. When they returned to the kitchen he could see that his mother was not only afraid but was also very sad and he knew it was because of his father. She never looked that way except when it was about his father. It was the same way Mrs. O'Connor had looked when her husband was killed in the pit.

Then Angus the Barraman came in and his presence made Alan sure that something terrible had happened, for he should have been down in the pit at this hour. A few minutes later they were joined by old Mr. MacIvor who had not been inside their house for more than a year. Alan stood by the kitchen window pretending to look out while he listened. Angus the Barraman said something and he heard his mother shushing him and Angus stopped what he was saying in mid-sentence. Then she touched Alan on the shoulder and led him into the parlor. She took a book of pictures and laid it on the table before him, but it was a book he had looked at so often he knew it by heart.

"Now be a good boy and stay in here. We have things to talk about together and you are not old enough to understand."

When she went out she closed the door behind her and Alan heard the kitchen door close, too. He crossed to the window and looked out, feeling the fear grip the inside of his stomach. It was a lovely day after a night of rain and the sun was shining over wet ground. A stalk of wild grass was bearded with raindrops glistening like rainbows in the sun, but his fear prevented him from enjoying them. He left the window and opened the parlor door without a sound, tiptoed to the kitchen door and put his ear against the crack to listen. Angus the Barraman was talking, and his voice was more lugubrious than usual.

"He did what he could, Mollie. No man can do more than that whatteffer now. The paper said he wass the better man till he got so tired. I haff been tired my ownself and I know how it feels."

Mr. MacIvor said, "Yes, indeed, Mollie, the paper said he did good. The crowd could not believe it, he stood on his feet so long."

Then Alan heard his mother say, "To think that thousands of people paid money to see such a thing!"

There was a long silence, and Alan could hear the rocking chair creak as Angus the Barraman moved back and forth in it.

"Now perhaps Archie will come home," Mrs. MacDonald said.

"Yes, indeed," said Mr. MacIvor, "and for Alan it whill be a fine thing to haff his father with him again. The other night I prayed to God that Archie might win, but if I had stopped to think I would not haff prayed, for if he won he would not come home at all."

Alan heard his mother speak again, her voice sounding a wild note that scared him. "Four years, Mr. MacIvor. Four years Alan and I have been alone here. I wrote him a letter to Trenton, but now he will not answer it. Four years! Each time his picture is in the papers I must burn it so Alan will not see what they have done to his face. It is awful, those men he is with. I knew they were awful, and the doctor himself says there are no words for them. It is those men who have changed him."

"Indeed," said Angus the Barraman, "when my brother wass home from Chicago last year he told me there iss bad people in the States. There iss people so bad he hass been there ten years already and he does not know yet how bad they iss. There iss good ones too, and Chicago iss a fine city, but the bad ones in Chicago iss real buggers."

There was another silence. Then Mr. MacIvor said, "Holy Chesus, but Red Whillie MacIsaac whill be mad today. He lost two dollars on it."

"And where whould Red Whillie be getting the two dollars to lose?"

"He took it owt of the old woman's stocking the night before last, and he bet it before he could spend it, moreoffer."

Somebody got up and a chair moved. The voices blurred and Alan realized as he heard more feet moving that more neighbors had come in the back door. It was like the wake the day after Mr. O'Connor died. He went back to the parlor and closed the door, and after about an hour he heard the people leaving. When it was quiet again his mother came to him, and this time he was too frightened to ask her any questions at all.

"Run out and play," she said. "I'm not feeling well today and I will have to lie down."

Alan did as he was told and went out to the road, but when he saw some of the other boys in the row playing in the field, he knew he didn't want to hear whatever they might say. All he could think of now was his father and what might have happened to him last night. He wished his mother would tell him everything and not say he was too young to understand. The doctor had answered every question he had asked. Alan decided to go up the road to the colliery property. From where he stood outside the wire he could see the Newfoundlanders breaking up coal on the ground and the tipples working and the little pit engine shunting the cars around. When the whistles blew for twelve o'clock he saw Mr. Camire come out of one of the sheds and cross the yard. He turned away, not sure whether he liked Mr. Camire or not, and went back down the road to his own house.

The house was empty, and this was the strangest thing of all today. His mother always worked on her rugs in the morning and the moment the whistle blew she got up and prepared their dinner. He wandered from one room to the other wondering where she was and what had happened to her and remembered somebody saying that when bad luck came it never stopped with one person but spread like the smallpox. She had said she was not feeling well and was going to lie down. Perhaps when he was away she had become so sick they had taken her off? It might even be like the time Mrs. Jim Jack MacFarlane had been sick and the black wagon from the hospital came up to the door and Dr. Ainslie stood by while a pair of men in white carried her out of the house. Mrs. MacFarlane had never come back again.

In sudden panic he ran outside and trotted up the row. The boys had disappeared. Then he went back the way he had come, hoping his mother might return. He saw nobody. At this hour all the women were busy inside giving their children a midday meal and the men were still in the mine, eating from their black pails. At last he saw old Mrs. MacCuish who lived alone, sitting with gaunt knees on her own doorstep. He stopped to speak to her, even though his mother had told him that Mrs. MacCuish had been queer ever since her husband's death.

"Where is my mother?"

The old woman stared at him and narrowed her eyes. "And how would I be knowing where she iss?" She put her hand to the small of her back and got groaning to her feet. "Come here, boy!"

Alan approached cautiously, and the old woman looked down at him with her gaunt face set in bitter lines.

"So she went away and left you with nothing to eat, did she?"

"Yes, but she didn't mean to."

"Heh! What makes you so sure of that? Come inside with me now."

Alan stood in the doorway and looked about. It was dark and dirty and it smelled of the old woman.

"Is my mother sick?"

"Body and soul, that iss what I say, body and soul! But I am a Christian. Would I be telling what I know of her to a little child?" She pushed a chair towards the kitchen table. "You sit on that and be quiet."

She took a bottle of molasses from a shelf and screwed off the top. Then she lifted a dirty plate from the sink, wiped it with her apron and set it in front of him. She picked up a loaf of bread and cut two slices, both very thin.

"There!" she said. "Say your grace and eat that."

Alan shivered as he sat down and picked up the bread. It was stale and there were little marks of mold at the corners. But before he could touch it the old woman cackled at him.

"Say your grace before you put that fud into your mouth or it whill poison you."

Alan looked at her wide-eyed, frightened and puzzled.

"Heh!" she cried at him. "And what else would I be expecting but this? You do not know your grace whateffer. Now then, you will say it after me." She fixed her narrow eyes on his. " 'Most merciful God' – go on, say it now!"

"Most merciful God," Alan repeated.

"I am a misserable sinner and I know I whill be damned."

"I am a miserable sinner and I know I will be damned."

"But I thank Thee for this fud."

"But I thank Thee for this food."

"And for Thy efferlasting mercy."

"And for Thy everlasting mercy."

"Now then," the old woman said, "you can eat and it whill not poison you. Pour out the molasses. Pour it out good and wipe the staff of life in it."

Alan did as he was told, but when he tasted the thick brown syrup he could hardly bear to swallow it, for it was not like the creamy molasses his mother gave him. It was full of crusty lumps and the moldy bread was dank and sour.

The old woman kept staring at him. "Iss what I haff in my house not good enough for the likes of you?"

Alan did not know how to answer, but as she continued to stare he murmured that it was very nice.

"It iss blessed by the good God," said Mrs. MacCuish, "and that iss more than can be said for the bread where you come from."

Alan forced himself to eat the two slices while the old woman stood on the other side of the table watching him with compressed lips. When he had finished he looked around for a cloth to wipe his fingers.

"Lick them," the old woman said. "Hass nobody told you it iss a sin to waste fud?"

Alan licked his fingers and held them stiffly in front of him for fear of smearing his pants. "What is sin, Mrs. MacCuish?"

"Aha – and what else whould I be expecting? So she did not tell you, eh? She iss one of the ones that say to themselves in their vanity there iss no hell, but her sins whill find her owt, don't you worry over that. Be sure your sin whill find you owt – that iss the words of the Good Book. And you whill find owt it iss true on the day when the sheep are parted from the goats. Sin!" the old woman went on. "What are you your ownself but a lump of it whateffer? And the time whill come when you whill pay, and when you whill remember everything you haff done, but then it whill be too late whateffer."

Alan licked his fingers again. "Do you think my mother is home now?"

"How whould I be knowing if the Lord did make up Hiss mind He had stood her as long as He could? Go and see for yourself if she iss home. I whould not be knowing."

Alan went to the door with his head hanging and the old woman following him.

"Now you haff had my fud you whill come again?"

Frightened still, he murmured, "Yes, thank you, Mrs. MacCuish."

"Heh! Don't try to lie to me. You whill not come unless you haff to."

The moment Alan reached the sidewalk he began to run, but when he reached home the house was still empty, so he walked out into the sunshine again. This time he saw somebody he liked. Mrs. MacDonald was walking up the road with a basket on her arm and she smiled as he ran towards her.

"Whell now, and aren't you the silly boy fretting yourself like that, when all your mother iss doing iss in to the store to market?"

He looked up at the woman's ruddy, smiling face and there was no fear. The fear had lifted from his shoulders and gone sailing up to the sky like a kite. Then Mrs. MacDonald began to laugh and he laughed with her and the laughter was wonderful even though she was making fun of him a little. He ran off down the road and over the bridge, climbed the slope on the far side and turned off into the woods near the doctor's house. He walked through the firs and birches and down the slope of the interval to the doctor's brook, and there he sat on a stone watching the pouring water and wondering where it all came from. Tadpoles flickered along the bottom of a shallow near the brink and he caught one and held it in his hand but it struggled so much he knew it was frightened, so he dropped it back into the water and was glad to see it scuttle away. A man with shaggy hair under a broken-peaked cap came along the uneven path carrying a bundle with a stick thrust through the loop where the ends of the cloth were knotted. He looked at Alan speculatively, put one hand on the side of his nose and blew a jet of matter to the ground, scratched his behind and passed without a word. A dog came out of the underbrush and nuzzled against Alan's legs, but after a time the dog went off to follow the man. The boy took off his shoes and put his feet into the water. It was warm, not sharp and challenging like the water of the sea, but warm and soft, and he remembered it was not fit to drink because chemicals had poisoned it. With his feet in the flowing water, his chin in his hands and his elbows on his knees, he sat there on a flat stone and tried to think.

About one thing there was no doubt at all. Things had gone very badly with his father in the States and now perhaps he would never come home. If he was a prize fighter, as the boys said he was, then he must have been beaten in a fight. But why was that so bad he wouldn't come home? And why was his mother so ashamed? Maybe she would talk to him about his father now, and he could stop trying to keep her from knowing that he understood what a prize fighter was. She always looked so frightened whenever he almost gave it away, and he hated to see her afraid of anything. But he wanted very badly to talk to someone about his father and find out what awful thing had happened to him in the States.

Then he remembered Dr. Ainslie. Yesterday in Louisburg the doctor had answered every question he had asked. Perhaps if he went up the hill to the doctor's house, the doctor would tell him what the prize was for a fighter and what happened to you if you lost it. The doctor knew everything and did not think he was too young to understand what older people said.

Alan dried his feet on the grass and put on his socks and shoes. When he climbed the bank and came out through the break of the trees the doctor's house stood there before him big and alone, and he thought how important and different the doctor was to live in a house like that. An empty buggy with the shafts on the ground stood on the gravel in front of the surgery door, but the horse was not in sight. He crossed the gravel and circled the buggy, but there was no sight or sound of anyone, so he turned back and made his way through the brush at the edge of the woods.

He couldn't think what to do next until he remembered the spring in the woods which his mother said had the sweetest water in the world. He found the path leading to it and walked along silently over a carpet of brown pine needles until he came to the place where the spring bubbled out of a gnarl of roots and stones that made a small pool with dead leaves on the bottom. He lay on his stomach and stared into the spring and watched his own face. He smiled and the water smiled back at him. He tried to look tough and the water moved underneath and he thought it made him look tough, too. Then a squirrel ran along a branch of the soft maple over his head and he could see its movements in the water. After the squirrel had gone he put his mouth down to the surface of the water and tried to suck it in, but the water was so cold it hurt his teeth.

He thought about his mother again and wondered why she was afraid. He continued to lie on his stomach watching the sky upside down in the water. He heard an angry shout, but it seemed to be a long way off and he paid no attention until he heard it again, much nearer. So he scrambled to his feet and ran back along the path to the edge of the wood where the gravel began on the doctor's drive and then he stopped and hid behind a wild cherry bush and watched.

Two men were running up the drive, panting heavily, one of them very small and the other very big, and he recognized them both. The small man was Levi the peddler and the big one was Red Willie MacIsaac. Levi was only a few paces ahead of Red Willie, but he had time to duck underneath the doctor's buggy when he reached it, and there he crouched between the wheels, the whites of his eyes gleaming when he peered up. Red Willie drove at him with his boot, the biggest one Alan had ever seen. The whole of Red Willie was big and angry, and Alan remembered Angus the Barraman saying he would be mad today because he had lost two dollars. Then Alan remembered that it was on account of his father that Red Willie had lost the two dollars, and he hoped Red Willie would not see him. So he stood very still, watching.

He could feel the fear that came out of little Levi's white eyes. Red Willie was after him hard, going round and round the buggy, shouting and kicking underneath it, but each time his boot went out to strike, the peddler dodged behind the spokes of the wheels and crouched in a new position, looking up like a fox. Alan wondered what Levi had done to make the big man so angry, because he had heard his mother say that Levi was a nice little man. He watched Red Willie's boot swing back once more and drive forward, and then he quailed as a roar of pain followed. But it was Red Willie who was roaring as he hopped up and down on one leg and held the injured foot in both his huge hands and shouted what he was going to do. It would be something special, for now Levi would have to pay extra for making Willie smash his shin against the wheel.

And then suddenly the roaring stopped. The surgery door had opened and Mrs. Ainslie was standing at the top of the steps. One look at her told Alan that she was angry, too, and that her anger was much more important that Red Willie's. Even the big man was afraid of it, for he took off his cap after he had dropped his injured foot and stood facing Mrs. Ainslie with the cap passing from right hand to left hand and back again.

"It wass him that started it," Red Willie said at last, pointing under the carriage with the cap.

Mrs. Ainslie looked him up and down before she answered. "So you're a bully as well as a drunkard! Why don't you pick on someone your own size to fight with? And some other place to make so much noise?"

Red Willie's face turned as red as his hair and his huge lumbering body came erect with rage and injured pride.

"You haff known me all my life," he said, and bent down with his hand held a foot from the ground to show how small he had been when Mrs. Ainslie had first seen him, "and you whould say a thing like that against me, that I whould be fighting with a little bugger like that, under there!"

"What else were you doing?"

"I wass only trying to kick the guts owt of him."

"You were, indeed."

"And why not, when he says I cannot even beat Archie MacNeil any more, and him a broken-down fighter than can stand up to nobody any more. I'll show him – as soon as Archie comes home."

Alan watched and listened intently, his mind bursting with what he was hearing. So his father *was* coming home! But what was a broken-down fighter? And could Red Willie really beat him? If he could, then his father wasn't the strongest man in the world after all.

Little Levi had sneaked out on the other side of the wagon and now was tiptoeing down the drive, looking over his shoulder as Red Willie still protested to the doctor's wife. But she was watching little Levi, and finally she broke into a ringing laugh.

"You overgrown child!" she said to the big man. "Now go on home. Your quarry's reached the road."

Red Willie stared at her without comprehension and then her meaning began to inch into his mind. He turned to see the last of Levi as he disappeared in the direction of the mine.

"You let him get away on me," he muttered.

Mrs. Ainslie stopped laughing. "Be on your way, MacIsaac. And thank your lucky stars the doctor wasn't here when you put on that exhibition."

She turned and went back into the house and closed the surgery door, and Red Willie stood there like an ox. Then he put on his cap with both hands, pulled it down hard over his right ear, shoved his hands into his trousers pockets and slouched off. Halfway down the drive he saw a fair-sized stone and swung back his leg to kick it. The stone shot high and rang against a tree.

After Red Willie had disappeared Alan came out of hiding and walked boldly over to the carriage, hoping Mrs. Ainslie might see him and come out again. But the surgery door remained closed. He studied the ground where the scuffle had taken place, and then turned to follow Red Willie down the drive, trying to figure out the meaning of what he had seen. Apparently Red Willie thought it was all right to kick a little man but wrong to fight one. It must be very bad to be small. He looked down at his own legs and wondered how long it would be before they grew heavy with bone and muscle. Someday they must be like his father's. At the edge of the road he saw a stone like the one Willie had kicked and he swung back his leg and let go the way Red Willie had done, but when his toe hit the stone he had to suppress a yelp of pain. Why was it that nobody thought much of Red Willie, though a lot of people were afraid of him?

When he reached the main road the first of the men were coming back from the mine. All the way up the road he met them walking with black faces and staring white eyes, their lunch pails under their arms with the gray metal showing through in the spots where the paint had been rubbed off. His house was still empty when he got home, so he sat on the front step, feeling very tired and a little queer, and drew pictures in the dirt with a twig, watching occasionally as a woman brought out a washtub to scrub the coal dust off her husband.

Angus the Barraman waved when he reached his own house, and then he came over and sat on the steps beside him, his face and hands still black and his eyelids red.

"There iss hell in my legs today, Alan. Where iss your mother?"

"I don't know."

"She whill be home soon, howeffer?"

Again Alan said he didn't know, and Angus the Barraman took out a plug and bit off a chew. He looked down the road and saw two of his own boys chasing each other around the house.

"My kids iss making so much noise I ought to get up and beat the hell owt of them, but I whould sooner sit here a bit." He chewed ponderously for a minute. "We haff heard your father comes back to town soon," he said finally.

Alan looked at the dirt and continued to draw pictures.

"We haff heard also that he does not come home at all."

Still Alan said nothing and Angus continued to chew, breathing through his nostrils like a dog and stopping occasionally to calculate whether or not he had worked up enough juice for a worthwhile spit.

"Mr. MacNeil?" Alan said. "Could Red Willie MacIsaac beat my father?"

Angus the Barraman's eyes made two white circles in his black face as he stared at Alan with apparent lack of comprehension.

"Could he kick the guts out of my father, Mr. MacNeil?"

Angus's shoulders began to shake with amusement. "Ho, ho, ho," he said. "But that iss so funny you do not even know the beginnings of how funny it iss."

Alan began to laugh too. "Then you mean Red Willie isn't telling the truth when he says he can beat my father?"

"Och!" said Angus. "Och now, but that whould be fine! By Chesus, I whould like to see Red Willie drunk enough to try, and then we whould see how far he whould bounce when your father let him haff the right cross."

Alan squirmed with pleasure. "What is a right cross?"

"It iss your father's favorite punch. After he makes hiss man drop hiss guard with the cleverness, he giffs him the right to the side of the jaw or to the face maybe, and when he lands it good that iss usually all there iss to it."

Alan was feeling more lighthearted every moment. "Then my father is still the strongest man in Cape Breton, isn't he, Mr. MacNeil?"

Angus turned slowly to feel Alan's biceps. After his fingers had probed the frail muscle, his face became solemn and he shook his head.

"You whill haff to grow like a son of a bitch to be as strong as your father." He took his fingers from the biceps and felt Alan's head. "Maybe you whill haff the big brain, like the doctor."

"But is my father the strongest man in Cape Breton, Mr. MacNeil?"

Angus thought this over for such a long time that Alan was beginning to believe he had forgotten the question. Finally he squeezed his chew into the side of his left cheek and let go a squirt.

"There wass Captain Livingstone from Boulardarie," he said, "who wass so strong that once when he wass buying a suit of clothes in the Boston States the man in the store asked wass they too loose, so Captain Livingstone swelled out the muscles of hiss back and shoulders and burst every seam in them just to show a little of what he could do."

"Is my father stronger than that?"

"Whell now, in the muscles he iss not. He might beat the captain with the clefferness, but the captain iss dead now, so who knows?"

"If the captain was so strong, why did he die? Did somebody kill him?"

"Whell now, nobody effer told me abowt that, Alan." Angus scratched his head. "I would not be surprised howeffer if he was drown-ded. Maybe he wass drown-ded and the Jamaica sharks ett him. They tell me them sharks off Jamaica hass bites so big they can bite the head off you."

Alan looked down in the dirt and began to scratch a skeleton while Angus the Barraman chewed steadily beside him.

Then Alan said, "Mr. MacNeil – what happened to my father last night?"

"Och!" said Angus, and began to squirm in his pants. "What whould you be asking a question like that for?"

"You were talking about my father this morning. I heard you."

"Och, and what iss talk? Och, now! It iss what I said beforehand moreoffer – there wass dirty tricks in Trenton on Friday night. Withowt the dirty tricks – och, there whould haff been no question at all whateffer abowt it. But don't you be asking me any more abowt that, for I haff promised your mother I whill not say."

Alan kept after him. "Mr. MacNeil – what are dirty tricks?"

"Whell now, I did not promise her I whould not talk abowt that. So listen and I whill tell you. There iss all kinds to them. But suppose you wass fighting a fella and you hit him in the balls – that whould be the dirtiest trick you could do."

"Did a man hit my father like that, Mr. MacNeil?"

"That I do not know for sure, but I haff my ideas on it. But I am not going to talk any more abowt your father, Alan, so be a good little bugger and don't ask me."

At last Alan's face broke into a smile. "Without the dirty tricks, is my father stronger than anybody that ever lived in Cape Breton?"

"No," said Angus the Barraman decisively, "he iss not, and you can't blame him for it, eether. For nobody that effer lived anywhere wass so strong as Angus MacAskill of St. Ann's, who wass four hundred and twenty-five pounds of bone and muscle, and wass so strong he did not haff to fight at all to prove it. MacAskill was so strong that Queen Victoria her ownself invited him all the way to her palace in London just to haff a look at him, and when he wass finished with walking up and down before her, she had to buy herself a new carpet to make up for the holes hiss heels had cut into the old one." Angus the Barraman shook his head solemnly. "But what he did there wass nothing to what he did right here in Cape Breton, for the Queen wass a lady, and it whould not be polite for MacAskill to show off to a lady what he could really do."

Angus stopped to let go a long spit.

"He showed it once and for all the day the Yankee sea captain put into St. Ann's for water and boasted there wass stronger men in the Boston States than they wass in Cape Breton."

Angus stopped again, and for nearly a minute Alan waited for the story to continue. Angus shifted his cud. Then he took out his plug and bit off another chew and settled himself.

"You see, Alan, it wass like this. MacAskill wass so gentle he whould neffer be the one to start anything. It wass the sea captain that started it, for when he saw the size of MacAskill he began to laugh."

Again Angus paused, and worked hard on the dry tobacco until he could feel the slime beginning to grease his gums.

"What did MacAskill do?" Alan said.

"There iss men here that saw him do it," said Angus the Barraman, "and if you do not believe me, you can ask Big Alec McCoubrie."

"But what did he *do*, Mr. MacNeil? What did MacAskill do?"

"Whell now, it wass yourself that asked me." Angus let go another squirt. "When that sea captain laughed, the giant did not think it wass funny at all. So he stood up and he looked across the bay and measured the distance, and the bay wass so wide not even a rainbow could cover it. Then MacAskill put owt his hands, and he picked that sea captain up, and he bent over and he pointed hiss ass across the bay like a big gun, and nobody effer saw the like again of what happened then. For MacAskill fired such a blow owt of hiss ass that the sea captain sailed most of the way across the bay, and he landed with a big splash in the water right in front of Englishtown. He whould haff gone all the way across moreoffer and busted hisself on the beach, but MacAskill wass such a nice man he did not want to hurt him."

Angus the Barraman began to laugh and slap his legs, but the moment he hit himself he winced and groaned.

"Keep owt of the pit when you grow up, Alan. It iss fine work when you are young and your own boss, but it puts hell into your legs when you get old. By Chesus, if there iss not a strike soon I do not know what I whill do whateffer." He got slowly to his feet and began to rub his back and his eyes showed white in his coal-black face as he stared down the road. "Whell now, and here iss your mother!"

Alan jumped up to look and saw his mother coming down the road with Mr. Camire. He could see that his mother was happy again and it made him want to laugh and do something to show Angus the Barraman that he had never really been worried at all. His mother was smiling as she talked to Mr. Camire and the Frenchman was carrying his guitar in its case. That meant he would stop for supper and there would be songs.

"Don't you think it would be fun, Mr. MacNeil, to be a Frenchman and play the guitar?" Alan said.

"Some of them foreigners iss clever little buggers," said Angus the Barraman. "But the trouble with them iss, you can't always believe what they say."

Alan's mother and Camire came up and asked Alan what he had been doing all day and then they began to talk to Angus, but Alan wanted his mother to himself. He pulled her skirt until she followed him into the house, leaving the two men outside.

"Mummy, Mr. MacNeil said that Father might be coming home."

She turned her back while she took off her hat and laid it on the parlor table. Then she turned back and looked down into his face. With an impulsive movement she put her hands on his shoulders and held him.

"Alan dear, maybe he comes and maybe he does not. Now we do not know any more."

In a small voice, muffled by her dress, he said, "Is Father dead like Mr. O'Connor?"

"Of course not." She thrust him away and he looked up at her and saw that her eyes were smiling. "Your father is alive and well. Now then, go out and talk to Mr. Camire while I fix the supper. It will be a fine night after all. You will tell me all about what you have been doing today and after supper Mr. Camire has promised to sing for us."

Nineteen

L ONG AFTER it had grown dark that night Alan lay in bed
 with his eyes open listening to Louis Camire downstairs
singing French songs to his mother. He had been at it for
hours and Alan wondered when he would stop. He was less
sure than ever if he liked Mr. Camire or not. Part of the
evening had been fun. Mr. Camire had brought a bottle of red
wine and he had talked about strange countries. There was a
city in Italy, he said, where the streets were made of water and
people went from house to house in boats and every night
there was music and singing from the balconies. There was
no coal anywhere in Italy and nothing was black in the whole
country except the hearts of the rulers. There were mountains
in Italy with snow on their tops in the summertime, and
below the mountains were green hills covered with olive
orchards which turned gray whenever the wind blew the
leaves backward. On the plain between the hills and the sea
there were trees with walnuts and oranges on them. If a man
was hungry he could pick the walnuts and crack them in his
palms and eat them, and if he was thirsty all he had to do was
to reach over a stone wall and pluck an orange from a tree. At
least, that was all a man need do, Mr. Camire said, if it were
not for the police, but soon there would be no police, for

there was going to be a revolution in Italy and the rulers were going to be hanged because they had kept the people hungry. Mr. Camire said that the wealth of the world was like a pie. There was plenty of pie but only a few people were cutting it and of course they cut all the big pieces for themselves, but when the rulers were hanging from the lampposts there would be plenty of pie for everyone. Alan wondered if this was true, and he was not sure who a ruler was and had no idea what a revolution was, but he hoped that nobody would be hanged in Broughton. He fell asleep remembering Angus the Barraman's warning that it was not safe to believe everything a foreigner said.

He woke up later, how much later he did not know, and heard Mr. Camire's voice talking very loud downstairs and his mother speaking much more quietly. Alan sat up in bed, listening.

"No, Louis, Alan is upstairs and he must not be ashamed of me."

"Name of God – ashamed! It is natural and it is necessary."

"It would not be right now."

"There is always something. First it was your 'usband. Now you think he will not come home, so now it is the boy!"

"I am all he has, Louis."

"So! Then you do not like me!"

"But you know I do."

"The first time I saw you I said to myself, That is my girl." Alan could hear the sound of muffled movements. "Now I want my girl."

"Please be quiet, Louis."

"Why? Why not? We both want it."

"Who can have what he wants? Isn't that always the way?"

"*Nom de Dieu*, who told you that?"

"Please, Louis – not so loud!"

Camire's voice dropped, but only slightly. "Why do you drive me crazy? You look at me and it means only one thing when a woman looks that way. And then you say no! What is the matter with you that you are not honest?"

"Louis!"

Camire's voice dropped low, Alan heard his mother speak again, and then he heard the sound of the front door closing. He hunched himself up in bed wondering if he could hear his mother crying. A few minutes later he heard her in the parlor, then she shot the bolt in the front door and then the stairs creaked. As her steps mounted slowly he snuggled down under the covers and pretended to be asleep. When the bed tilted and he knew she was sitting on the side of it he opened his eyes.

"Have you been awake, Alan?"

"No, Mummy. I just woke up now." He felt very bad about telling her a lie, but he knew she would feel worse in a different way if he didn't.

"Have you been asleep all this time?"

"Yes."

She sighed and he knew she was glad to believe him.

"Is anything the matter, Mummy?"

He felt her small breasts strain against him as she held him and he wanted to struggle free, but he was afraid she would be disappointed if he did.

"It is hard when you are older, Alan. Sometimes everything gets mixed up."

"Does Mr. Camire get mixed up?"

She let him go. "Sometimes. But he is more sure than most. And he likes us very much. More than some people do."

"Everybody likes you, Mummy."

He could see that his answer had disturbed her, so he tried to change the subject. "Do you like Mr. Camire?" he said.

"Of course."

"Dr. Ainslie doesn't."

"I know." She was troubled again. "But the doctor does not know everything. Poor Louis has had a hard life. In France he had a fine education and when his father dies he will have a business in France all his own, and then he will show everybody what he is." He saw the smile return to her lips. "It must be beautiful in France. People don't fight with each other like they do here. I should think maybe we can go there someday."

Long after she had left him to sleep Alan thought about what she had said. It was the first time he had ever heard her talk about going to some other place. At school the teacher had told them about boys from Cape Breton who had gone away from home to the States and become famous. But Alan did not want to go away from home. He wanted his father to come home instead so he could see him fight and watch people pay money for a prize and then read about how famous his father was in the papers.

Twenty

THE WEEK END PASSED, Monday and Tuesday followed, and Margaret discovered that a sudden lull had fallen in Daniel's practice. There were no night calls, no operations and fewer people than usual came to the surgery. Sometimes it happened that way.

There was also another thing Margaret noticed. Daniel seemed almost frightened by this rare opportunity to rest and enjoy himself a little. With less work at the hospital, he made more work for himself at home. The moment dinner was over he went into his study and plunged into Homer. When she asked how the translation was coming along, he accused himself of stupidity and said he would never be able to finish his self-appointed assignment before Christmas. It was then that Margaret understood how deeply worried he was about something he was keeping to himself. His eyes told her that he longed to talk to her, but she knew him well enough to be aware that his Highland nature was probably deceiving him about the nature of whatever might be troubling him. She even sensed a measure of hostility to herself, though she was sure Daniel was unconscious of it, for in little things he was more solicitous than usual. He asked if she wouldn't like to take a holiday with her sisters. He tried to persuade her to go to Halifax for a few days to buy herself some new summer clothes. He even talked of getting a girl to help her in the house, though she had assured him long ago that without children she preferred to manage both the house and the calls alone. Meanwhile the lonely, longing look in his eyes remained, and Margaret wondered how she was going to find a way to help him.

When they were drinking their coffee after dinner on Wednesday night she said, "Dan, why don't *you* take a holiday? You could easily manage a week in the Margaree. You haven't had a rod in your hands in years."

He looked annoyed. "Of course not."

"Why not, Dan? This is a wonderful chance. Collie McCuen could take over your work for a week and in the fall you could take his for a week and let him go hunting."

"No," he said, "I can't go off like that now."

She knew there was no point in pressing further at the moment, so she got up from the table and went out to water her roses. As she stood with the hose in her hand watching the geometric pattern of shadows lengthening over the gravel drive, she wondered why the place where they lived no longer meant anything to her husband. It was entirely his creation. He had selected this site on the verge of the intervale above the brook. He had planned and helped to build the house himself and had lived alone in it the year they were engaged. He had cut the undergrowth out of the wood, torn up the saplings and burned out their roots and now the grove of birches and pines was like a small park. When they were married he had given her the whole place as a gift.

Margaret shut off the hose and bent over the rose bushes one by one, examining the newest shoots for aphids. Then she strolled to the edge of the bank and looked down the slope of the intervale to the brook. She loved the brook's curve as it came out of the grove for the run through the intervale and she loved the sound it made.

Still puzzling over Dan's present state of mind, she remembered with something like surprise that he had not always been like this. He had always been intense, but when she had first known him he had laughed a great deal. She asked herself if the change was her own fault. Self-analysis was not easy for Margaret and it generally made her uncomfortable. Her mother had taught her that sensible people get rid of their troubles by laughing at them. Now her common sense told her that the situation between Dan and herself needed more than a joke and a smile. She told herself that she was thirty-five years old, not unintelligent, and married to one of the ablest men in Nova Scotia. Why had her marriage turned out like this? Was Daniel now resenting her as a person in the way he had always resented her family? Once his acid comments about her mother had made her smile. Later on they had annoyed her, and her refusal to accept them had finally forced him to keep his thoughts on her family to himself. But in the last month Margaret had begun to wonder how much she herself resembled her mother in Daniel's eyes. She thought of the murderous weight of overwork and responsibility he endured as a matter of course and she realized that no member of her own family could have tolerated a quarter of it without feeling abused.

Tonight she felt painfully useless. Her own world was too neat, too small and secure. His was the world of the sick and frightened. She had grown up comfortably without worry or struggle. Daniel had struggled from the day he was born. Her mother had reared her with the notion that there was a smooth-edged solution for everything. But how many times had she lain in bed hearing Daniel's feet pacing the floor and known there was no solution for him at all? How many times had she lain beside him, hearing him think aloud in the medical terms she could not understand, helpless to aid him as he tried to grope through darkness to the unknown, sure of nothing except that time was running out on his patient? Not once had he reminded her that a human life depended on his ability to think clearly. To say that a life was at stake would have seemed to him both sentimental and unprofessional. She was proud of him because she knew he saved people who would have died under other doctors, but had she ever understood, had she ever felt even a fraction of the price he paid?

She turned to the house, saw that the light had come on in his study, and supposed he was back at his Homer again. Why did he do it? What was Homer to him? Why didn't he take a holiday and go home to the Margaree, instead of trying desperately to overcome this academic giant of his own contriving?

Then the thought came to her that perhaps he didn't want to go because the Margaree was a home no longer. She remembered the look on his face when he had taken her, only six years ago, to see the old farm. There was no one left within a mile of the place. A fence he had once built himself now ran into a grove of young spruce. The house was a ghost house, unoccupied, with rattling shingles and broken panes. His father's gravestone was overgrown with young spruce and it had astonished Margaret to find it there alone on the top of the mountain instead of in the churchyard in the valley. She remembered a large, granite boulder at the head of the property, also surrounded by spruce. "I used to be able to sit here," he had said, "and look down on the whole valley. Now you can't see anything except trees." And she had imagined how that valley must have seemed to a boy of sixteen who had never been any place else. She recalled now the sweep of the noble stream between the hills with the islets of white stones in the channel and how the moon had looked climbing the sky over the opposite mountain. She heard again, with a shudder at the beauty of it, the evening in the Margaree when they had heard wild distant music in the sky and Daniel had pointed up the hill to a cottage so small it was only a white dot and said it was old Angus Fraser piping as he walked back and forth before his door. No wonder, she thought now, growing up with those wild, solemn, Bible-reading Highlanders all around him, looking out at the glory of an innocent world, Daniel had been unable to prevent a need growing in him until now that need was higher than a mountain.

When Margaret went into the house it was already deep twilight and the cirrus clouds had lost their color. Quietly she entered his study. His back was towards the door, but she knew he heard her, for his head lifted slightly. She slipped her arms about his neck and pressed her cheek against his hair.

"Let's harness the mare and go for a drive," she said.

She felt tenderness and even some of his deeply controlled passion in the impulsive movement with which he seized her hand and pressed it to his cheek.

"I'm not much to live with, am I?"

"If you only thought a tenth as much of yourself as others do, you'd never say things like that. Let's drive to the cliffs by Dr. Dougald's? It's still early."

To her surprise he pushed back his chair. "All right, but I don't want to see Dr. Dougald tonight. Let's go to your mother's instead. I haven't seen any of them for two months."

Margaret, too surprised by this suggestion to know what to say, went upstairs to put on her hat and a light coat while Daniel went outside to harness the mare. She came downstairs, passed through the surgery and had already closed the door behind her before she saw that a small, wiry little man was standing on the gravel of the drive talking to her husband. It was too dark to see his face, but his posture and manner of gesturing told her it must be Louis Camire. She waited by the door. When Daniel started towards her, then brushed past and went into the surgery, she knew it was another emergency. She sighed as she watched him bend over the leather bag he always left packed, snap it open and hastily check its contents. He was wholly the doctor again and almost unaware of her existence, and in this kind of situation Margaret knew her role.

"I've got to go out on a case." His back was turned. "Will you call Miss MacKay right away and tell her to have the OR prepared for me? It's probably an appendectomy."

From the undertones in his voice she thought the case must be more serious than a simple appendix, but she never asked questions at moments like these. She stood aside as he rushed past her with the bag in his hand. Camire had lighted the carriage lamps, and as Margaret stood in the surgery door she saw the two pools of light move away into the darkness. Then she closed the door and telephoned the hospital.

Twenty-One

"WHEN did the boy get sick?" Ainslie snapped at Camire as they drove out to the main road.

"Yesterday 'e was not feeling good and today 'e felt terrible. But it was after dinner the pain got bad."

"Why wasn't I notified before?"

"*Docteur*, poor people 'ave not got the telephone."

Ainslie looked at the Frenchman's profile. "You've got two good legs. You should have come for me at once."

He cracked the whip and the mare reached the main road. He sat in tense silence while she trotted hard down the hill and braced for the pull on the opposite side. The miners' row looked, as usual at this hour, like the flank of a ship that had run aground with all her lights burning. The mare hauled hard towards the center of the row, and when she reached the MacNeil house, Ainslie jumped out with his bag in his hand, calling to Camire to hold the mare's head. He opened the door of the house without knocking and encountered a woman in the hall he remembered as Mrs. MacDonald.

"Is he upstairs?"

"Oh, Doctor, we are afraid for him. All day he has been vomiting."

Ainslie brushed past her and mounted the stairs. Since all these houses were identical, he knew where to go. He found

Mollie sitting by the side of Alan's bed looking unnaturally calm. The boy's face was flushed and his cheeks were stained with tears.

Ainslie crossed the room and put his hand on Alan's forehead. The boy looked up at him and smiled, and as though in answer to a challenge, Ainslie smiled back. "Well, you're warmer tonight than you were in the fog at Louisburg, aren't you?"

When he turned to open his bag he heard Mollie whisper to Alan that everything was all right now the doctor was here. He slipped a thermometer into Alan's mouth, drew down the covers and examined the boy's right side, pressing gently and stopping when he saw the wince. He replaced the covers and took the pulse, removed the thermometer, registered in his mind the information it gave him and added it to the whole. When he snapped his bag shut again he nodded to Mollie and went into the outer hall. She followed him and Ainslie closed the bedroom door.

"I'm afraid it's an acute appendicitis," he said quietly.

"That is what Mr. Camire said."

"You'd have done better to consult me sooner. Has Alan had a pain in his side before?"

"Last winter he talked about it sometimes."

"Why didn't you call me then?"

"I thought it was only a stitch."

"And the vomiting – has he done that often?"

"Sometimes, Doctor, but I did not want to be bothering you if it was only something he ate."

Seeing the anguish in her eyes, Ainslie suppressed a rebuke. "All right," he said, "I'll get Mrs. MacDonald to help you. Wrap him warmly in several blankets and I'll drive him into the hospital myself. There's no time to waste."

She grew pale and her breathing came so quickly he could see she was swallowing air. "Are you going to cut him open, Doctor?"

It was a question he had heard many times before. As often as possible he answered it with a calculated laugh to brush away the layman's primitive fear of the unknown, but this time he had no laughter to spare. He found himself tensing his muscles as he had done years ago before his first operation, and he recognized the similarity of the reflex, without taking time to inspect its implications.

She clutched his wrist with a strength that surprised him. "Please, Doctor! He is so frightened. Would you speak to him? He thinks you are so wonderful. If you tell him everything is fine he will believe it. It does not matter if everything is fine or not, I don't want him to be afraid."

All ages of women were in her face and the boy was every sick child Ainslie had ever seen. For a moment he felt dizzy. Mollie's face, the spirit of love emerging through her fear, shook him, but years of meeting emergencies had provided him with reflexes which he obeyed with certainty. He turned and walked down the stairs with calm steps. When he reached the open air the dizzy feeling left him and in its wake was a gnawing sense of his own unworthiness.

In front of the house he saw Camire holding the mare's head.

"Was I not right, *Docteur?*" Camire said.

"Yes, you were right. Stay here with the mare. I want to be ready to get under way as quickly as possible. I only hope it doesn't rupture before we reach the hospital."

He returned to the house, climbed the stairs again and saw that Mrs. MacDonald was about to lift the blanket-bundled Alan from the bed.

"I'll do that," he said. He bent forward, placed his hands carefully under Alan's back and thighs and lifted him. "Tell Mrs. MacNeil to hurry along," he said to the woman. "I want her to go with us."

With Alan in his arms, bearing him downstairs with scrupulous care to avoid any sharp movements, Ainslie was once more totally the doctor. He stood holding the child while Mollie climbed into the carriage. Instructing Camire how to help him, he transferred the weight of the boy from his arms to Mollie's knees. Camire held Alan's head while Ainslie went around to the other side of the carriage and took his place in the driver's seat. Alan's head then rested on his thigh and Camire tucked the blankets closely about the boy's body.

"Good!" Ainslie said, "Good!"

He picked up the reins and set the horse in motion. When they rounded the corner he cracked his whip loudly, and the trained mare, knowing the whip crack came only when there was need, began to trot and make the wheels hum in the dust. They passed the long wire fence of the colliery property with Alan silently watching the bulge of the doctor's elbow, and high above them a skyful of stars.

To go into the dark, Ainslie was thinking, to go into the dark and share the patient's fear. Had he heard those words from some other doctor or were they his own? To become everybody – father, mother, child and old man – to become everyone in order to be a doctor. Osler with his drooping mustache on hands and knees woofing like a bear in order to give a child the curiosity which turned into the germ of a will to live. Was it sentimental? His hand dropped to Alan's forehead and rested there, feeling the high temperature and sensing through the heated skin the boy's fear, sensing it and knowing that while the pain was the boy's, the fear had probably come from the mother.

"How is it now?" he asked.

Alan was trying not to whimper. When he answered he said, "It's worse."

"That's good," Ainslie said. "That's a good sign." He held the mare steady and watched the road. "Alan, can you hear me?"

"Yes."

"I'm going to tell you what's going to happen so you won't be surprised. You have a useless little thing inside of you called an appendix and I'm going to take it out. It's been hurting you and making you sick, but in a few weeks you'll be telling all your friends about it and they'll be wishing they'd had an operation, too."

Ainslie looked at the nearest landmark and calculated they would be at MacDonald's Corner within another twelve minutes.

"This is what will happen when we reach the hospital," he went on. "You'll be carried up to a big shiny room with a high table in the middle of it, and there'll be doctors and nurses waiting for you. One of the doctors is Dr. Grant. He's the one who will put you to sleep so you won't feel the pain any more. When he tells you to breathe deeply, you'll open your mouth and breathe as hard as you can. Open your mouth as wide as a codfish if you feel like it. You'll hate the smell of the stuff, but it won't hurt you. Just at the moment when you're thinking how much you hate it, you'll drop off to sleep. And you'll like Dr. Grant. He has the reddest hair you ever saw in your life."

After a while Alan said, "As red as Red Willie MacIsaac?"

"Compared to Dr. Grant's, Red Willie's hair is as dark as mine. Dr. Grant's hair is red enough to set the woods on fire."

A moment later Alan said, "How long will I be asleep?"

"Oh, I wouldn't be surprised if you were asleep all night, just as if you were in bed at home. And you're going to have wonderful dreams. When I had *my* appendix out, I dreamed I was at the circus on a merry-go-round full of pipers."

Alan's voice brightened. "Did you have yours out too?"

"Indeed I did. What's more, I've got it pickled in a bottle in my surgery right now."

There was almost a laugh in the boy's voice. "Can I have mine in a bottle, too?"

"You wouldn't think much of it. It's an ugly little thing."

"I want it in a bottle so I can put the bottle on the fence and throw stones at it."

"Well, we'll ask Miss MacKay to save it for you, then."

The wheels hummed as the mare kept up her pace. They crossed the bridge and drove up the half-empty main street, turned through MacDonald's Corner, and then they left most of the lights behind as the mare slowed for the pull up the hill.

Ainslie glanced down again and saw Alan's face staring up at the stars. "They're fine tonight, aren't they."

Alan nodded.

"When I was seventeen I went to sea for five months all one summer and fall. One night I crawled forward on the bowsprit and lay on my back the way you're lying now. The bark had all her sails spread and it was like flying through the air chased by a pack of clouds. There was phosphorus in the water and every time the sprit lifted I could see the waves of the ship's passage blazing away from her sides like fire. Each time the sprit dipped, I could look up – just like you're doing – and see Orion swinging in and out of the gap between the jib and the fore-topmast staysail." He pointed up. "Do you see that cluster of very bright stars? That's Orion. Orion was a great hunter."

"But a star isn't a man."

"No, but that cluster looks like a hunter with belt and sword, so the old people named it after a great Greek hunter called Orion."

"Greek," said Alan, "like Mr. Petropolis that sells the bananas?"

Ainslie laughed. "Petropolis? He's just a little fellow, but Orion was a giant."

"Was he stronger than Giant MacAskill?"

"Where did you hear about MacAskill?"

"Mr. MacNeil told me."

"Did he tell you about how he picked up the ship's anchor that weighed a ton and threw it?"

"No, but he told me how he blew the American over the rainbow. Was he stronger than Orion?"

"I wouldn't think so. Orion used to break the tops off

mountains and throw them at people. Or perhaps that was the Cyclops." The mare had turned into the hospital yard now. "When you're better I'll tell you about both of them, but now we're going up to the operating room to see Dr. Grant."

When the carriage stopped, two orderlies came down the steps with a stretcher. They lifted Alan out and placed him on it. Mollie, still silent, walked beside the stretcher holding his hand while the men carried him in. Ainslie tethered the mare and went in by another door. He was washing his hands in the alcove off the common room when he heard Grant come in and ask what the case was.

"Appendix," Ainslie said without turning around. "An eight-year-old I'm rather fond of. His father's Archie MacNeil."

"If the kid's half as tough as his father," Grant said, "a little thing like an appendix won't hurt him."

"He's not like his father in any respect whatever," Ainslie said, and left the room.

When he was in the hall the strange feeling of being about to perform his first operation settled upon him again. He looked at his hands and saw they were trembling. He stood still and breathed deeply several times, leaned his head back and closed his eyes. Slowly he brought his nerves under control, but when he looked at his hands again he saw they were still tighter than they ought to be. He walked on down the corridor and stopped at Miss MacKay's desk.

"That case I just brought in – is the boy's mother still with him?"

"She went upstairs with the orderlies, but I don't know where she is now."

Ainslie looked down at his hands as he massaged the fingers of his right hand with those of his left. Then he separated his hands and articulated them.

"I want one of the private rooms prepared for them," he said. "His mother will spend the night with the boy when the operation is over."

Miss MacKay's voice showed her surprise. "Isn't that unusual, Doctor? I mean, isn't it unusual for a patient from the collieries to have a private room?"

"The bill for the room will be sent to me," Ainslie said shortly.

"But, Doctor . . ." Miss MacKay smiled. "That's quite out of the question. I was just thinking that if she didn't know . . ."

Ainslie flushed in sudden irritation. "Miss MacKay, it's unusual for me to have my orders questioned. If hospitals were run by intelligent people no child would ever be left without its mother after an operation. A child alone in such circumstances is a frightened child, and so long as we do things like that to children the world is going to continue to be the sort of place it is now."

The nurse flushed under her gray hair and Ainslie hurried off, annoyed with himself for having betrayed his emotions. But after he had climbed the stairs and reached the operating room, he was cool and aloof. As he articulated his fingers once more he knew they were as strong and delicately sensitive as those of a concert pianist. Grant, his head flaming over the white sheet covering the patient, was bending down to give Alan the benefit of the routine jokes he always reserved for the moment before he held the mask over a patient's face. Ainslie nodded to him to begin and turned his back. As he inspected the instruments he heard a whimper from Alan, followed by Grant's soothing voice telling him it would not be long, and finally he heard the heavy breathing that meant Alan had gone over the frontier and no longer cared. When Ainslie approached the table he had forgotten what Alan's face looked like. All he saw was the exposed abdomen and flank of a slightly built child with delicate skin. He picked up the scalpel and made his incision.

"A good long one," he muttered to Grant. "I've no patience with this nonsense about leaving a neat scar. I want room to work, and when I close up, I want to be sure there's nothing left inside."

Grant smiled, knowing the implicit criticism was of Ronnie Sutherland. One of the nurses also smiled, but Ainslie saw nothing except the work of his rapid fingers. When he stood back from the table Grant was dangling his watch in his hand, nodding appreciatively as if at a private joke. Ainslie knew Grant was complimenting him on the rapidity of his work, but he disregarded it. After checking the pulse and the pressure he passed his hand over his face. His cheeks were as wet as if he had been swimming. Then he caught sight of the houseman, whose presence he had forgotten completely.

"Everything seems to be all right, Weir," he said. "There's no likelihood of peritonitis, but I'd appreciate it if you'd look in on the patient several times tonight."

"Certainly, Doctor."

Ainslie thanked Grant and left the room. On his way to the common room he stopped at Miss MacKay's desk to apologize for his rudeness before the operation, left before she could answer, and ran upstairs two at a time, took off his gown and gloves, washed his hands and face, ran downstairs again and left the hospital. He climbed into his carriage and drove the mare hard down the hill, but when he reached MacDonald's Corner he charged right through it instead of turning in the direction of home. The mare was galloping as she dashed down the narrow street towards the sea, and late leavers from Jimmie MacGillivray's saloon stopped to stare and wonder who was sick in that part of the town.

The mare kept on going, past the last houses and on down a little used road. This area was no part of Broughton harbor. The smell of salt water and drying fish finally struck Ainslie's nostrils as he approached a wharf reputedly used by smugglers. He pulled back on the reins and drove out onto the deck of the wharf. Then he jumped out of the carriage, drew the reins in a clove hitch around a bollard and walked to the end. There he dropped down on the coaming and let his legs dangle over the side. The tide was going out and the noise of waves ebbing back and forth around the pilings filled all space.

For a while Ainslie thought the shaking of his body was caused by the quivering of the wharf over the pounding surf, but he knew his mind was pounding with its own rhythms and his body was out of control. There were no sea birds, no other human beings, no sign of habitation, only the docile mare waiting, yet Ainslie kept muttering "No!" over and over again, without knowing what he was saying no against. He was still shaking as if with a malaria chill, then he stopped muttering and shouted "NO!" as loudly as he could at the empty, noisy space, and suddenly he felt the tears burst down his face.

After that he stopped shaking and he began to see the white breakers and feel the rhythm of the surf, and finally he took out his pipe and his trembling hands broke several matches before he got it lit. Puffing on it, he stared into the soft darkness over the water while a confusion of scenes and voices tumbled through his mind like barrels bursting loose in the hold of a ship.

"She'll never let me!" he heard himself cry out once, and recognized that "she" was Margaret, cool, detached, sensible, devoid of all trace of wild Highland imagination. Again he saw Mollie leaning over the sick Alan in the miner's cottage, and the three figures began to blur and come apart again. He tried to hold on and keep them separated long enough to understand what had happened to him this night, but it had happened first in Louisburg and he had been afraid of it then and ever since, terrified to think about it, terrified even now to shout it at the empty sea.

How long before he was able to say it quietly to himself he could not tell. But after he had said it again and again, it was his and he was no longer afraid of it. His life was a barrenness because he had no son. And now a son had been found.

There it was. All of it. It made no difference that Alan was the child of two people as dissimilar from himself and Margaret as were Archie and Mollie MacNeil. A man's son is the boy he himself might have been, the future he can no longer attain. For him, Alan was that boy.

For quite a while Daniel Ainslie sat with his face buried in his hands. He knew he was sobbing, but it made no difference now. He might as well stop trying to bolster his fierce inner pride. He let his mind go where it would, freed of the restraints he had put upon it for so long. He saw Alan growing up, year by year moving to manhood in dignity, himself being a companion to him, helping him, teaching him to be the kind of man he himself was not, thereby giving himself a continuance out of the ancient life of the Celts into the new world. He saw Alan as a young man crossing the grass of an Oxford quadrangle with young Englishmen as his friends, sitting in the college hall under the portraits of great men who had sat there before him, and he saw himself an old man with Alan in middle life understanding him, the two of them counseling together, watching Alan's children grow up in a world unknown to the pits.

There was no ending to such dreams. He raised his head as a last shudder passed through his body. The admittance of the one fact had brought him face to face with the other he had known all the time would be waiting there to trap him. He loved Alan, but he also loved Margaret and the two facts could not be held at once. If he clove to Margaret he would lose the boy because Margaret would never forget that he was another woman's son. Why was he trying to forget it himself? Why was something within him saying that Mollie MacNeil was unimportant, that her feelings did not matter? Why did something within him say that she could be disregarded, so that it was

Margaret's censure, not Mollie's loneliness, that he feared?

How much longer he sat on the coaming of the wharf he did not know, but finally a kind of panic began to grip him. Now that the problem had a form he must find a solution for it, but there could be no solution. He began to shake again and he asked himself of what he was afraid. Alan might be in trouble in the hospital and the nurses might be trying to find him. That's what he was afraid of. He pulled himself to his feet, relieved to have an immediate objective, and began to run up the wharf to his carriage. How would anyone find him if he were needed badly? He must hurry.

Before he realized that his feet had caught in something soft he plunged forward, an explosion of light burst in his head and his right temple hit the boards. For a moment he lay half stunned, trying to understand what had happened. He rolled to get up, and as he did so, the hair on the nape of his neck prickled. He had stumbled over something alive, and now this living thing was rising beside him. He could smell, feel and hear it, and as he jerked his head around he saw the outline of a broken-peaked cap appear against the residual light from the sea. It rose on a pair of huge shoulders and stood over Ainslie like a tower.

"Who's there?" he said.

The tower moved. "There wass dirty tricks in the States last Friday night, and by Chesus, I am going to kick them back up your ass."

Ainslie recognized the voice. "You drunken swine, MacIsaac – don't you know who I am?"

The huge figure swayed as Ainslie came to his feet. Then the truculent voice became plaintive. "Doctor, how whould I be knowing it wass yourself?"

"Get out of here!"

Red Willie swayed on his heels. Then he belched in the doctor's face, put his hand over his mouth and excused himself. "I would invite you to a drink, Doctor, but all the rum I haff is inside of myself."

"Och!" said Ainslie, and turned from him. He walked to the mare and felt his hands trembling as he untied the reins. By the time the mare had pulled the carriage off the wharf, he knew he was unfit to enter the hospital. "Oh, God damn that drunken blackguard!" he said to himself.

The mare pulled him up the hill. Overhead the post-office clock banged a single note and Ainslie knew he was in MacDonald's Corner and it was one o'clock in the morning. The mare hesitated, waiting for the pull of the reins that would tell her whether the destination was home or whether she was to continue up the hill to the hospital. With a sudden jerk of the reins, Ainslie sent the mare around the corner and down the main street. He took out the whip and cracked it savagely, the mare broke into a gallop as though she were pulling a chariot, and the sound of her crashing hoofs and the rattle and bang of the carriage clattered so loudly through the empty street that windows went up as wakened sleepers tried to see what was happening. She charged over the bridge and was continuing home, when Ainslie again bore hard on the left-hand rein and sent the carriage lurching on two wheels into a dirt track. Tossing her head with fright, the mare galloped over level ground and through a brake of pines to the end of the track. She stopped panting in front of a high, gaunt house with a widow's walk on its roof. Beyond the house, guarded by a low stone wall, a cliff dropped sheer to the open Atlantic.

Ainslie jumped from the carriage, slapped the mare's neck and saw foam on the bridle. He tethered her and went around to the front of the house, ran up the steps and pounded on the door. He waited nearly a minute and pounded again. Then he heard heavy steps inside, the door opened, and Dr. MacKenzie stood there, huge and gray and apparently undisturbed.

"Dan," he said quietly, "what's the matter?"

Ainslie lurched inside and dropped into a chair in the high-ceilinged, gloomy hall.

"Dan, are you all right?"

Ainslie looked up. He spoke in a voice unnaturally quiet. "Dr. Dougald, would you mind doing me a favor? Call the hospital and ask if the MacNeil boy is all right?"

"Surely, Dan. That's easily done."

Ainslie sat motionless while MacKenzie rang the operator. He did not move when the doctor asked for Weir or when he put his question a moment later. MacKenzie hung up and turned around.

"Weir says it was a perfect operation. He added that it was the swiftest appendectomy he's ever seen."

"But the boy – is Alan all right?"

"He came out of the anesthetic without even vomiting. He's asleep now."

MacKenzie left the room and Ainslie seemed to sink further into the chair. The last time he had been in this house – how long ago? – he and the old man had argued about religion and MacKenzie had insisted that it was entirely possible for a scientific medical man of experience to believe in the efficacy of prayer. Was that three months ago or three minutes ago? It was hard to know. He could hear his own voice saying over and over, *But how can you?*, then MacKenzie asking him what he thought of when he imagined God. Was that then, or now? There jumped into his mind the image of a tight-skinned dog with green eyes, standing before him with muscles rippling under its tawny hide. Then it disappeared.

"Dan, whether you like the stuff or not, you're going to drink a glass of brandy with me."

Ainslie looked up and saw MacKenzie holding out a glass. He took it, tossed half its contents down his throat, gasped at its sharpness and continued to sit there, holding the glass tightly.

"It's smuggled brandy," MacKenzie remarked. "It goes against my principles to drink any other kind. The rule of the majority may be all right, but injustice from a majority is just as bad as injustice from anybody else. Since Confederation, the central provinces in this country have treated us very badly. So – speaking philosophically, mind you – it is no sin for Nova Scotians to drink smuggled liquor." MacKenzie took a long pull from his glass. "Now, what have you been up to?"

Ainslie swallowed the rest of his brandy and coughed. "I'm not sure. I'm not sure of anything any more. Can we go outside? It's a warm night. Let's go up to the widow's walk – if you can put up with me for a little while."

"Excellent idea." MacKenzie downed the remainder of his brandy and set the glass on the table beside a tray of old calling cards. "As a matter of fact, that's where I was when you came along. I never go to sleep any more until three or four in the morning. That's all I seem to need."

An hour and a half later they were still on the roof and Ainslie was still trying to understand his problem by hearing it put into his own words. He had tried to tell MacKenzie how he felt about Alan and how impossible he found it even to discuss the subject with Margaret, but when he was finished he knew he had failed to make himself clear, had failed to relieve even a fraction of the pressure inside himself. So he stopped talking abruptly and listened to the surge of the sea. Ground swells snored somberly in the darkness at the foot of the cliff, retreated and snored in again with primeval rhythm.

"It's the weakness in myself I can't forgive," he heard himself saying. "Tonight I cracked up and I'm ashamed to have lost control. I suppose it's a tendency I inherited from my mother. She died when I was ten, but –" Ainslie stopped and passed a hand over his forehead, brushing back the dark hair that had fallen forward over it. "My father was always afraid I'd be like her. He warned me often enough, heaven knows. I'm afraid she was a weak character."

MacKenzie shifted his position and Ainslie went on with his explanation. "Did you ever know my father? No, I don't suppose you could have. He was a remarkable man even though he had no education besides what he learned from the Bible and Bacon's *Essays*. I remember the year the barn on our farm burned down. I was eight or nine, I think. For a year and a half after that we didn't have enough to eat, but my father never complained. And what's more, he never borrowed. To borrow seemed to him like theft, for it would have meant mortgaging what he meant to save for our education. So we all went hungry and he made us keep on studying. I have two brothers, you know. They're both ministers. One's in Philadelphia now and the other's in Toronto. All of us well educated, thanks to my father. Mother thought it was more important for us to eat than to learn. She had none of his will power. She died shortly after the barn was rebuilt and we were more or less on our feet again."

Down below the sea smote the cliff a heavy blow. The tide had turned and now it was rising. The long diminuendo of the wave traveled away down the coast like a freight train rumbling through a valley.

"Some people can go on living with no purpose ahead," he jerked out. "Living in a kind of vacuum. But I can't. Even if work for its own sake were important, which it isn't, I couldn't go on indefinitely the way I have been. It's no better than being a miner in a pit, boring into the black till the seam runs out."

MacKenzie coughed. Then Ainslie heard the comfortable sound of the old man's pipe knocking against the heel of his shoe and the crunch as he pressed home a new charge of tobacco into the empty bowl.

"I'd never meant to tell you this, Dan," he said when the tobacco was glowing. "But I think now maybe I should. I knew your father and mother in the days of my smallpox crusade around the island. I knew you, too. You were about the same age as Alan MacNeil, or maybe a little older. You didn't recognize me when we met again because I'd grown a big mustache by then and my hair had turned gray, and besides I doubt if your father ever mentioned my name in your hearing. He never forgave me." A match flared as the old man relit his pipe, his profile leaped out of the darkness and disappeared again. "I attended your mother – very briefly – at the beginning of her last illness. She was dying of pernicious anemia. The direct result of the eighteen months when your father's ambition forced his whole family to go hungry. Being your mother, she ate much less than you boys did, and in those days there was little one could do for pernicious anemia, once it got under way. You may not owe your life to her, except as one always owes it to one's mother, but you certainly owe your health to her. I wouldn't talk about her lack of will power if I were you. When I gave your father my prognosis he dismissed me, and I never saw either of them again." MacKenzie coughed again. "I remember that she had very gentle eyes. You would do well to honor your father less and your mother more. She was a very loving woman."

When it was plain that MacKenzie had said all he meant to say Ainslie roused himself from his stiff posture. He got to his feet, moved forward and grasped the railing with both hands and stared out to a blink of light in the east, no more than a faint presence in the darkness. He thought of the expression in Mollie's eyes as she comforted Alan, lost sight of it in a welter of images, then recovered it again. Then it was not Mollie's eyes he was looking into; they were the eyes of his own mother. Mollie and his mother became confused and he was confused with Alan.

Behind him the old man was saying, "You aren't looking for a son, Dan. You're looking for a God."

It took a while for the import of the words to reach him. He felt alone as he had never been alone in his life as he stood with his hands on the railing and heard the rumble of the sea at his feet. It surged against the cliff, broke, fell back and surged again, and still Ainslie stood motionless, staring into the night. As his father had denied his mother, so was he trying to deny Alan's mother, to disregard her, to dismiss her as of no importance. And yet the little boy he once had been still longed to be loved by some human being as Alan was loved by her. It was all too confused. If he couldn't stop trying to understand it, to come to grips with it, he would lose his reason. What did MacKenzie mean by saying he was looking for a God? Once again his mind blurred.

When he turned around his face was dark with anger. "You don't understand," he said. "All I want to do is help the boy. Mollie MacNeil is a good woman, but she'll never be more than what she is now, and Alan deserves far better than that. I'm the only one who can help him and nothing is going to stop me. Nothing!"

Twenty-Two

AFTER HIS FIRST NIGHT in the hospital Alan began to enjoy himself. Everybody seemed to know that Dr. Ainslie had a special interest in him, and this made him a privileged patient.

After three days he was transferred to the children's ward, an appendage of the men's ward, and his mother went home. There were only two other boys in the children's ward, both younger than himself. They had had their tonsils removed and the day after Alan joined them, they went home. So it was the convalescing men who kept him entertained. Whenever the nurses would let them, they came to sit on the side of his bed and talk about their children. Bill Blackett took a fancy to Alan, at first because it was Dr. Ainslie who had helped them both, but later because Alan was an insatiable listener to Bill's stories about whaling and cod-fishing off Newfoundland, Negro women in the West Indies with baskets on their heads, his brother Garge, and sharks, sailfish and second mates.

To Alan, the hospital became the most exciting place he had ever dreamed of. To begin with, there were the smells. Had he been blindfolded he could have told the time of day from the odors. The carbolic smell was there at every hour, but the odors that told the time came and went, were different throughout the day. In the early morning it was the smell of hot toast. About ten o'clock the first whiffs of smoke came into the windows from the nearest colliery when the offshore breeze sprang up. At noon it was the dinner smell from trays that came into the wards on carts, and about four in the afternoon, especially on hot days, feet began to smell in the men's ward as the patients grew restless and threw down their covers and all the doors were left open to allow air to circulate. There were also the smells peculiar to special people: sharp soap from the nurses' hands and sometimes the odor left on their linen by a too hot iron. Whenever a doctor entered from the operating room there was the terrifying smell of ether which still made Alan's stomach turn.

Even more exciting were the sounds of the hospital. The nurses rustled and the housemen padded about on rubber soles; the tires of the wheeled stretcher whirred on the linoleum whenever a patient was taken to the operating room or brought back again. There was the happy sound of rattling dishes at mealtimes, Gaelic voices of the nurses joking with patients as they bathed them or brought them food; and after dark, while occasional sounds entered the open windows from the town, the ward quivered with heavy breathing, with the irregular breath of one man predominant, the man who was going to die.

When Alan first heard that terrible, snoring sound he was frightened, for he thought an animal was loose in the ward. The next day he was sure it was an animal, for in the far corner of the men's ward was a bed with an iron guard around it. Inside the guard was a huge, squat figure that moaned and flopped, covered with hair and naked except for a pair of diapers. It was only when he saw a nurse come in and change the diapers that Alan realized the figure was human. A little later Bill Blackett told him the flopping man was a sailor who was eighty-one years of age. Even after Dr. Ainslie explained that the old man was too far gone to know where he was, the sounds he made haunted Alan. Finally Dr. Ainslie decided to eradicate his fear. He took a pencil and paper and sketched a human figure, drawing in the heart and brain and the main arteries. Then he explained that a blood vessel had broken in the old sailor's brain so that his brain no longer functioned and the nerves controlling his muscles were not good any more. "It won't hurt you," the doctor said, "to see a man like that. He's very old and he's had a good life. Now he's just fading away." Dr. Ainslie smiled at him. "I don't want you to grow up afraid of things. Most of what we're frightened of are things we don't understand." He smiled again. "What's happened to the old man couldn't possibly happen to you for another fifty or sixty years, and probably won't happen at all. And even if it did, by that time you'd be old and tired and you wouldn't mind going to sleep. When you hear the old man moan, don't feel unhappy about it. It's only breath coming out of his mouth. Just think of him as if he were asleep and snoring."

Alan lay in bed and watched the doctor go away with his brisk step to see one of the patients in the outer ward. It seemed that every time Dr. Ainslie came to see him he made everything feel better. Now Alan could look at the old man with interest and think how nice it was of his wife to come into the ward every day with a bottle of alcohol to rub his body, even if the old man didn't know who she was.

But Bill Blackett took a different view of the matter. Alan repeated what the doctor had said, but it made no difference to the Newfoundlander.

"Thet 'airy old man," he said, "'ow do the doctor know 'e can't feel? Floppin' and gruntin' like a seal on a clamper of ice. Seals feel, even if they can't talk. You ought to 'ear 'em moan when you swats 'em. Thet old woman ought to give 'im the alcohol to drink, 'stead of rubbin' 'im down with it."

Bill turned and saw something new on the small table beside Alan's bed. It was a colored globe of the world which the doctor had brought the night before.

"Wot's thet you got theer?"

Alan told him what it was, and how Dr. Ainslie had explained the movements of the earth.

"The doctor do give me the creeps sometimes, like thet moanin' old man. It ain't 'uman for a man to want to larn everything." He reached across the bed and gave the globe a spin with one of his four surviving fingers. When it stopped, he leaned across Alan and peered at it, looking for familiar names, but he still found reading difficult and Alan had to point out Newfoundland. Even then Bill didn't believe it. "Thet chart ain't right," he said. "I bin all around Newfoundland, and it don't look like any pork chop."

Blackett began to spin the globe again, and he was still spinning it when Dr. Ainslie came in. Alan saw the pleased smile on the doctor's face when he thought Bill might be interested in geography, too.

"It be immense, zurr," Blackett said, jumping smartly to his feet, "to think of us goin' round and round and not even feelin' it."

Ainslie laughed, and then Blackett's face fell when he heard the doctor say he had a free half hour. That meant a spelling lesson for Bill. So Alan watched him follow the doctor out through the main ward to the reception room at the end where they could be alone. When the half hour was up, both men came back.

"Bill tells me he's been down in the West Indies," the doctor said, "so I've asked him to tell you what the islands are like. I was there myself once, but Bill saw more of them than I did."

Again the doctor left, but when Blackett was alone with Alan he became interested in the plate of fruit that Mollie had brought the day before. He ate an apple, seeds and all, and when there was nothing left but the stem he turned back to the globe. When they discovered the dot named Dominica he got to his feet and pushed back his cowlick and grinned broadly.

"I knowed a girl in Dominica oncet told me I 'ad the longest 'un she ever did see." Then he went off down the ward, rolling in his walk as he always did, and Alan knew he would lie in the sun behind the hospital until suppertime.

The days passed and they were into the second week of July. Every afternoon Mollie came to see Alan, and though she tried to laugh with him, the boy sensed that she was uneasy. He wished he knew why. She never mentioned his father any more, and the afternoon before his operation seemed a long way back, so he made no reference to his father either.

One day a huge doctor with white hair and a drooping white mustache came through the ward. Alan sensed that he was someone special because the nurses were especially polite to him. He stopped at the door of the room where Alan was, smiled at him and said that his name was Dr. MacKenzie. Then he joked with him for twenty minutes. But all the time he stood there, Alan had the peculiar feeling that the doctor was giving him some kind of test.

A day or so later Mrs. Ainslie came especially to see him. She brought some flowers and some more fruit and before she went away she kissed his forehead. In her, too, the boy detected an unspoken question.

It was still another day when Louis Camire appeared with a paper bag in his hand. He looked at Alan sharply, drew up a chair beside the bed, told him that his mother was not feeling well but sent her love, then opened the bag with a flourish and dangled a large bunch of grapes in front of Alan's eyes.

"Better than ice cream," he said. Drops of water glistened in the cluster and the grapes smelled cool and sweet. "I made that Greek, that Petropolis, give me the best 'e 'ad. With Greeks, you 'ave to know what to do." He laid the grapes on the counterpane. "The *docteur*, 'e will be 'ere this afternoon, no?"

Alan shook his head. The doctor never came into the wards in the afternoon, he said. Sometimes he came back in the evening if he happened to be in the hospital anyway. Camire looked relieved and Alan wondered why he didn't like the doctor. They began to eat the grapes in silence, and then Bill Blackett came rolling down the aisle in the men's ward. When he saw the grapes he grinned and came on towards them and sat on the side of Alan's bed opposite Camire. The Frenchman looked at him sharply, but Bill merely stretched out the surviving fingers of his right hand and broke off a small cluster of the grapes.

"This *docteur*," Camire said, his forehead wrinkling. "'E cut off your 'ands, no?"

Blackett stuffed his mouth with grapes and held out his stump. "'E be the smartest one of the lot," he mumbled through his chewing.

Camire grunted. "What for do you thank 'im? Maybe it was not necessary to cut off your 'ands at all, eh?"

Blackett swallowed his grapes half-chewed and answered amiably. "You should of seed 'em before 'e got his knives in 'em. They was so bad squatten it makes me creep to think about it. Thet accident was a lucky thing. Now I got no proper 'ands left, I got to use me brains."

Camire shrugged, dismissing Blackett as a person of no importance, and turned to the globe by Alan's bed. "The *docteur*, 'e give you this, too?"

"Yes," Alan said.

"Why? What does 'e want from you?"

"Nothing. He just likes to teach me things."

"Nobody does something for anybody without they want something back." He reached out and turned the globe until the blue shape of France was uppermost. He peered at it and then pointed with his finger to the spot he took to be the city of Avignon. "That is for me," he said. "It is a place so much better than all this I make a blasphemy to make comparisons at all. One day I will take you there. You and your mother."

He looked at Alan obliquely as though to catch his response on his face, but Alan kept his attention on the grapes. Blackett was chewing placidly and seemed not to be hearing a word.

"You and your mother," Camire went on. "You are too good for 'ere. Nothing counts 'ere but the size of the muscles. When you grow up you will be small, like me. This place will drive you crazy. But in France there was Napoleon and 'e was smaller than me. In France there is everything. In Avignon everything is veree old and beautiful." A wistful note entered the little man's voice. "When a man fights in Avignon, it is for something that makes sense – for a woman, or for money. But 'ere they fight for nothing because there is nothing else to do."

Blackett was chewing Alan's grapes vigorously and crunching the seeds in his teeth. He said amiably to Camire, "I never seed any Frenchman knowed the first thing about 'ow to fight."

In a flash Camire turned on him. His dark eyes grew larger. And then he began to chuckle ominously as he pressed a forefinger into the middle of Bill's chest.

"You never? You try me and you will see something."

Camire's expression frightened Alan, but the Newfoundlander went on chewing the grapes stolidly.

"The great MacIsaac," Camire said, still excitedly, "the big Red Willie – I showed 'im once the end of a broken bottle in the face. After that 'e made me no more trouble." He turned to Alan. "You want go to France with me, sometime?"

Alan was still frightened by Camire. France was a place he had no thoughts about, but he remembered the night he had heard Camire shouting at his mother, and his mother saying how beautiful France must be. He felt a quick chill of fear.

"My father is coming home soon," Alan said, "and when he comes home everything will be different for Mummy and me."

Camire got to his feet. A look of bitterness crossed his face. "Your father!" he said scornfully. "Me, I told your mother 'e would never come back here again and she did not believe me. Then the *docteur, l'enfant de chienne*, 'e tell 'er the same thing and she believed 'im."

Camire turned and left without saying good-by, and Alan lay back in bed and wished he could keep from feeling frightened.

"Some of them Frenchmen," Blackett said, "is sons of bitches with broken bottles. I seed one oncet. 'E gouged a man's eye out before 'e 'ad 'is neck broke on 'im. Up in St. John's, thet were."

But the next day all the fear Camire had produced in Alan dissolved when Dr. Ainslie arrived. This time the doctor had a large book under his arm which he laid on the bed and said it belonged to Alan from now on. It was a book filled with pictures of famous sailing ships, with a colored print of the *Flying Cloud* on the cover. There was a text inside describing some of the ships and sectional drawings showing how they had been built.

Dr. Ainslie laid the book on Alan's knee and pointed to the picture of the *Flying Cloud*. "The sea, Alan, is the mightiest thing we know. The sky is the most changeable and mysterious." He pointed to the royal yard. "Think of it – having to stand up there and set sail between sea and sky! Think of an instrument like that ship – she probably had as many as three thousand separate ropes and every one of those ropes had its purpose! Think of handling a ship like that – it was like turning yourself into a force of nature!" A note of pride entered the doctor's voice. "The man who built that ship, Alan, was a Nova Scotian like ourselves, even though he had to go to Boston to show what he could do. Donald McKay was his name, and he was the greatest shipbuilder who ever lived. I want you to remember the names of great men. I want you to realize – and to realize when you're a boy – that nothing of the slightest value has ever been accomplished by a crowd of people. Individual men, following ideas of their own, have given the world everything we value." He pointed to the picture again. "When experts saw that vessel under construction they said she'd never sail. But look at her!"

The doctor left to make his rounds and Alan forgot Camire and the feeling of apprehension about his father and mother. For the rest of the day he was lost in the book of ships, and when the nurse came in that afternoon to take his temperature he was singing some words from the book to a tune of his own. *O Susanna, darling take your ease, for we have beat the clipper fleet, the Sovereign of the Seas!*

The nurse told him the place in his side where the stitches had already been taken out was almost healed and if the doctor said so, he could leave the hospital in a few more days.

The few days passed and now they were beginning the third week of July. Dr. Ainslie gave Alan a final examination, his mother arrived, and that afternoon Alan was driven home. When he got back to the house in the miners' row it seemed much smaller than he remembered it, and his mother seemed much younger and even prettier. He wanted to be measured because he was sure he had grown several inches in the hospital. But when she stood him up beside the panel where all his marks of growth were kept, they found he was only half an inch taller than the last time she had measured him, and that was three months ago.

"Father won't be so pleased with me when he comes home," he said, and watched her face.

But she turned her back and pulled something from a cupboard and he couldn't tell what she was thinking, or even if she had heard him.

Twenty-Three

I F GOD LOOKED DOWN on them that summer, the kind of God their ministers had told them about, He must have been well pleased, for by summer's end all of them except Alan were conscious of their sins. Longing to do their best, they had discovered there is no best in this world. Yearning for love, they had found loneliness. Eager to help one another, they had made each other wretched. Dreaming of better lives, they had become totally discontented with the lives they led.

If an omnipotent and interested God looked down on them that summer, irony must have been one of His pleasures. For here in Cape Breton were these innocent ones, eager to make themselves worthy of the great world of Europe from which their ancestors had been driven long ago; and there across the sea was that great world of Europe, enjoying the final summer of its undisturbed arrogance. For this was the year before 1914.

In Cape Breton it was a lovely season, the kind people talk about for years afterwards. There were no storms throughout the whole of August, the Bras d'Or was golden in long afternoons, the shadows of cumulus clouds moved with stately grandeur across the hills of the Margaree and the tides rose and fell under the spell of the moon. In such a summer even Broughton became almost beautiful.

During Alan's days in the hospital, Ainslie had watched a child's mind respond like a plant to the nourishment he gave it. The joy he found in Alan was a real joy, and for a time it was almost an assuagement of his inherent loneliness. Alan would succeed where he had failed. Instead of looking forward each year to another blank wall of work, each year now he would see Alan grow, change and develop, and the future would become a garden instead of a desert. Alan would become more than a foster son; he would become a purpose in life.

It was only when Alan went home from the hospital that Ainslie was opposed by the strength of recalcitrant facts. How was he to see the boy without creating a crisis?

He solved this problem by persuading Mollie that he would like to keep an eye on Alan for a few weeks in order to build up his strength, and to that end Alan must have his noon meal with them, then a nap, and in the afternoons some supervised exercise. He noticed – and refused to let himself think about it – that this suggestion disturbed Mollie profoundly, but he was the doctor and she was the patient's mother, and whatever her objections were, she did not voice them. He also noticed that Margaret showed no enthusiasm for his arrangements.

But Margaret did not interfere with his plans. She saw that Alan had the food Ainslie prescribed and she made no comment on his excessive preoccupation with the boy. She herself was subject to a sense of guilt this summer. Hers was the subterranean guilt of failure which every childless woman knows. Now it was sharpened by her husband's growing fondness for another woman's son and by a return of the conviction she had tried so hard to bury: that it was more his fault than hers that they were childless. Dr. Dougald had told her that the operation performed on her had been both necessary and honorable, but this did not remove her knowledge that for several years before that operation, in the early part of their marriage, she and Dan could have had at least one child and perhaps two, if he had really wanted one enough. But those were the days when she had taken life as it came and when Daniel had determined to put his profession ahead of all other things in his life. This summer was made no easier for her by the realization that she could become as fond of Alan as her husband was, were it not for her own pride and her constant awareness that Alan was Mollie's son, not hers.

So they lived in a miasma of unspoken hopes, fears, hurts and misunderstandings. If either Margaret or Mollie had shown the doctor her inner dismay over the manner in which he was taking them both for granted, he might have decided his dilemma by the ruthless opposition of one duty to another and by making a clean choice. But neither woman, for separate reasons, said anything to bring him face to face with the facts. So Ainslie made the mistake of thinking that their silence signified surrender to his will. Like most men who appear outwardly strong, he had overlooked the strange and mysterious strength of the weak.

It was Mollie who overthrew him. One morning after he had left for the hospital, Mollie presented herself at the surgery door. She had left Alan in her own house, studying a boy's history the doctor had given him. When Margaret opened the door and saw who was on the step, she suppressed an impulse to shut it again, for her instinct had long ago told her that so far as Daniel was concerned, Mollie was her enemy. But Margaret believed in looking problems in the face once they had forced themselves upon her, so she invited the girl in.

Then Margaret had to wait while Mollie tried to explain her visit through the usual Gaelic reticences, until finally the girl broke into tears.

"It's only because I am so frightened," Mollie said, dabbing at her eyes.

Margaret looked at the girl for a moment and resisted an impulse to despise her for her helplessness. "Come into the kitchen with me," she said. "Let's make some tea. As a matter of fact, I'm frightened, too."

Mollie said nothing more while Margaret moved about the big sunny room and set out cups and saucers on the scrubbed pine table. She left the girl in silence while they both drank the fragrant liquid as they sat on opposite ends of the table, and Margaret thought how alike – apart from the girl's difference in education – Daniel and Mollie were. Both were capable of the infinite self-deception of the Celt. Both were alarmed by plain words and clear-cut alternatives. Both resembled animals in the mediumlike way they managed to sense others and take it for granted that others would be equally capable of sensing themselves.

"I'm going to string some beans," Margaret said. "Perhaps you'd like to help me. Here – put them in this bowl and we'll put the strings on the paper. Now – what has made you frightened? We may well be frightened by the same thing, you know."

Eventually Mollie found her way through a number of hesitations until she was saying the words she had come to say. "Archie left me just like my father said he would, Mrs. Ainslie. We married because we had to marry, or my father would have died of the shame. But Archie liked me once and I always thought he meant it when he said he would come back. Now the doctor says it would be a terrible thing for Alan if he does come back, and about that the doctor is right. I wanted Alan to be proud of Archie and to think he had a wonderful father because to the other boys he did not seem to have a father at all. But the doctor is right – if Archie came back now I don't know what would happen to Alan. So I wrote and told him I never wanted to see him again."

When her husband's name was mentioned, Margaret glanced up, then looked quickly down at the beans again.

"It is wonderful, Mrs. Ainslie, what the doctor has been doing for us. He is so clever and so much older, and Alan is growing fast. It is only – Mrs. Ainslie, Alan comes home from here every day and talks to me about the fine things the doctor says he is going to do for him. He even talks about going away to school someday and then going to a college in England. And now – now I am frightened!"

Again Margaret glanced up. She remembered the evening of their drive into Broughton two months ago. The girl had seemed so gay and fresh then. She had possessed the graciousness of all things living within their own right. She had been warm, loving and beautiful. What difference did it make if she was only a child living with an illusion? Her ignorance gave Daniel no right to tear away her illusion and leave her with nothing in its place.

"Go on, Mollie," she said quietly.

"It used to be his father Alan looked forward to, but now – Mrs. Ainslie, how can Alan have those things the doctor tells him about? When he finds out he cannot have them, it will be terrible for him. I do not want Alan to go into the mine, and I am going to find a way so he will never have to do it, but now he talks always about the doctor, saying he is going to be famous one day. And that is not right because it is not true." She began to cry again. "I do not mean to be saying these things. The doctor has meant to be good to us. But I am so frightened, for the doctor has never thought about me in what he is doing to Alan."

Margaret stopped stringing the beans and put her hands on the table, as though the sight of their firmness would help to calm the girl. For she realized that she herself was afraid no longer.

"Since you've told me this much," she said, "perhaps you'd better tell me some more."

Mollie looked at her with tragic eyes. "I did a bad thing once, Mrs. Ainslie. But after Alan was born, I thought it could not have been wicked after all. For how could a boy like Alan come from what was bad? But now I don't know what to do, for the doctor has made it so I hardly know where to turn. I have been living alone so long, and everyone knows it and knows I don't count."

"Tell me about Louis Camire," Margaret said quietly. "He's a friend of yours, isn't he?"

Mollie dropped her eyes. "Before this summer he was just a friend and that was all."

"What do you mean by that? Are you living together now?"

"He would like me to. And he would like to take Alan and me to France."

A light shone in Margaret's mind. At last she seemed to see a way out of the intolerable confusion of this summer. As it was her nature to abhor confusion of any kind, she was quick to take the opportunity offered. Gaelic as she was, Mollie was in quest of her advice and moral approval, and Margaret knew it.

"Well, you'd like that, wouldn't you?" she said. "It would mean that Alan would never have to go into the mines. From what I've seen of Louis Camire, he seems a decent man of some education. So all your troubles would be over."

"Except for Archie. Louis says if he does not answer my letter it will mean he has deserted us and then I can go with him and take Alan away from here. Louis says anyone here who is any good goes to the States, so why should not Alan go to France?"

Margaret looked up at the clock and again set to work with the beans. When they were finished and she had put them on to boil, she smiled at Mollie and put her arm about the girl's thin shoulders.

"Everything is going to be all right," she said. "Alan will be here soon and you don't want him to know we've been talking. We won't tell him our plans, either. It will only confuse him to think about something else right now."

Mollie looked relieved as she left the house, and Margaret returned to the kitchen to finish preparations for the lunch. She found herself humming for the first time in weeks, and then she began to sing. It was only when she was setting the table in the dining room and pouring Alan's milk into a tumbler that her sense of guilt returned to the surface of her mind, and returned with violence.

Now she could pin it directly upon an act of which she was acutely ashamed. She, the doctor's wife, had used her author-ity to send Mollie away with tacit approval of an act which would be momentarily convenient to herself, but which in its final results might damage them all. She told herself it was Daniel's blind obsession which had driven Mollie to Camire this summer. That was true enough, but she knew it had been her own words which would seal the relationship. How would Alan fare with that conceited little Frenchman as a stepfather, in a country so far away? And what of Archie in all this, Archie, the broken-down fighter? He was still Mollie's husband. Undoubtedly he was barbarous, but he was a Highlander like the rest of them here. If Daniel Ainslie, four generations removed from Scotland, could still think of Scotland as his sacred mother country, Archie MacNeil would hardly forget Cape Breton. Why did they all assume that he would never come home just because he had been away four years and living a savage kind of existence nobody in Broughton could understand? What, most important of all, had she done to Daniel? What kind of despair would he be thrown into when he discovered that she had helped Mollie reach a decision which would send her off with the little Frenchman he despised, and remove Alan from his influence forever?

But Margaret soon calmed herself. Daniel might rage. To those who did not know him he might at times seem hyster-ical, but deep in his core was a hard rock which had not been cracked. He had never in his life failed in a crisis. After the frenzy passed he would bury himself in his work. And later in

London, if Dougald MacKenzie's plans worked out, when at last he found himself with men of his own professional stature, away from Cape Breton with its memories and haunted Calvinism, they could begin a new kind of life together.

So Margaret reasoned with herself, but her feeling of shame remained, and with it a ponderous foreboding. She sensed, without having to put the thought into words, since the religion common to Daniel and herself had performed that task for her in her childhood, that the essence of sin is a willful and inextricable involvement of the self in the lives of other people.

Twenty-Four

E VER SINCE HIS FIGHT with Packy Miller, Archie seemed to have been living in a steam bath. It had been hot in Utica, where he had gone in hope of a fight which had not materialized. It had been hotter still in Buffalo, where something peculiar had happened to him on the street, and he had come to himself in a precinct station with a kindly man in police uniform bending over him and asking his name. Now he was in Montreal, had been here a fortnight, and it was the hottest place he had ever known in his life.

As Archie walked down the curving slope of Beaver Hall Hill his open pores were saturating his only suit of clothes. The worsted between his shoulderblades showed a dark patch of sweat and he could feel the cloth clinging stickily to the insides of his thighs. He walked through Victoria Square and turned into St. James Street, entered a large, cement-fronted building and rode up five floors in an elevator to the office of Raoul Picotte, the chief boxing promoter in the Province of Quebec.

He gave his name to a dark-haired girl and sat down in the outer office waiting for Picotte to receive him. Over his head was a framed photograph of a hockey team, with Picotte standing at the end of a line of bulky players, wearing a fur cap. Two stenographers sat behind a wooden railing with idle machines in front of them and chattered in French while

Archie waited. He sat there still and loose in his sweaty clothes. He looked over the girls' heads through the window to the gray flank of a large grain elevator. Though the distance between himself and the elevator was barely a hundred yards, it looked flat and its edges seemed fuzzy.

The door of the inner office opened and a well-groomed man with iron-gray hair stood there. Raoul Picotte had carefully manicured hands and small feet in pointed shoes. When Archie saw him he thought he must have come to the wrong office, for he had never seen a fight promoter who looked like this.

"So you're Archie MacNeil?" Picotte's English was perfect. "Come inside."

Archie went through the open door and took a chair facing Picotte's desk. It looked more familiar here, for the walls were hung with photographs of boxers in fighting stances. They all looked indistinct to Archie, but he recognized Jack Johnson by his color and Jack Dillon by the stance he had studied for years. Picotte sat behind his desk and looked Archie over with a long, appraising stare.

"So you think you deserve a chance at Eugene Masson's Canadian title, eh?"

"It iss what I came here for."

"It's a pity you did not come two years ago when I wanted you."

"I am here now. Iss that not good enough for you?"

Picotte smiled. "Tell me, Archie – why did you break up with Downey?"

"Because he iss a son of a bitch."

Picotte gave him a penetrating stare. "Have you ever seen Eugene fight?"

"I haff been in the States four years. How whould I be seeing him fight, when he hass fought no place but here?"

Picotte smiled again. "Just tell me something, Archie – what gives you the idea you're worth a shot at Eugene's title?"

A slow anger kindled the redness around Archie's eyes. "While he picked the safe ones, I wass fighting the best there iss. By Chesus, in one year I fought more than he did in hiss whole life."

"There's not much argument about that," said Picotte dryly. He opened a silver case and extracted a cigarette. While lighting it, he said with his eyes screwed up against the smart of the smoke, "Eugene's fast. Nobody has ever knocked him out."

"Sure he hass neffer been knocked owt. Why should he be knocked owt, when he fights nobody with a punch and does nothing but dance?"

Picotte's shrewd eyes softened. He got up and went to the window. "Come over here, Archie."

Archie got up and joined him. His suit was still clinging to his skin and he felt dull and heavy in the head. He remembered having felt that way in Buffalo before he woke up in the police station. What he needed was a spell of training and regular meals to get the lead out of his bones. He had never been in so bad a shape as he was in now. It took most of what he had to get out of bed in the morning, and the last two weeks of stevedoring had left him exhausted. He did not notice how Picotte's shrewd eyes watched him as he lumbered around the corner of the desk.

"Ever been in Montreal before, Archie?"

"I haff been here two weeks already."

"This is quite a city." He pointed to a square building nearby with the words OGILVIE OATS written in white letters around a black water tank on its roof. "What does that sign say, Archie?"

Archie stared, following the pointing finger. "What sign whould you be meaning?"

"Right in front of you where I'm pointing. Can't you see it?"

"That iss pretty far away," Archie said.

Picotte went back to his desk, and Archie, slouching around after him, slumped in his chair.

"It iss time Masson met a man willing to fight," Archie said. "What iss the Canadian title worth, with him holding it?"

Picotte picked up his cigarette and leaned back in his chair, the cigarette between his fingers and a wreath of smoke drifting away from it. "Tell me something else, Archie – how long is it since you've seen a doctor?"

Archie thrust out his jaw and his bronze hair bristled above his scarred face as he looked angrily at Picotte. "Why whould you be asking me that?"

"Because your left eye is completely blind, and your right eye is losing its sight, too."

Archie slumped back again. "I can see good enough with one eye to look after Masson."

Picotte got up again and came around the desk. This time Archie did not move. Picotte put his hand on Archie's shoulder and felt the pack of muscle, nodded admiringly, then leaned back against his desk and surveyed the fighter with crossed arms. His jaw looked lean and shrewd as he tightened his lips over the tip of his burning cigarette.

"Archie," he said in the voice of a man talking to a child, "you've done your fighting. Why not hang up the gloves for good?"

Archie stared back without moving. His body was still trim and powerful, but after his fight with Packy Miller, the scar tissue over his eyes had become infected and it was still rough and angry-looking. The flesh over his cheekbones was battered and mashed, his nose was a sponge with hardly any unbroken bone left in it and his ears were like the handles of a jug.

"Listen, Mr. Picotte, since my last fight I haff improved. I haff been thinking about things. Look – I whill show you." He got up and sprang into a fighting stance, crouching and holding his fists close together before his chin with the elbows guarding his heart and solar plexus. He danced around the office, snapping out quick, vicious, short punches. "You see,

Mr. Picotte," he said, stopping suddenly. "With the big punch I haff, it iss not necessary to fight so open. From now on I whill fight out of a crouch and wear them down with the short ones. I whill save my strength for the big punch when they are ready."

As he slumped back into his chair he realized he had made no impression. "So you whill not make the match for me with Masson?"

Picotte took the cigarette from his lips and snubbed it out in an ash tray. Eying its ruin, he said, "I still have some conscience."

"Then maybe you haff something else for me? A semifinal or a preliminary, maybe?"

Picotte shook his head.

Archie stared at him, trying to think. Then he got to his feet. "All right. You can go to hell."

"Sit down again." Picotte's voice was quiet and authoritative. "I want to talk to you some more."

Archie hesitated, but finally he did as he was told. He watched dully while Picotte put his hand into his breast pocket and took out his wallet. He watched Picotte count out five ten-dollar bills, eye the ceiling while he made a rapid calculation, replace one of the bills and leave four tens lying on the table.

"Are you married, Archie?"

"I haff a wife."

"How long since you've seen her?"

"Four years."

"That's a long time."

"I whill go home when I am the champion."

Picotte smiled. "What does a championship mean? Who even remembers some of the champs? But everyone remembers Sam Langford from your own province. Everyone remembers old Peter Jackson from Australia and Peter Mahar from Ireland. What's a championship?" He pushed the four bills across the table. "One night two years ago you earned a lot of money for me, though you don't know it, maybe. Let me pay your way home. That's where you ought to go now, Archie – home."

Murky thoughts blundered through Archie's mind as he sat there watching the dapper French-Canadian with his money. What was the idea of offering him money? Who had ever offered him anything for nothing in all his life?

"So you think you can get me owt of Montreal that way and keep Masson for the easy ones? Whell, I am no fool. Downey used to giff me money like that, in bills too, but I found owt what he wass up to."

Picotte's shrewd eyes narrowed. "Did he? So that was how Downey worked you, eh? In New York they call him the son of the original bitch." He pushed the four bills so far in Archie's direction that they protruded over the edge of the table. "You need this money bad, Archie. Take it."

"How whould you be knowing if I need it or not? And what makes you think I take money I haff not worked for? Do I look like a bum?"

Picotte smiled. "Listen, boy – don't make it too easy for me to take this back. I like money. But I told you before – I owe you something. You remember Timmy O'Leary? The night you stopped O'Leary I was there. I didn't think you had a chance, but you were a Canadian and I backed you at one to four. From what they told me afterwards, I made more on that fight than you did yourself. That forty dollars is 10 per cent. Call it your commission on the deal, if that makes you feel any better."

Archie glared at him. "There iss a place where you can put that money, and you whould be knowing where it iss. All I want iss a chance to show what I can do again."

"The night you whipped O'Leary," Picotte went on, ignoring him, "you were great. Any man in the world you could have taken. Jack Dillon, Philadelphia Jack O'Brien – it would have made no difference, you would have whipped them. Nobody can take that night away from you, Archie." Picotte gave another encouraging smile. "Take that fare money and go home to your wife. She doesn't care if you're the champion or not. Four years is a long time to leave a woman alone."

Archie rubbed his forehead roughly with his right palm and wondered what it was, the queer feeling that came over him so often these days. Picotte looked blurred and he felt dizzy and slow.

"You whill not fool me that easy," he said, and got up and blundered out of the office.

A few minutes later he was in St. James Street, walking back to Victoria Square with his hands in his pockets. This was a godforsaken city in the heat. It was almost as bad as Trenton. He reached the square and found an empty bench under a tree and sat watching the carriages and motor cars and horse-drawn drays moving noisily around the oblong island of grass where he sat in the center. He glanced up at the statue of Queen Victoria, but the pigeons had made such a mess of her face that he did not know who she was. He felt in his pocket and took out his money to count it. All he had was two dollars and seventy cents left from a fortnight of stevedoring. Next week he would keep out of the taverns and save his pay, but this was a godforsaken town and he liked nobody in it. Next week if the foreman gave him any more of his lip he would have to show him what he could do, and that would be the end of his job on the docks.

Archie sprawled on the bench with the sun in his face. The heat made him drowsy and the drowsiness sent his mind a long way back behind the arenas and gymnasiums and cigar-smoking, gravel-voiced crowds among which he had lived these past years. He remembered Mollie the way he had seen her the first time. He remembered her strange, exciting timidity, her gentleness and how she had made him laugh and how good he had felt to know that a girl like Mollie would take up with the son of a man like his father. For a moment he felt a pang of guilt for having left her alone. Then he remembered her letter saying she never wanted to see him again. By Jesus, he thought, and passed his hand over his scars. "By Chesus," he muttered aloud, "I haff taken it here in my flesh and body, and who iss she to complain?"

Twenty-Five

L ABOR DAY marked the end of summer but not an end to the unusually warm season, and Alan went back to school. About the same time Ainslie's practice became so crowded that he had time for nothing but work. There were many operations and more people than usual lying sick in their homes. Each morning he set out with the mare at seven-thirty and seldom returned before midnight. He ate his lunch in the hospital or went without it, and Margaret was instructed how to dispense the routine quotas of medicine to the miners who called at the surgery to receive them.

Then finally a break came in the rush of work, and Ainslie managed to be at home one night for dinner. When the meal was over he pushed back his chair and said, "How do you think Alan is faring at school? He's probably wasting his time. I'd better take a walk and drop in on him this evening, because I see no prospect of being here for lunch for a while yet."

Margaret watched him search his pockets for his tobacco and matches. "I wouldn't do that if I were you," she said.

"It won't hurt," he said. "I need a different kind of exercise." He began to hum out of tune as he went into the kitchen to get some matches.

When he returned to the dining room, she said, "Alan hasn't been eating his lunches here since school began."

He stopped humming and looked at her. "Why not?"

"His mother wants him at home."

For a moment he looked relieved. "I'll set her straight on that. School or no school I want him here every day. It's the only way I can be sure he's being properly fed."

"But his mother has forbidden him to come here for any reason."

Slowly his face became an angry red. He watched her for a moment, as though testing her words in his mind to be certain he had heard them correctly, then he turned and left the room. Margaret waited, heard him stop by the front door, and then she got up and followed him.

"Please, Dan – don't go up there," she said as he was about to close the door behind him.

He waited but he did not return to the hall. She opened the door wide and stood on the step above him. Still he refused to turn, but she knew his curiosity was greater than his anger, so she said, "If you'll stop to think instead of rushing off into the night, you'll realize that you've brought this on yourself. Mollie has decided to take her boy back and there isn't a thing in the world you can do about it."

"That's nonsense!" he said.

"Perhaps. But it might have been easier for you if you had consulted her in the first place, instead of simply giving her orders as though she were a patient."

"She wants the boy's good as much as I do."

He had turned around and was trying to read her face.

"I'm sure she does," Margaret said. "But you haven't come to an agreement, have you, on what *is* Alan's good?" She pretended to pluck some lint off his shoulder. "Mollie happens to think it will be best for Alan if she leaves here and marries that Frenchman, Louis Camire."

For half a second she wondered if her husband might be going to faint. His eyes became round and large and his face paled as slowly as it had flushed. But there was nothing she could do to help him, though she knew she was more sorry for him than she had ever been before.

He turned his back again and looked down the dark drive.

"Are you sure?" he said tonelessly.

"Yes, I'm sure."

He brushed her restraining hand from his shoulder and went out into the darkness and she could hear the sound of his feet going down the gravel drive.

Twenty-Six

D AN AINSLIE walked out to the road, down the slope and over the bridge, then up the slope in front of the miners' row. It was a cool evening with a smell of kitchen fires in the air, but there were several miners and their wives sitting on front steps. Ainslie felt that the eyes of all of them were watching him as he approached the MacNeil house, so he lifted his chin defiantly and quickened his gait to that of the visiting doctor they all knew so well.

Mollie answered his knock on the door.

"Where's Alan?" he said without preliminaries.

"He is upstairs doing his lessons, Doctor."

"I'd like to see him."

But Mollie stood there in the door without speaking and with no apparent inclination to ask him in. Immediately he felt a fool, for everyone must see that the doctor was not going inside on a professional call.

"I want a word with Alan," he repeated. "I've been too busy lately to see how he was getting along."

"Alan is fine."

"May I come in?"

"You are the doctor and I could not say no."

Her face was naked. He saw its delicacy, its tenderness, its love. She was the mother Alan had known all his life. And there was something else he recognized, a last reserve of strength which she was calling upon. To oppose him – to oppose his father? He passed his hand over his eyes.

"I've come as a friend," he said. "Not as the doctor."

"Yes, I know."

He straightened his shoulders. "I trust Alan is feeling stronger all the time?"

"You have been good to us, Doctor. We will always be grateful."

This girl had only to look at him and say she was grateful for what he had done; she had only to look at him and express her thanks while deliberately ignoring what she knew he had been trying to do, and he was helpless against her. There was a rock in her as there was a rock in them all, buried deep in the past of his whole race. But he knew in that moment she was stronger than he was because he was ashamed of something and she was not. Her features were dim as she stood with her back to the lighted hall, and she seemed to him incredibly poignant and beautiful.

"Then it's true," he said. "You're going away."

"Yes, Doctor. We are."

He looked beyond her to the stairs, but there was no sign of anyone else in the house. "Tell Alan I send him my love."

"Yes, Doctor. That I will do."

He turned away and heard the door close behind him. With his chin down he began to retrace his steps quickly down the board sidewalk in the direction of the bridge.

"Good evening to you, Doctor," a voice said in the night.

Ainslie kept on walking. A few steps on he stopped and turned.

"Did I hear you say somebody is sick?"

"No, Doctor. No indeed. I wass just saying good evening to you."

"Good evening to you, Angus."

He crossed the bridge and climbed the slope on the other side and started up his own driveway. A half-moon rode overhead and its light filtered through the trees. He turned off the driveway among the birches, reached the grass of the interval and saw the brook. There were dancing pin points of light where the moonbeams struck the broken water near the bridge. The sky was a radiant dome, the firmament glowed and there was not a breath of wind. On such a night, he knew, the sea would rest in shining silence all around the island and sailing ships would be as still on its surface as protruding black rocks.

Ainslie dropped onto a patch of grass by the brook, stared up at the sky, then lay on his back and closed his eyes. A terrible fatigue, an exhaustion of the whole spirit, engulfed him. His vision of Alan growing up twisted itself into a mockery of what it once had been. He saw the lad in a scholar's gown crossing an Oxford quadrangle under the moon, saw the gown flutter and disappear, and there was Alan again with coal dust black on his face, a metal lunch box under his arm, a cap with the broken peak on his head. Then Louis Camire's face came into his mind, but the Frenchman's part in Alan's future crushed his imagination and he could not think about it. It was he alone who had driven this girl to Camire. How then could he blame her or hate her? God forgive me, he thought.

A shaking rage began to mount within him. There is no God, he kept repeating to himself. God is nothing but an invention of mad theologians who have told generations of men that He is the all-seeing Ancient of Days who at the same time damns men and loves them. The theologians, not Jesus, have tried to convince us that God, out of His infinite loving-kindness and tender mercy, out of His all-wise justice, has decided that nearly all human beings are worthless and must be scourged in the hope that a few of them, through a lifetime of punishment, might become worth saving.

Now he had something specific to be angry about, and Ainslie let his rage build upon itself. Underneath all his troubles, he told himself, lay this ancient curse. He thought desperately of Margaret and desperately of himself, and he knew that it was his fear of the curse which had hobbled his spirit. The fear of the curse had led directly to a fear of love itself. They were criminals, the men who had invented the curse and inflicted it upon him, but they were all dead. There was no one to strike down in payment for generations of cramped and ruined lives. The criminals slept well, and their names were sanctified.

For nearly an hour more Daniel Ainslie lay on the grass and tried to come to terms with himself. If there was no God, then there was nothing. If there was no love, then existence was an emptiness enclosed within nothing. He felt as though his spirit had hurled itself against the window of his life like a wounded bat and broken the glass. It had been caught in a prison and now it was free. But its freedom was the freedom of not caring, and the things it witnessed now were different from those it had seen before. Now his spirit flickered like a bat over a dark and sinister landscape as lifeless as the mountains of the moon, its bat's eyes contemplating a world older than the human race; a world where there were no gods, no devils, no laws, no certainties, no beginnings and no end. A world without purpose, without meaning, without intelligence; dependent upon nothing, out of nothing, within nothing; moving into an eternity which itself was nothing.

With a slow movement, as if coming out of a deep sleep, Ainslie sat up and looked at the sky. With longing for continuance brimming in his blood, he had looked ahead on his days and seen total emptiness. He had reached his core. And there he had stopped. He got to his feet and looked down at the brook. In that moment he made the discovery that he was ready to go on with life.

For many minutes he stood there looking down at the brook in the moonlight. Now Alan and Mollie MacNeil were two people he had known and loved a long time ago. "God bless them!" he said, and turned towards the house.

When he opened the surgery door Margaret was sitting behind his desk with the telephone in her hand. He smiled at her tentatively. Her answering smile reached him and he knew that if he had not come home, he had at least returned to the surest haven he had ever known.

"Miss MacKay has just called," she said. "The tonsils case you operated on this morning. She says bleeding has started again. Weir would be more comfortable if you could see it."

He nodded and began to check the contents of his bag.

"I spoke to Mollie," he said and cleared his throat. "What you told me was quite true."

Now he could once more think about the people around him. He knew Margaret would never understand what had wrought this change in him, as he knew it was not in his power to explain, but he was grateful for her calm silence which no longer seemed to be accusing him. Once more it was a strength against which he could lean.

"You might call the hospital and tell them I'm on my way," he said as he reached the door with the bag in his hand. He turned around and his eyes went to three photographs on the wall behind her head. They had hung there in the same place for years. Tonight he was seeing them as though they were new. Lister, Osler and Dougald MacKenzie. What qualities did they share which he lacked? It seemed important to take time to find the answer right now. Perhaps it lay in the fact that they were all three supremely fortunate human beings. They were all men who had lived out their careers before the world had become conscious of its own nerves. They had lived with a sense of continuance and permanency which he had never known. Within that permanency their wagons had been hitched with reason to stars. During their life spans the great and obvious evils had been attacked and conquered – fevers, plagues, the kind of death that came from dirty hands. They were men the Romans would have called *beati*, secure in their age and in themselves. As Ainslie looked at their photographs he realized why he could learn nothing from MacKenzie any more. He was now alone with his own skill, surer of his fingers than of his soul. Even here in Cape Breton he could guess at vistas of skill and knowledge which old Dougald lacked the imagination to contemplate. So he would go to Europe, as MacKenzie had said he must do, and there he would reach the top of his profession. Perhaps MacKenzie and Margaret had known he would come to this decision all the time, but it was his own path, not their pressures, which had led him to it.

"One thing more," he said to Margaret. "I may be at the hospital all night, so I'd better tell you while I think of it. You might write to Halifax tomorrow and see what kind of shipping space you can get. It doesn't matter whether we land in Southampton or Liverpool, so long as we leave soon."

Twenty-Seven

I N THE SECOND WEEK of September the weather broke at last. A storm that had begun off Cape Hatteras roared out of the sea and tore across the whole province from Yarmouth to Cape North. It made the spruce forests whistle like banshees and it turned the dirt roads to splashing brown mud. It shook the wooden houses and rattled the windows. It lifted the ocean against the shores and in the bare places along the coast it drove the flying spume half a mile inland. Under Dr. MacKenzie's house the sandstone cliff trembled for three days as the ocean entered the caverns it had made and rumbled volcanically. Fishing schooners homeward bound from the Banks to Lunenburg and Gloucester ran battened down under bare poles while the seas crashed over their bulwarks. Cape Breton changed from an island of shining waters and sunlit green to a granite-gray outpost smoking with cold rain as it threw back the sea.

On the third day of the storm a freighter with a flooded engine room fired distress signals in the night, and just after dawn a small group of watchers on the cliff near MacKenzie's house saw her hit. A huge sea rolled her over, lifted and beam-ended her on a reef, and there she hung impaled. From the way she wallowed it was clear to people who knew ships that her after-bulkhead was gone. She jerked up on the incoming sea and lay level with the ocean fuming across her, then crashed down with the ebb, so that her stern was under and her bows pointed skywards like a gun aimed for the highest trajectory.

The men on the cliff fired a line across her and watched a seaman go overboard as he came out of the shrouds to make it fast. The line was hauled in and fired again. This time it caught on the foremast shrouds and the crew belayed it. A breeches buoy was run out and one after the other the seamen were pulled in to the top of the cliff until nineteen men were accounted for, five unconscious and lashed to the buoy and four others with nothing worse than broken bones.

Ainslie and McCuen were called to work on the survivors, who had been carried to MacKenzie's house. When they arrived they found the old doctor at work in his shirt sleeves, so all three of them administered first aid as they could, set bones and sent the serious cases on to the hospital. MacKenzie's housekeeper gave the doctors their breakfast and shortly afterward Ainslie and McCuen drove off in the blowing rain to begin their regular rounds of the day.

During the next night the gale blew itself out and left a coldly shining sky over the province and a sea roaring angry green around it. The summer was over. Men began to think of the autumn run of salmon and of crystalline days when they would stalk deer and bring home partridge to be hung. Their wives counted jars of preserves and vegetables on cellar shelves and hoped for one more week of warmer sunshine before a killing frost left gardens black in the dawn.

For Dan Ainslie there was no respite from work. Although he and Margaret were making their plans to leave Cape Breton within a month, there was little time for either of them to savor the coming change in their lives. Margaret thought she had never seen Dan work so hard before. For years he had driven himself and wasted energy through nervous frustration. Now he wasted nothing.

When he returned each evening from the hospital he ate his dinner quietly and usually spent the length of a burning pipeful of tobacco talking to her about getting the house ready for the Doucettes from Louisburg, who would be coming up to take over the practice while they were away. Or they talked about Ruth's engagement to the bank's Mr. Toast. But neither of them spoke the name of Mollie or Alan MacNeil.

Then he went into the surgery and buried himself until midnight, and sometimes long after, in journals and medical textbooks. He was determined to recapitulate what he knew of neurology and neuropathology before he reached London, and each day confirmed his belief that there was no field of medicine in which more was mysterious and less was actually known. On three nights out of four his work was likely to be interrupted by a call. He made the call and returned to his work. Those were the times when a clear evening under the new moon or some remembered smell in the air reminded him of his childhood, and he thought of Alan with renewed pain. Those were the nights when neither Margaret nor anyone else could help him, because no one knew how much he needed help, and he was powerless to tell.

Over his books in the surgery a conviction gradually developed from an old hunch that the sciatica which plagued so many miners in the Broughton area was not caused by the dampness of the mines, as most of the textbooks said it was. His imagination grew on the problem until there were moments when he felt the answer was only just beyond his reach. He studied carefully the incipient pains in his own sciatic nerve which he knew were caused neither by dampness nor by cold. Nor was such a condition caused by too much muscular strain, or by a nerve lesion, though this last theory seemed to draw him closer to the answer than anything else he could find.

Then there were hours when he realized that he was nowhere near a solution of the problem, but he felt himself drawn forward into the mystery, and the longer he studied the more eagerly he looked forward to the advanced clinical work he would be doing in London the following year.

Twenty-Eight

T HE FREIGHT TRAIN that Archie MacNeil had boarded in
Moncton was slamming and banging on the curves that
outlined the Bras d'Or as it rattled on its way towards Sydney.
Far ahead of the car where Archie sat the whistle kept wailing
at the crossings, and there were many crossings to wail at on
this section of the line. He leaned against the side of the open
door and watched the dark green spruce go by. The heavy
odor of balsam told him that he was coming home at last. The
fights were over and he was going to a place where people
would like him. When he got home the nightmares would
stop and the pains in his head would go away. He would go
down into the mine again and show those men who had never
left Broughton how a trained fighter could work. And the
coal dust covering his face would hide the scars and lumps so
that when he came home from work with the dust on him he
would no longer have a face that frightened children and
made men laugh.

The train passed Iona and pulled out into the open, and
as he sat in the doorway of the rattling car Archie could see
the waters of the Bras d'Or sparkling in the sunshine. There
was no kind of country he had seen anywhere in the United
States which he thought could equal what he had seen today
in Nova Scotia, and the farther north he had come the better

it had been. There was no lake in the world as pretty as the Bras d'Or and if anyone wanted to deny it he would make them prove it. There were no people anywhere in the world like the people here. When he got home they would all be good to him because he had come back and once he had made them proud.

The train swerved away from the lake and ran through more spruce, then it came out of the woods into a blueberry barren. He could see the low dark blueberry bushes and wished the train would stop long enough so he could pick some berries. It made him hungry to think about them. They passed into the spruce again and the land darkened as though a curtain had been drawn. Behind the train the sun had set, so he left the open door and went back to the bales of cloth where he had slept all the way from Moncton. It was cloth on its way from Montreal to Sydney and Broughton. It was clean and dry and better to sleep on than the bags of feed he had traveled with to Moncton from Montreal.

He crawled into a nest between the bales and unwrapped the newspaper in which he had kept the last of his food. He ate the last scraps of bologna and dry bread and washed it down with cold tea in a whiskey bottle which a waitress had given him at an all-night stand in Moncton. When he finished, he took aim at the square opening of the door and hurled the bottle out, but the fine sound of its smashing was lost in the clatter of the train. Then he lay back and closed his eyes and thought about the old days when Mollie had been able to make him laugh. He would sleep awhile and be fresh for her tonight, for after all these years this night would be even better than the night after they were married. She did not really mean that she never wanted to see him again! He would show her how that was a mistake.

Archie slept only a short while on the bales, for he had scarcely closed his eyes before the pain started in his head again and he sat up, terrified by a nightmare. Fierce men were coming at him as his muscles tightened to protect himself and he struck out instinctively. So he propped his back against the bales and stared at the open door and let the darkening rush of the landscape make him feel numb. The train kept on bucketing around the curves while he lurched with it, but he did not mind the motion so long as the nightmares stayed out of his head. The sky through the open square swayed to the motion of the train, it swung and tilted on the banked curves, but even when it grew quite dark and the stars came out, it still seemed like a friendly sky because he knew it was over Cape Breton.

Twenty-Nine

EXCEPT in the vicinity of the slowly moving train, the September night was so still that in the forested hills of Cape Breton a snapped twig could startle a deer at a distance of half a mile. The deer were out that night with polished horns, but they moved so stealthily no one saw them come or go. The autumn salmon were furtive in the deep pools of the Margaree and the Baddeck, and halibut lay flat, black and icy-cold on the bottom of St. Ann's Bay. All around Cape Breton, in the coves and at the foot of dark promontories, the sea ringed the island with a thin line of astringent foam as the ground swells broke in the darkness, retreated with long throaty sighs and broke again.

In the bedroom where Alan slept the lamp was out, but moonlight entered the window and made a bright cross-barred rhomboid on the floor. He woke up and opened his eyes to the light and then he saw a mouse crouching delicately on its hind legs in the bright center of the rhomboid as it nibbled on a crumb of bread. Its whiskers moved nervously up and down as it held the bread in its forepaws, and Alan was glad because the mouse had found something to eat. The house seemed very warm because his mother had built a big fire in the kitchen stove. Alan thought about the way the embers had glowed red through the draft under the stove box as he closed it the way he was told to do before he came upstairs to bed.

His eyes took in everything he could see in the room, the wooden chair on which his clothes always hung, the table where the globe of the world now stood, the lighter square on the wall which was the calendar the butcher had given him, and the book of ships lying beside the globe. He lay still, watching the mouse.

The metal alarm clock ticking in the kitchen could be heard through the floor. Its sound made Alan wonder why the mouse wasn't frightened by it. He guessed it must be very late, maybe almost twelve. But there was still a murmur of voices in the parlor. Mr. Camire and his mother thought he was asleep and he knew they hoped he was. Mr. Camire had been in the house every night now for more than a month. It made a difference which Alan felt but could not put into words, not even to himself. His mother was as kind to him as ever. She did for him the same things she had always done. It was the way she did them that was different, as though she were no longer thinking about him at all. Alan knew that was on account of Mr. Camire. Tonight Mr. Camire had brought a bottle of red wine when he came and he made Alan understand that he wanted the wine and his mother to himself.

So Alan lay in bed and wondered, trying to understand what had happened in the past weeks since he had gone back to school. The biggest difference was not seeing Mrs. Ainslie and the doctor any more, even bigger than the change in his mother. It seemed to Alan as if he had begun to grow backward instead of forward, as though it were last year instead of this year. At first, when he was told he must not go to the Ainslies' any more, he had thought the doctor was angry with him or disappointed because he was not clever enough, but his mother had said it was only because the doctor was too busy to see anybody except his patients.

And then there was Louis Camire. Alan's ponderings stopped because he couldn't find a satisfactory pattern for thinking about Mr. Camire. He remembered the little Frenchman talking to him in the hospital, saying that one day he would take them away to France. Maybe that was the trouble. Alan sat up in bed. Was it on account of Mr. Camire that the doctor no longer wanted to see him?

Wide awake, Alan stared at the windowpane and listened intently for sounds from below. There was an occasional movement in the parlor but the sound was very faint and he could hardly hear it. Mr. Camire and his mother were not even talking together. He lay back on the pillow but his eyes remained open. It was certainly on account of Mr. Camire that the doctor did not like them any more, just as it was because of Mr. Camire that Mrs. MacCuish said hateful things whenever his mother walked past her house. How could his mother really like Mr. Camire? Sometimes she refused to talk about him, and when Alan asked more questions she averted her eyes. What did Mr. Camire want of them, to make him return every night? Alan had no words for his feelings, but he knew that Dr. Ainslie had come to give, as Mr. Camire had come to take.

So the boy lay with round eyes staring at the dark ceiling where the moonlight showed a crack in the plaster that twisted and turned like a river in a geography book.

Perhaps it was the thought of the geography book that made Alan suddenly remember his father. His mother never talked about him any more, but Alan was sure his father would come home one day because that was what he had learned and repeated for years. His father was away in the States and things had gone hard for him there, but someday he would come home, and when he did that would be the end of Mr. Camire. His father was a fighting man, a man so wonderful at fighting that people wrote about him in newspapers, a man so mighty that when Alan had asked if Red Willie MacIsaac could beat him, Angus the Barraman had roared with laughter. Why was his mother ashamed because Archie MacNeil was a prize fighter? What was the matter with that, when his father was so brave and strong that even strange Americans paid money to see him fight and every man in Broughton was proud to have known him? Archie MacNeil would come home someday and show Alan what he could do, and then his mother would be the way she used to be and he would have a father like other boys in the school, and Mr. Camire would go away and the doctor would be friends with them all again. He wondered if the doctor knew his father. He wished he had remembered to ask someone.

Downstairs a door opened and closed. Alan jumped out of bed, for it was the outside door and its closing could mean only one thing – Mr. Camire was leaving.

In his bare feet he went to the bedroom door, opened it and stood at the top of the stairs to wait for his mother. He wanted to ask her right now if the doctor knew his father. It was dark, for there was no light burning in the hall below, but the foot of the stairs caught the light that shone from the open parlor door.

Suddenly Alan's heart began to beat faster, even before his mind took in the fact that strange sounds were coming from the parlor. He stood stiff and silent, listening intently. There were heavy steps, and sounds of metal hitting wood, and then all at once grunts and scuffles and above it all his mother's piercing scream. Before the scream died away there were more strange sounds of furniture being knocked about, and Alan was running down the stairs as fast as his bare feet would take him. When he reached the lighted square of the parlor door he stopped like a fawn caught in the headlight of a train.

Everything that was happening in the room he saw quickly and completely, understanding none of it, yet feeling all of it, so that for the rest of his life all the violence of the world would be the violence of this night.

An ugly man with a great body in a soiled city suit, his face battered and lumpy and his nose mashed square, was standing sideways to the door. His arms were bent at the elbows and thrust forward, his huge hands half clenched, his shoulders poised and on guard, and in the split second while the boy watched, not taking a breath, the big man's clenched fist shot out and smashed into Mr. Camire's head.

As the Frenchman's white body fell backward, Alan heard his mother scream again. This time the sound of her voice in terror not only made his heart beat faster still, but it froze him where he stood in the doorway, unseen by the three struggling people within the room. In the next few seconds a table was knocked over, Camire got to his feet, and Alan saw that he was holding a wine bottle by its neck. The big man was looking at something on the floor that Alan couldn't see, in the direction of his mother's scream, and it was in this fraction of time that Alan knew he was watching his father. He felt the fact, rather than knew it, perhaps because he had so often dreamed of the day when his father would come home and rid them of Mr. Camire.

Like a fox, Camire made a sudden darting movement, smashed the wine bottle on the leg of the fallen chair and shot forward with the fangs of the broken glass jabbing at Archie's face as the remainder of the wine dribbled out. It was then that Alan saw what his father could do. So that was what it meant to be the strongest man in the world! Archie shifted backwards and aside, smoothly and easily, and the broken bottle jabbed viciously towards his left ear. His hand shot out and closed on the poker beside the grate, the pack of muscles under the cloth of his jacket shifted, the poker shot up and Camire seemed to stand quite still, staring at the upraised arm.

It was then that Alan saw his mother. As the poker came down she was suddenly there between the two men, thin and frail as she tried to stop them. When the poker hit her head her large soft eyes rolled into her head and she seemed to sink down into the melting white wax of her own thighs and calves. The two men stared down at her. Alan stared at her. Then the house shook with the thunder of Archie MacNeil's voice. He roared as the poker swung up again and Camire darted back and forth across the room, trying to find a place to hide as he gave mouselike squeaks of terror.

Seven blows landed on him, but Alan was no longer there when the Frenchman was silenced at last. The boy had fled.

Thirty

JUST FOR AN INSTANT Archie knew what had happened, but the knowledge got mixed up with the pain in his head. Then he heard the rain of blows on the outside door and heard men calling in Gaelic voices to open up for the love of God. It was like the roar of the crowd yelling at him to come on when he was already blind with blood, pain and exhaustion. Now, as always, he answered it. He staggered into the hall and reached for the knob of the front door. He tried to open it, but it was locked. He had locked it himself, a long time ago. The shouting outside kept on, so he unlocked the door and pulled it open and stood there facing the street with the light from the parlor at his back and himself in the frame of it.

"What the hell do you whant?" he said.

He took them in all at once, the forgotten familiar faces he had come home to see. Angus the Barraman was in front of the crowd. He reached out to touch Archie's arm.

"We hear you are haffing trouble, maybe. We haff come as your friends only."

The figure in the door stood motionless, back to the light.

"Och, Archie, there iss trouble everywhere, and four years wass a long time for her to be alone. She whould neffer haff done it but she thought you whould neffer come home at all."

The figure in the doorway swayed, then stood still.

"The doctor hiss ownself thought you whould neffer come home, moreoffer. And the Frenchman hass been seeing her only lately."

When Archie still gave no sign that he had heard, Angus reached out again. Then Archie hit him. To the men behind Angus, the punch seemed powered by a superhuman force, it came so fast. Before they could catch him, Angus fell to the ground. Archie closed the door and they heard him lock it behind him again.

"Now we must get Big Alec McCoubrie," one of them said.

"But we must also get the doctor, fast."

Two men started off on bicycles towards Broughton and another was already running towards the doctor's house. So, long before the policemen arrived, they could see the doctor coming up the hill on his bicycle. He had dressed so hastily a scarf was around his neck in place of a collar and tie. One of them ran to take his bicycle and the crowd stood back when he took his bag from the handlebars and ran to the door and tried to open it.

When he turned around to face them they felt his authority as he looked them over by the light of the moon. "Tell me again what you saw through the window," he said quietly.

After they told him once more, he said, "What about the boy?"

"We haff not seen him, but we are sure he iss somewhere inside. Archie would not touch the boy, surely."

He studied them for a moment longer, then he said, "Matheson and MacDonald – you're big men. Smash in that door."

The two men named stepped forward, braced themselves and lurched against the door. On the third try there was a crack of splitting wood and they heard Archie's voice inside.

"The first man who comes in, I whill kill him."

The two men turned to look at the doctor.

"This is Dr. Ainslie speaking, MacNeil," his voice called out. "I want you to understand that the first man to enter will be me."

He motioned MacDonald and Matheson against the door again and this time they smashed it. The door jumped from its hinges with a crash and the two men went down with it. The crowd saw Ainslie step forward, his bag in his left hand, and then Archie loomed under the overhead light. The doctor and the fighter stopped as they recognized each other. Matheson and MacDonald picked themselves up and stood back, but Ainslie and Archie MacNeil stood a yard apart with their eyes on each other's faces.

At that moment Archie seemed of more than human size. Standing in the doorway with the light over his head, he was a good foot higher than the doctor. In the imaginations of the crowd he was higher still because of what they knew he had done. They saw him draw back his right fist, but only Ainslie was close enough to see and understand the expression in Archie's eyes. They were as full of pleading as the eyes of an overwhipped child. At the same time the doctor's trained glance told him something else. One of the eyes was blind and the other was glazing. The battered face was loosening as a process of profound disintegration was occurring in the fighter's whole organism.

The men said afterwards they had never heard the doctor speak so gently. "It's all over now, MacNeil. Nothing you or I can do can change what's happened."

They saw Archie's fist loosen and his cocked arm fall loose at his side. They saw his face contort in a spasm of pain and his one good eye suddenly stare and they saw the doctor drop his bag and put both hands on the boxer's shoulders and catch him as he lurched and fell forward.

Matheson and MacDonald helped Ainslie carry the unconscious man out. They lowered him to the ground and propped his back against the wall of the house while behind them Angus the Barraman began to groan and move. Ainslie entered the house and the crowd at the steps saw the window of the parlor brighten as he turned on another light, but no one made a move to enter. They heard him leave the parlor and then the sound of his feet running upstairs and they heard his voice calling out to Alan asking where he was. Still they remained standing outside.

There was a sound of horse's hoofs and a carriage drove up and stopped on the fringe of the crowd. They recognized Mrs. Ainslie in the carriage and one of the men crossed the ditch to hold the head of the mare, but none of them said anything to her and she asked no questions. A moment later the doctor came out of the house with Alan in his arms.

They watched him as he crossed the ditch and they saw the boy in his nightclothes stiff with fright, his eyes averted from the doctor, his ears apparently deaf to the comforting words the doctor was saying. When Mrs. Ainslie stretched out her arms to take him from her husband, Alan gave a little cry; and with a convulsive movement both his arms went about her neck as he buried his face in her shoulder.

They saw Ainslie stand stiffly beside the carriage and heard him clear his throat. "He was hiding upstairs in a cupboard, but he's not hurt," the doctor said to his wife. "Whether or not he saw what happened I don't know. Give him a bromide and stay with him until he goes to sleep. It may be morning before I get home."

One of the men jumped into the carriage to drive the mare so that Mrs. Doctor could hold the boy and keep him warm. The doctor himself re-entered the house and the crowd broke up a little, men muttering together in small groups as they waited. Archie sat motionless with his back to the wall and his head hanging forward on his chest, and Matheson crouched beside him, holding him upright with his arm so he would not sprawl sideways with his head on the ground.

Later there was the sound of a clanging bell, then the surge of hoofs as a team of horses drove the ambulance fast around the corner. The horses pulled up panting with foam on their bridles and two men in white jumped out and ran around to the back of the ambulance to open the doors. They rolled out a stretcher, the crowd parted for it to go through and parted again when the stretcher came out the door with a small covered body on it.

The doctor followed and touched one of the orderlies on the arm. "There's still another one," he said, and pointed to Archie.

The second stretcher was rolled out of the ambulance, Archie was placed on it and the men panted under his weight as they rolled it in.

Ainslie turned to the crowd. "When the police come, tell them I've left the Frenchman inside. There's nothing to be done for him. But none of you are to touch his body until the police come."

Then the doctor stepped into the ambulance and crouched on the floor between the two stretchers. As the driver closed the doors, they could see his fingers search for the pulse at Mollie's wrist.

Thirty-One

T HE ORDERLY who drove the ambulance had once driven a sulky at the Cape Breton County Exhibition and was proud of being the best driver in Broughton. He drove his team fast and kept the pace smooth, and he knew every break and pothole in the road between the colliery and the hospital. He also had a new bell, softer than the bell on the fire wagons but loud and musical, and he clanged it at every opportunity on the way in. The dirt road was empty all the way to the bridge, but he had his opportunity in the main street and from the Nickel Theater to MacDonald's Corner the bell rang constantly. The post office clock struck the half-hour between eleven and midnight as the team of bays turned through the corner. The driver rang his bell again, and was delighted to see Mr. Magistrate MacKeegan, crossing the street, jump clear of the horses and turn to shake his stick, then lower it when he recognized the ambulance. All the way up the steep hill to the hospital, as the hard-working bays passed knots of men on their way home from the saloons, the orderly had to suppress a longing to call out to them that he had Archie MacNeil and his wife aboard and that he was driving from the scene of a murder.

He reached the hospital, saw Dr. Weir waiting on the steps, and reined in. By the time he and the orderly beside him had jumped from the box and run around to the back, Dr. Weir had opened the doors. Inside Dr. Ainslie was still crouching between the two stretchers. When they peered in and then stood waiting for orders, the doctor seemed not to know he had reached his destination. The driver was crestfallen, for he had hoped the doctor would praise him for his performance. He had beaten his record from that particular colliery by forty-five seconds.

Dr. Weir waited a moment, then said, "Everything is ready, Doctor."

Ainslie looked up as though he had no idea where he was. He shook his head, breathed deeply once or twice and shook his head again.

"Never mind," he said as he got out. "She died on the way in. The other has a clot in his brain. If he's lucky, he'll not recover consciousness."

Then Ainslie began walking down the drive.

Weir ran after him. "Doctor!"

Ainslie kept on going and Weir fell into step beside him.

"Doctor, aren't you coming into the hospital?"

"No."

"But –"

"There's nothing to be done for him. Put him in bed. Keep him quiet. You know what to do as well as I."

"Yes, Doctor, I suppose so."

They had reached the street and Ainslie turned to walk down the hill.

"Dr. Ainslie – you have no carriage!"

"I have two legs. And the trains are still running."

Ainslie continued to walk and Weir watched him go.

When he reached MacDonald's Corner he turned into the main street and walked to the harbor bridge. Here he stopped and looked at the riding lights of the moored schooners and smelled the drying fish and the salt air. When he closed his eyes he saw the beast again, the tight-skinned, tawny, green-eyed dog with the small ears. It was standing over the blood and its eyes were on his face.

He left the bridge and continued walking under a sky quiet with stars. His feet plodded along the dusty road over which his carriage had drawn him on so many thousands of cases and the land around him was very dark. He met nobody, or if he did he was unaware. After a while he reached the enclosure of his own colliery, saw the black mass of the bankhead loom against the lighter mass of the sky, plodded past and turned down in front of the miners' row. There he stopped and scanned the road. A few lights were still burning in the cottages, and in front of the MacNeil house he saw Alec McCoubrie the policeman sitting on the steps talking to a pair of miners. He took the far side of the road and went by without speaking. He knew their eyes were on him as he passed, but none of them spoke until he was out of earshot. He crossed the bridge and mounted the slope on the far side, turned into his own driveway and disappeared among the shadows of the trees.

The lights were burning in the surgery and in one room upstairs, and a carriage he recognized as MacKenzie's stood at the door, the horse with a feed bag over his nose.

Ainslie had no sense of the distance he had walked or what time of night it was. He stood in the darkness outside his own house for a long while, hearing the sound of the broken water in the brook. Then he took the path by Margaret's rose bed around the house to the front door and went in that way. He avoided the surgery and climbed the stairs. He opened the door of their bedroom, but the room was dark. Then he remembered where he had seen the light from the outside. He crossed the hall and opened the door of the spare bedroom and saw Margaret in a large rocker with the sleeping boy in her arms. She smiled at him over Alan's head and her brown hair was lustrous in the light that shone behind her chair.

"He's all right," she said. "Dr. Dougald looked him over and he thinks the effect of the shock will wear out in a little while. He must have seen or heard nearly everything."

Ainslie leaned against the door. "How could you tell? Did he talk about it?"

"No. Not at all. But he didn't relax or stop shaking until after we got the bromide down, and then he began to cry. I'm glad you weren't here. It would have broken your heart."

Ainslie looked down at the boy, but Margaret could detect no emotion she could recognize in the expression of his face.

"You must be tired," he said.

"Well –" She smiled. "I couldn't leave him alone until he fell asleep." Her eyes fell to the drooping figure in her arms and her face softened. "Poor child, he'll have to be loved very much to make up for this."

It was then that Ainslie began to cry. He made no sound, but the tears welled up and overflowed and he made no move to brush them away. It was the first time Margaret had ever known him to be unashamed of showing such emotion. Under other circumstances she would have tried to help him by pretending she hadn't seen the tears, but now she could do nothing but sit with the sleeping boy in her arms.

After a few moments the tears stopped and Ainslie came over and stood beside her.

"Here, let me take him now." He cleared his throat and blew his nose. "He's quite heavy. Your arms must be paralyzed, holding him so long."

She smiled again. "They're not numb at all." Their eyes met and held. "I like holding him."

"Mollie is dead," he said.

"Yes, I know. Dr. Dougald called the hospital and they said you had gone." She looked down at Alan again. "Do you want us to keep him and raise him as our son?"

She was afraid Daniel might cry again, so she indicated that he could relieve her of the boy's weight. He reached down, and as she shifted the burden, Alan whimpered. Ainslie took her place in the chair and tried to hold the boy in a comfortable position. Alan opened his eyes. Through the drug, his vision focused on the man who was so close to him. For several seconds he stared. Then he became rigid and began to scream in terror.

"It's all right, Alan. It's all right. You're with us now. There's nothing to be afraid of now. It's the doctor. Don't be frightened. You're going to stay with us."

The screaming stopped but Alan's body remained stiff and unyielding. Ainslie tried to talk to him. Every time he spoke the sobs began anew and the boy tried to hide his face from the doctor's eyes.

"Do you want me to hold you again, Alan?"

The boy looked up at Margaret, then at Ainslie, and when she held out her arms he slipped off the doctor's knees and moved into them, nestling down against her shoulder when she returned to the chair. Over the boy's head Margaret looked at her husband, but all she saw was his back going out the doorway.

Downstairs in the surgery, MacKenzie opened his eyes when he heard Ainslie's steps approaching and he was sitting upright when the doorknob turned and Ainslie entered.

"I've brought over some of my smuggled brandy," he said. "Over there – I've already poured it out for us."

He rose from the leather couch where he had been lying, crossed to Ainslie's desk and picked up two small glasses charged with brandy and water.

"Here!" he said, and thrust one out.

Ainslie dropped into the Morris chair and leaned back. If he saw the glass extended in MacKenzie's hand, he gave no sign of it.

"Margaret tells me you know she's dead," he said tonelessly.

MacKenzie nodded and replaced the rejected glass on the desk.

"I killed her as surely as my father killed my mother," Ainslie went on. "You told me the truth once and I wouldn't listen. Through arrogance, the both of us. Through total incapacity to understand that in comparison with a loving human being, everything else is worthless."

MacKenzie lifted his glass of brandy to the light, put back his head and poured it down. Then he wiped his long white mustache and sat down facing Ainslie on the edge of the desk.

"Keep a grip on yourself, Dan," he said sharply.

"What else have I done all my life but keep a grip on myself?" Ainslie shuddered. "Alan is terrified of me now. He isn't afraid of Margaret at all."

"That's only shock." MacKenzie's shrewd eyes probed his friend's exhausted face. "It was you who found him hiding and he's still terrified by what he saw tonight. It's only shock and it will pass."

Ainslie closed his eyes. "But I love the boy."

MacKenzie rose, set his empty glass beside the untouched one and put his hand on Ainslie's shoulder.

"Yes, Dan. Now I think you do."

Afterword

BY ALEC LUCAS

As a body Hugh MacLennan's fiction might well be entitled the anatomy of contemporary Canada. No other series of Canadian novels has been written with a greater sense of a national identity, and no other author has tried harder to define and demonstrate the forces that have determined it. *Barometer Rising* (1941), the first of MacLennan's novels, dramatizes Canada's fight against corrupt colonialism. His next book, *Two Solitudes* (1945), focuses on problems of race and religion in the province of Quebec. Even his most intimate novel, *The Watch That Ends the Night* (1959), describes the depression of the 'thirties and comments on the Canadian left-wing movement. *The Precipice* (1948) and *Each Man's Son* (1951), however, differ from his other novels, emphasizing ethical rather than sociological issues. Both are studies of Puritanism, the *bête noir* for MacLennan of Canadians and Americans alike. In *The Precipice* he makes it the basis for an examination of the moral and social attitudes of Canada and the United States, and in *Each Man's Son* he takes a close look at the inner world of the Puritan conscience.

Whether correct or not, MacLennan undoubtedly sees Calvinism as the albatross of the Canadian character. His speeches, essays, and novels repeatedly confirm his aversion to the "iron in our hearts" that thwarts the joy of living.

"America's crisis," he observes in *Cross Country* (1949), "and therefore the crisis of the rest of us, consists in this: puritanism has conditioned its members to act rather than to think, to deal with means rather than with ends, to press forward with ever-increasing speed and efficiency toward a material goal." Canadian Puritanism, MacLennan holds, manifests itself as a "futile, haunting sense of guilt" that has "enormously inhibited the Canadian character."

Although MacLennan bases Canadian identity on Calvinism, he also stresses the importance of racial groups in Canada's development. He selects the English, the French, and the Highland Scots as the most significant, and in *Barometer Rising* and *Two Solitudes* makes the first two central to his themes. In *Each Man's Son* the Scots come directly into the foreground, where MacLennan can examine both their Calvinism and their predicament as a betrayed race, berating and praising them simultaneously. If they brought the dry rot of a negative morality with them, they had been "poets once before the damned Lowlanders got to [them] with their religion," says the fatherly Dr. MacKenzie, Ainslie's confidant and the novel's choric character. If brutalized by circumstance, they were still a people of hardy courage and almost desperate resolution.

After books on Quebec and Ontario, MacLennan went home again in *Each Man's Son*, since he had already written *Barometer Rising* out of his knowledge of the Maritimes. Yet he seems even more at home in *Each Man's Son*. He was born in Cape Breton, the setting of the book, and even when his family left Sydney (probably the Broughton of the novel), it moved no farther than Halifax. The subject, too, is one that MacLennan feels on his pulses, since he is of Highland Scottish descent. Furthermore, Dr. Ainslie suggests the author's father, Dr. MacLennan, a man of similar high seriousness and respect for learning.

Although both *Barometer Rising* and *Each Man's Son* are regional fiction, they differ in that the first stresses place and the second people. Despite the specific setting in a mining community, *Each Man's Son* depends largely on the tippling, squabbling, yarn-telling Scots for its local colour. They form a living and (to mention an element lacking in MacLennan's earlier novels) a frequently humorous backdrop for the story, and emphasize its theme, not specifically as Mrs. MacCuish does, but more generally. While MacNeil, like a shadow, waits in the wings, they keep his world before the reader, most significantly through their attitudes. Like MacNeil they have their ideals and express them in terms of the passionate and the physical. Moreover, they suggest the forces that control MacNeil and torment Ainslie. Natural men, the miners are damned according to the Puritans since they do not live by the light of faith and doomed according to Ainslie since they do not live by the light of reason. MacLennan himself implies that as they work in darkness, so they live in darkness, their ungodliness deriving from the unsatisfying nature of the Puritan God. For MacLennan they are lost, not because they neglect this austere God, but because, like Archie, they have set up instead the ideal man of brawn. Their gods are the muscular men, the Archie MacNeils and the giant MacAskills. The miners never know that the physical has no meaning beyond itself, nor that fighting it on its own terms must be a losing battle.

Even though less geographically and historically precise than in *Barometer Rising*, setting in *Each Man's Son* is no less important. Aside from its usual functions, it isolates a pure culture of the Scot in Canada. Moreover, it reflects the major issues of the story – even in the very first pages. The promontory like a giant casts its shadow over Alan and Mollie; the moon and the tide destroy Alan's sand castle; the conch shell evokes an imaginary world; and the black bankhead looms over all. Although not symbolic, these details suggest MacNeil's looming presence, which broods over the whole story and Ainslie's attempts to dominate the mother and her son. They suggest also the immediacy to the mining community of the natural world, the sense of the past, and the Puritan fear of sin and damnation. All of these contribute to the major conflict of the novel, man's struggle against the forces that inhibit him in his search for freedom of spirit.

Other details of setting amplify this conflict. The hospital becomes the beacon light of science for a troubled world; although it ministers only to physical need, it stands out boldly against the Calvinist church, which ministers to man's spiritual need by preaching his weakness and God's strength. The mine, too, is not simply a mine – MacLennan sets no action *in* it – but a means of developing theme and examining the characters of MacNeil, Camire, and Ainslie. As a mine it is for MacNeil a hateful place to work, for Camire (a socialist who dreams of inheriting private property) a social evil exploiting the labourer, and for Ainslie a corrupting force, maiming men's bodies and stultifying their minds. The mine also represents the natural world dreaded by Ainslie and Puritan alike, since they believe it dooms man to a purposeless life, the lot of the unenlightened as Ainslie, and, of the nonelect, as the Calvinist see it. Finally, as the heart of darkness, the mine challenges each man to find the hidden meaning of life itself. MacNeil tries to discover it in the physical; Ainslie, in the rational; and Camire, in the sentimental. None finds it, nor, MacLennan implies, can he find it in Calvinism.

The world of Margaret Ainslie, a gentler Puritan, and of Mollie and Alan MacNeil acts as a foil for the mine and the three men, the narrowness of whose outlooks, set against love and kindness, becomes patent. MacNeil's concept of love is limited to passion and the flesh; Camire's, to an affair of the heart and romantic escape; and Ainslie's, although seemingly less self-centred, to the head and the "good" of the individual. Dreading both the physical and the emotional (a Puritan legacy) and trusting to the rational, Ainslie destroys his and his wife's happiness and undermines Alan's and Mollie's. Each man attempts to fit human relationships into the world of hand or heart or head that he has tried to establish in his personal life as a way "to lick" the mine.

The narrative that sets up these struggles depends on the efforts of each man to come to terms with Mollie and Alan and to escape the menace of the mine. MacNeil seeks success as a boxer in the United States but, betrayed by the "business world" there and his own "weaknesses," and defeated in the ring, he returns home. Camire, dreaming of his boyhood in France, manages, through his love-making (and as a result of Ainslie's meddling), to persuade Mollie (with Alan) to leave Broughton with him, only to have his plans thwarted when Archie returns. Studies in the failure of self-gratification as a *modus vivendi*, both men reveal values that Ainslie has rejected in his search for happiness; at the same time they define more clearly the nature of his problems. Simply put, his is the story of a childless man seeking to "adopt" another man's son. Yet it is no less the story of a man hounded by a sense, inculcated by his Calvinist father, of man's sinfulness. Taught that the successful must be godly since the godly are successful and that the senses are in league with the devil, Ainslie makes his own life into a fight against failure and against human frailty in himself and others, a battle that he can win only by hard work and the sternest denial of the sensuous and emotional. Fearing failure, he wants to subjugate all to his will. Fearing the flesh, he tries to live above it in the depersonalized world of the rationalist and the scientist. In the hospital, a refuge paradoxically for his maimed spirit, he can feel at home, for there his objectivity forms part of his professional code of ethics. Outside the hospital, however, he is cut off from the world by this same objectivity, his love for his wife twisted, his relationship with Mollie and Alan misguided, and his attitude toward man, except as a creature to be improved or a patient to be cured, almost contemptuous. The episodes in Ainslie's life have a double focus, for through them MacLennan examines both the Puritan conscience and the stages by which Ainslie moves from his fear of life to a recognition of its beauty through the great liberating effect of unselfish love.

The events of the narrative derive from Ainslie's decision to take Alan MacNeil under his care, for when the novel opens Ainslie is a successful doctor but an unhappy man who longs for a son to give meaning to his empty life. On the professional level, the only one he understands, he succeeds. A series of cases that emphasize the categories of hand, heart, and head into which Ainslie (and the thematic organization of the novel) divides life culminate in Alan's appendectomy, by which Ainslie does "beget" a son. Totally involved for once, the surgeon becomes a man. On the personal level, however, Ainslie's rational ethic fails him. Unaware of Alan as an individual, he dreams of moulding the boy into a projection of his own ideal self. He wants both to play God, a just but dispassionate Jehovah, and to create God in his own image to fill the spiritual vacuum of his agnosticism.

The incidents that reveal Ainslie's failure recapitulate his life and disclose the limits of his emancipation from his Puritan upbringing. In an external-internal drama in which the past is reflected in the present, Ainslie plays the role of both son and father. As the one he sees himself a boy again, growing up like Alan under the threats of the mine and the Calvinist Church; as the other, a man whose duty it is to remove these threats from his son's life. Ainslie only imperfectly understands the part taken by the villain Puritanism, but, in his soul-searching over Alan, he recognizes its crippling effect on his own life. Ashamed of sex and afraid of failure, he realizes, as the first step toward redemption, the harm that these attitudes have done to his marriage. Again the fact that Mollie and his wife occasionally become mother images suggests a second stage in his development, his growing awareness that because of his early religious training he is afraid to give love completely, since he has never felt free to accept it.

All this, however, is largely retrospection for Ainslie. In the present, except for his agnosticism, his father's Calvinistic precepts motivate his behaviour. Assuming that the same resolution and values that made the successful surgeon will make the successful "father," Ainslie disregards his wife's and Mollie's rights and feelings and Alan's hero-worship of his father and determines to make the boy his protégé. Thus he sets the stage for the spiritual crisis of his life. Mollie refuses to give up her son, and Ainslie perceives at last the strength of the weak.

Shocked by this defeat, he comprehends in his hour of agony the sterility of his attitude toward God and man. God either is or is not, but whether He exists as the God of Calvinism, or does not exist, as the free-thinker Ainslie holds, love has no place in human relationships. The loss of Alan has revealed but not resolved Ainslie's dilemma. It has disclosed the causes and results of his inability to love, but nothing of a way to overcome it. His spirit, released from the prison of agnosticism and Puritanism, is free, but in a purposeless world. Then in a flash of insight he moves out of his dark centre toward his salvation. He recognizes the meaning of the vitality of the natural world and the need to accept the simple fact of being as neither moral nor immoral. "He got to his feet and looked down at the brook. In that moment he made the discovery that he was ready to go on with life."

The denouement of the novel quickly follows Ainslie's crisis. Now a derelict, MacNeil, his semi-blindness a symbol of his spiritual plight, returns home to find Mollie with

Camire. Enraged, he brutally attacks his wife's lover. This fight, MacNeil's last, awakens Alan to the true nature of his father's world. MacNeil accidentally kills Mollie, murders Camire, and suffers a clot of blood in the brain, removing all obstacles from Ainslie's path. Fortuitous as this violent conclusion may seem, it is the plausible climax of MacNeil's career as a boxer and Ainslie's interference in Mollie's life. Yet the brawl functions as more than the escape hatch of plot. As the consequence of Ainslie's Puritanism, the basis of his meddling, it is integrated with the main theme of the book. Furthermore, it reveals that MacNeil's passion and Camire's old-world romanticism are not less selfish than Ainslie's possessive love for Alan. Neither cares for Mollie for her sake but for his own. Again the fight concludes the stories of Camire and MacNeil as allegories of love. In the struggle between the romantic (which ultimately cannot escape the actual) and the physical in love, the physical overthrows love altogether and comes to a dead end, its victory, like Archie's, meaningless.

This denouement also marks the final stage of Ainslie's salvation. For the third and last time the tight-skinned dog (his sense of guilt) growls at him, but not on this occasion because of the "sin" of sex or his denial of God. Now Ainslie, as a result of his spiritual crisis, sees the beast in a different light. He realizes that his determination and rational ethic are simply veiled Puritanism, based as they are on distrust of human "weaknesses." Even in his agnosticism he had not been free of its influence. Wanting God, but not the Puritan's God, he had set himself up as his own standard in the very same image, stern and unloving, and had thus been guilty of pride in self, the primal sin. Mollie had become his saviour. Crucified by his selfishness, she (like his mother) had given her life that he might be saved, for through her death he had come to appreciate fully his egotism. The final phase in Ainslie's regeneration develops from Alan's plight and his rejection of Ainslie. Led by this little child, he recognizes the need of sympathy for the human situation and of giving oneself in love, discovering at last the meaning in life he had so long denied himself.

MacLennan affirms life, and his novel deals dramatically with its ultimate values. Wrong in denying God but right in denying the Calvinist's oppressive God, Ainslie wrestles with problems that each man's son of us must face. Unable to live without an ideal, a religion, a god, man will accept one or find one for himself. Ainslie's great discovery is that God is love. No other answer, MacLennan implies, can long satisfy. Not the science of an Ainslie caring nothing for man's spirit and even denying it, nor the socialism of a Camire, setting man against man and seeing his salvation in materialistic terms, nor yet the "rugged individualism" of a MacNeil, struggling in a world where the law of the jungle prevails, answers the needs of man as a social being. Man can find no happiness within himself either, if he lives like the rationalist Ainslie, the sentimental romantic Camire, or the animalistic MacNeil. Unless he holds values spiritually greater than theirs, he exists in isolation and discontent, pointlessly trying to lift himself by his own bootstraps. Only by giving in love, not through restraint, can man break the barriers between self and society and self and God. Setting the Old and the New Testament concepts of God in opposition, *Each Man's Son* transforms a story about Puritanism into one of universal application. "Except a corn of wheat fall into the ground and die it abideth alone; but if it die, it bringeth forth much fruit. . . ."

BY HUGH MACLENNAN

ESSAYS
Cross-Country (1949)
Thirty and Three (1954)
Scotchman's Return and Other Essays (1960)
The Other Side of Hugh MacLennan: Selected Essays Old and New [ed. Elspeth Cameron] (1978)

FICTION
Barometer Rising (1941)
Two Solitudes (1945)
The Precipice (1948)
Each Man's Son (1951)
The Watch that Ends the Night (1959)
Return of the Sphinx (1967)
Voices in Time (1980)

HISTORY
Oxyrhynchus: An Economic and Social Study (1935)

TRAVEL
Seven Rivers of Canada (1961)
The Colour of Canada (1967)
Rivers of Canada (1974)